MADNESS OF THE MOMENT

Dominic undid the sash which bound Julia's dressing gown and slid the garment off her shoulders. She stood before him only in her chemise, the soft swell of her breasts just visible above the lace at the low neckline. He gently traced the curve of her breasts with one finger. Then he looked up at her face, compelling her eyes to his.

Julia felt a warm flush of arousal. She was intensely aware of the large bed which dominated the room. If she did not put an end to their lovemaking now, their passion would be unstoppable. She knew the choice was being given to her and she made it without hesitation. She lifted her arms to Dominic's shoulders and kissed him. . . .

ELIZABETH HEWITT, who comes from Pennsylvania, now lives in New Jersey with her dog, Maxim, named after a famous romantic hero. She enjoys reading history and is a fervent Anglophile. Music is also an important part of her life; she studies voice and all of her novels for Signet's Regency line were written to a background of baroque and classical music.

AIRS AND GRACES

Elizabeth Hewitt

SIGNET
Published by the Penguin Group
Penguin Books USA Inc., 375 Hudson Street, New York,
New York 10014, U.S.A.
Penguin Books Ltd, 27 Wrights Lane, London W8 5TZ, England
Penguin Books Australia Ltd, Ringwood, Victoria, Australia
Penguin Books Canada Ltd, 2801 John Street, Markham, Ontario, Canada L3R 1B4
Penguin Books (N.Z.) Ltd, 182-190 Wairau Road, Auckland 10, New Zealand
Penguin Books Ltd, Registered Offices: Harmondsworth, Middlesex, England

First published by Signet, an imprint of New American Library,
a division of Penguin Books USA Inc.

First Printing, September, 1990
10 9 8 7 6 5 4 3 2 1

Printed in the United States of America

1

The Earl of Morland gathered up a handful of the papers scattered across his desk and waved them for emphasis. "Look at all these damned bills! What the devil are you about, Julia? A thousand pounds for a court dress? You are never at court if you can prevent it, and you were presented a dozen years ago."

"And have worn the same stupid dress ever since," Lady Julia Halston responded, with neither concern nor contrition. "Eliza wished me with her for support when she presented Jenny, and it certainly wouldn't have helped your daughter if she had appeared with an aunt looking like a quiz."

"So now it is to be my wife's fault that you are extravagant?" he demanded, seizing upon this to fuel his anger. It was difficult to maintain his righteous indignation while his sister showed so little inclination to be either defensive or apologetic.

Julia gave him one of her lazy smiles. "No, indeed! Eliza specifically warned me against having my court dress made by Madame Céleste because her price was certain to be exorbitant. But you see, no one else makes my gowns." Her smile was a bit self-deprecating, as if commenting on her foibles, but in no way remorseful.

Morland let the bill drop to the desk and gave a short, sharp sigh. "Damme, Julia, I don't understand you, but then I never have. It is not as if Halston left you without a penny to bless yourself with. Your jointure is damned handsome."

A genuine smile lit up her cornflower-blue eyes. "A handsome jointure! Poor Hal, such a cliché. My jointure is adequate. Or," she added with a rueful glance at the paper-littered desk, "perhaps not."

"Your jointure is damned handsome," Henry Morland said emphatically. "It is your own fault that you cannot manage on what you have. I told you you were taking on more than you could handle when you bought that damned house. If you lived here with us, you would have the whole of your income to spend on dresses and other fripperies instead of seeing it eaten away by household expenses." It was clear from his tone that this was an old grievance. "You have wit, I'll grant you, Julia, but there are times when I doubt you have sense."

The first spark of anger flashed in Julia's eyes but was quickly gone. "I think you must be right, Hal," she said, her voice a silky, exaggeratedly fashionable drawl. "I did permit you and Papa to persuade me to accept Tony's offer when I was scarcely out of the schoolroom and had no notion of what I was about. Though I would have said that I was more biddable in my youth than lacking in sense."

Hal snorted. "If so, you outgrew it," he said. "If you ever do the least thing you are bid, I have no notion of it. And what the deuce do you mean by that remark about Halston? Your marriage to him was the one indisputably sensible thing you have ever done. Tony was a damned good husband to you. Too good, if you ask me. He let you have your head and a free hand in his pocketbook and this is the result of it." He waved one hand about vaguely, indicating not only the bills on the desk this time but her person as well.

As trustee of her jointure, Henry Morland theoretically had greater control over Julia's income than she did herself, for, with the exception of pin money, he was responsible for all of her financial affairs. But the control he sought was limited at best, for Julia rarely consulted him before committing herself to any purchase, be it a court dress or the house she had purchased on Half Moon Street four months after her husband had died in a hunting accident. Henry felt reduced to the role of accountant, merely paying bills, not sanctioning her expenditures, and he resented it greatly.

Julia knew this, but it did not overly concern her. The price she paid for her independence was having to sit in Hal's study at settling day each quarter and allow him to rake her over the coals for what he perceived as her extravagance. But Julia was not truly extravagant; she was merely determined to maintain her independence, and for her the house on Half Moon Street was a symbol of that, be Hal ever so right about the degree to which the expenses of it cut into her income.

As Lady Julia Halston while Sir Anthony lived, Julia had enjoyed the full use of an extensive income, and economy did not come easily to her. She was used to moving in the highest circles of society and to having only the best of everything. She had certainly made adjustments to allow for her altered circumstances, but there was a standard beyond which she would not allow herself to drop even if it did mean that she constantly skirted the edge of financial ruin.

But it was not only Julia's house and her penchant for expensive court gowns that her brother objected to. She sat before him in a walking dress of finest cambric styled with a deceptive simplicity that was unquestionably expensive. Her honey-brown hair was exquisitely and expertly dressed; a locket of intricate design adorned her throat, and small perfectly matched pearls glistened in her ears. No one regarding her would doubt that she was not merely a woman of fashion, but a leader of fashion as well.

Her brother's regard, though, was entirely without approbation. It was more than a matter of the amount Julia spent on her clothes and adornments; he disapproved of the manner in which she lived, and he had done so almost as much while Sir Anthony had lived as after Julia had become widowed three years previously.

Julia lived her life as it pleased her, without resorting to the opinions or expectations of anyone. Julia dressed in the highest kick of fashion and always daringly, in styles that emphasized her exquisite figure. She occasionally gilded her toenails, was suspected of dampening her petticoats, and drove a dashing high-perch phaeton and pair in Hyde Park during the fashionable hour for promenade.

Against all advice she had refused her brother's offer to make her home with him and his family in the conventional way of childless widows, and had compounded this by insisting on purchasing her own home, a trim Georgian town house on Half Moon Street, and living there quite alone except for a self-effacing companion, without even bothering to pretend that Lettice's presence was more than a sop cast to propriety.

It was not that Julia fanatically flouted convention: she merely skirted it at every opportunity. But Lady Julia Halston, the daughter of an earl, the wife and now widow of a very rich man, and a beautiful woman of style and taste, was forgiven much that would have been condemned in another, less fortunate woman; and Hal, who had all his life lived exactly as he ought, was envious of both her free spirit and the world's indulgence of it.

Julia understood this well enough, but she didn't give a damn for his approbation or, for that matter, anyone else's. She was blessed with both style and aplomb and her detractors were few except for those consumed with envy, and the condemnation of these, like that of her brother, was in general a matter of indifference to her.

Even her brother was not entirely immune to her charm, and in spite of his ranting, his threats and caveats generally were not to be taken seriously, but this time there was an implacability in his tone.

"I'm damned if I'm coughing up the dibs again, Julia. This time you can damn well stay in Dun Territory until next quarter, or dip into your capital. You need to learn the value of money and to live within your means."

Julia gave vent to a soft, silvery laugh. "Hal, Hal, please don't be such an old woman. You sound exactly like poor Groats, my old governess. If you must comb my hair over a stupid court dress, at least try to rehearse a few original phrases beforehand. It would be much more effective, I promise you."

"Laugh as you please, Julia," he said, waving an admonishing finger at her. "But I mean what I say. Not a penny will I pay for Céleste or your milliner or even your household accounts. You will see how you will laugh when your butcher refuses your orders in the future."

For the first time Julia felt a faint stab of alarm. Her smile became a bit more fixed perhaps, but otherwise she appeared no more than bored and a bit amused. "But, my dear brother," she said with a mild complaint, "as trustee of my jointure, it is your duty to pay my bills, since you and Papa persuaded Anthony when the settlements were drawn up that I was not to be given the freedom of my income myself."

Hal leaned forward across the desk, seizing upon her words. "That is it, isn't it, Julia? That is why you won't make the least push to economize; you resent my authority over your interests, but as it has turned out, it is certainly for the best. Left to yourself, you would likely have expended your capital and have no income left at all now."

"According to you, I do not anyway," she retorted, but still with a deceptive lightness. "Perhaps, if I had the management of my own funds, I would be more aware of the amount I spend."

"You are not obtuse. You know what you have for each quarter and how much you can afford to pay for things."

"Yes," she agreed, "but it hardly seems worth the bother to ask the shopkeepers for prices when I know I shan't ever see the bills anyway."

"Well, you had better begin to ask," the earl advised her curtly. "This is the end of it, Julia. Not another penny will I advance you before the next quarter."

Julia's smile slowly evaporated. "Then what am I to do? Hire out as a cook maid?"

"I can think of any number of things you might do to economize. To begin with, you could sell your house and come here or to the dower house at Plainfield to live as is more befitting your estate in life."

With equal slowness, Julia's smile returned. "Ah. I see. What a great deal of roundaboutation you make to come to your point, Hal. This argument is three years old, and my answer to you is the same as it was then: I am widowed, but I do not mean to be buried with my husband. Neither you nor Elizabeth nor Giles is going to push me into the role of dowager. I am very happy with my life as it is, and I would not for the world give up having my own establishment."

"Then you had better find some means of paying for it," Hal replied with a smile that was more of a smirk.

Though her exterior remained calm, inside Julia was seething with barely suppressed anger. When her husband had died so unexpectedly, his son by a previous marriage, the present Sir Giles Halston, had come personally to break the sad news to her, and in virtually the next breath had made it clear that he expected her to retire to the dower house at Plainfield Hall, the principal seat of the Halstons, as soon as she could manage after the funeral. When she had declined this generous offer and declared that nothing would convince her to live anyplace but in London, her brother, who like Sir Giles thought it the right and proper thing for her to live quietly, insisted that she come to Morland House to live if she wished to remain in town. But Julia found that offer even less palatable than her stepson's.

Sir Anthony had been a very generous husband, delighting in his young wife's ambition to cut a dash. In addition to the jointure that had been settled upon her and was indeed quite handsome despite her remarks to the contrary, she had a considerable nest egg from the excess of pin and household money Sir Anthony had bestowed on her in the ten years of their marriage. It was with this that she had purchased her house on Half Moon Street.

The efficiency with which she had managed her household and personal accounts during her marriage made it clear that Julia had neither the habits of a spendthrift nor an inability to practice economy. It was not precisely open defiance of the strictures of her family that caused her to live to the extreme of her income since her widowhood, but every word of unasked-for advice and every attempt to convince her of the error of her ways increased her determination to continue to live independently and well, and this was unquestionably expensive.

Julia's willfulness was ever amiable, though. She never argued or allowed her temper to flare in these encounters with Hal. But this time Julia recognized the adamant note in her brother's voice. Perhaps it was nothing more than that he had had a disagreement with his wife that morning or had lost at cards the night before, but she knew that, at least for now, he meant what he said. "Well, if my bills are not to be paid, then I suppose I shall end in the Fleet," she said quite conversationally, though it cost her something not to let her anger show.

"If you were not so extravagant—"

"My dear Hal," she interrupted, this time with a faint but discernible edge to her voice, "my extravagance, as you term it, consists of nothing more than living comfortably and fashionably, giving good wine and food to my guests, and dressing in the current mode. I assure you I live exactly as Tony would have expected me to live. He would be horrified at your pinch-penny ways."

"How you lived when he was alive was a different matter.

Now you have only your jointure to support you. You no longer enjoy the full extent of his income."

She leaned forward and said sweetly, "Then why didn't you negotiate a better settlement for me? You and Papa made every arrangement; I had no say in anything at all. I wonder you did not say 'I do' for me at the altar."

"I don't recall that you were coerced to say those words," he said aridly. "If you so dislike the present arrangement, I wonder you don't choose to alter your estate again. If you were to marry again advantageously, you might live as you please. Your jointure would continue, so you would even still have a degree of independence."

This too was an old argument, and Julia had no wish to be diverted from the present one. "I don't see any point in refusing to settle my accounts. If you do not do so this quarter, you must the next."

"Must I?" Hal said with a triumphant snort. "The terms of the jointure are that funds are to be distributed at my discretion."

"Is it discretion to cast me into ruin?"

"You have cast yourself into ruin, Julia," he replied in a pontifical way that made her want to throw something at him.

Julia sprang up from her chair, finally no longer able to contain her agitation. She took a few steps away from the desk and then turned abruptly to face him. "Let us be done with this stupid arguing, Hal," she said. "We both know you are not going to refuse to pay my debts indefinitely or allow me to be arrested and cast into the Fleet just to exact some sort of punishment because I purchased an extravagant court dress. If you imagine you can bully or frighten me into giving up my house and my independence, then it is you, I fear, who want sense."

"You are free to live as you please, Julia," Hal said with assumed indifference. "You are thirty years of age and responsible to no one but yourself. Lord knows there are enough in this town who do not regard a need to dodge their creditors as any check to their comfort. If you are of their number, then my concern is out of place; if not . . ." He paused and waited for her eyes to meet his. "If not, perhaps a bit of rustication at Plainfield or with Alicia at Dumphree would answer."

"In the midst of the Season?" she said, incredulous.

"London is at its most expensive during the Season," he responded blandly.

Julia was still uncertain whether or not he would carry out his threat to refuse to pay her debts. She did not want for common sense and knew that he was deliberately baiting her, but in spite of her words, she was a little frightened, and very, very angry.

Her situation was intolerable to her, but she had no choice but to accept it; it was Hal who held her purse strings. However much she might defy him with words, if he truly did refuse to pay her bills from her jointure, she would find herself virtually penniless. The residue of her nest egg would not be sufficient to keep her for a quarter, and when it was spent, there would be nothing at all.

But it was not her nature to bend easily, however forceful the gale. They might both know that he had the power to control her in this matter if he chose, but she would sooner hire herself out as a servant than acknowledge it. She smiled slowly and without humor. "I should have thought you would know by now that I can be led but not bullied."

"I have no wish to bully you, Julia," he said. "I am merely trying to manage your affairs to your best advantage. If you choose to ignore my advice, the consequences are on your own head."

She walked over to the table near the door where she had tossed her gloves and reticule when she had entered the room. With her back to her brother, she slowly drew on each glove. The only sound in the room was the ticking of the mantel clock, which seemed a bit louder with each passing second. She turned again with deliberation and said, "Go to the devil, Hal," and walked out of his study without waiting for his response.

During the drive to Half Moon Street, she kept her thoughts on a tight rein. Anger and fear were two of her emotions, but frustration at her own impotence was the uppermost. Whatever Hal chose to do—or not do—was completely out of her hands. Dwelling on their conversation would only aggravate her feelings and depress her spirits, and she would not allow that.

But her self-control was not as complete as she might have wished. She spoke pleasantly enough to Davies, her butler, when he let her into the house, but her assumption of serenity was short-lived when her companion followed her up to her room, ignoring Julia's hints that she did not wish to discuss her visit to Morland House.

Lettice Willoby was the sort of woman who looked exactly what she was: a dependent. If she had not been a companion, she would have been a governess or someone's maiden aunt. She was of medium height, medium weight, medium complexion. Her hair was neither brown nor blond; her eyes were neither blue nor gray. She smiled a great deal, not from humor but from a nervous habit; she was not stupid, but lacked wit; and there was about her an air of perpetual weariness that had nothing in common with the fashionable affectation of ennui.

Most of her friends marveled that Julia, who did not suffer fools gladly, would choose Miss Willoby as a companion, but in fact, she suited Julia quite well. They were not friends—there was too much disparity in personality and understanding for that—but Letty was generally self-effacing and tried her best never to give offense. It was certainly true, though, that Julia found her tiresome at times, but she could not help feeling sorry for Letty, who was only a few years older than she was but all her life had been dependent on the kindness of others. Given her own unwilling dependence on her brother to manage her affairs, Julia even felt a sort of empathy with her companion.

But Letty's principal appeal was that she was approved of by Morland. This was in no way an effort to please her brother but a means of stifling at least one objection to her living alone. More than once she had silenced his objections through the simple expedient of pointing out to him that she had a very proper companion to give her countenance with the world.

For the most part, Julia had no real difficulty getting on with Letty, but today her humor was considerably more exacerbated than usual. For once, Julia did not even attempt to keep back a sharp answer when Letty remarked for at least the third time that she hoped Julia was not put out of frame by any disagreement with her brother.

"Since I was in fair humor when I left the house and now I am not, the conclusion should be obvious," Julia said caustically. "With a bit of time for reflection I shall doubtless regain my temper."

Ignoring the hint yet again, Letty sat in a wing chair near

the fire and sighed unhappily. "Oh, dear. I am so sorry to hear you say so. I think it is such a sad thing for siblings to disagree, though it is not an uncommon thing, is it? And perhaps to be expected at times even in the closest relationships."

"Which mine with Hal is not."

"I know you and Lord Morland have a deep affection for each other," Letty said, ignoring or not hearing the acid note in Julia's voice. "He is always so helpful and protective of your interests."

"He is a damned interfering toad," Julia said unequivocally, the fine control on her temper escaping her at last.

"Oh, my dear Julia," Letty said with a nervous titter that, to Julia, was like nails raking slate. "You should not say so. I know you do not mean it."

"The devil I don't," Julia said with an unladylike snort. "He wants to bring me to heel and I'll be damned if I'll go meekly to his bidding."

"No, of course you should not," Letty agreed. "But I hope you said nothing to set up Lord Morland's back, my dear. I am sure he means only the best for you."

"I? Set up *his* back?" Julia said with outrage. "The man is insufferable."

"Perhaps he was just feeling out of sorts today," Letty soothed. "I have always found him to be very pleasant-spoken and kind."

Julia did not even attempt to retricve her lost patience at this ill-judged remark. "If you must be a damned fool, Letty, please do so elsewhere. It should be obvious to the meanest intelligence that I am out of temper, and your well-intentioned drivel is driving me out of my wits." Julia saw the look of hurt come into Lettice's eyes, and was instantly sorry that she had been so brutal.

Letty blinked her eyes rapidly to keep back starting tears. "I am sure I had no wish to give offense, Julia," she said with a faint catch in her voice that promised the beginning of a bout of tears. "It is only that I care for you and wish you would not be at outs with Lord Morland, for you know that he only wishes you to be happy and well."

"Oh, for God's sake," Julia cried in the accents of one goaded beyond endurance. "Letty, you know I have the devil's own temper when I am pushed too far. If you do care for me, have the good sense to leave me in peace before I say something unforgivable.''

Lettice's face began to crumple, but she made no move to get up from the chair and leave as requested. Julia was beginning to fear the worst: a bout of hysterics that she was in no humor to deal with. But she was saved this fate by the arrival of a footman with the news that Sir Royden Tallboys had called to see her.

Julia told the footman to tell Sir Royden that she would be with him in a moment, and then picked up her bonnet and her gloves again, which she had tossed onto a chair. ''Tell Midden that I shall be going out again, Letty,'' she said far more gently and as if there had been no quarrel. ''I am going to Lady Jeffers' rout tonight and will be back in time to change for dinner.''

With these words she turned her back on her companion and quit the room, not even looking to see if Lettice had heard her. She found Sir Royden in the front saloon and she addressed him with purpose. ''I am so glad you have come, Royden. Do you drive your grays today?''

''As a matter of fact, yes,'' Tallboys replied with a quizzical smile. ''Does it matter?''

''It does if you will take me out at once for a drive. I want to drive beyond the city and go like the wind.''

Tallboys laughed, but his expression was still bemused. ''With my very great pleasure. What has engendered this wish for speed and flight?''

''If I told you now, I should sound like a spoiled child in the throws of a tantrum,'' Julia said with a self-mocking smile. ''I shall tell you when we are halfway to Richmond.''

Sir Royden agreed to be patient and within the half-hour they were traveling at a speed that few other matched teams could equal. When at last the grays began to flag and Tallboys slowed them to an easy trot, Julia told him of her interview with her brother and subsequent guilt over her exasperation with Letty.

Julia always found Royden a comfortable companion. He had been a good friend of her husband's, though several years younger than Sir Anthony, and since his death, her friendship with Royden had grown considerably. He was also an exceptionally attractive man with dark-gray eyes and light-brown hair expertly cut in the style known as the Brutus. Julia was by no means immune to his attractiveness.

When Hal made oblique reference to her making another, advantageous marriage, she had no doubt it was Royden he had in mind. Julia was well aware that it was whispered in both ballrooms and clubs that she and Royden would make a match of it. No doubt Royden was equally aware of it, but so far he had given her no hint that he intended to offer for her, despite the increasing amount of time that they spent in each other's company.

Julia had seen something in his eyes that told her he found her equally attractive, even desirable, but she did not regard this as evidence that he wished to marry her. Julia was beautiful, bright, and vivacious, but since her widowhood had commenced, it was not offers of a permanent kind that most gentlemen had made to her. She was far from blind to her shortcomings. However much she might possess the reputation of an accredited beauty, she knew that many men were put off by her independence, her quick wit and intelligence, and her reputation for being expensive and just a little bit fast. Until very recently this had not concerned her in the least.

Though Julia's marriage had been arranged for her by her father, she had never held Sir Anthony in aversion, as was so often the attitude of heroines in similar circumstances in popular romances. She had liked Tony from the time they had met, and in a fashion, she had even grown to feel a more tender emotion toward him. He had been kind to her and generous, and she had thoroughly enjoyed her life as a fashionable matron. But she had had no illusions that she was in love with Tony or he with her.

Julia would have scoffed at any description of herself as a romantic, but she was never entirely unconscious of the fact that love, at least the love extolled by the poets, was an emotion of which she knew nothing. She had always had admirers, some of whom had unquestionably cared deeply for her and whose hearts she had severely wounded, if not broken; but her regard for these men, though sincere, was never returned to such a degree.

During her marriage she had blamed her inability to return the love of any other man on the values that, despite her love of the dashing and outrageous, would not permit her to break the vows of fidelity she had made to her husband. There were occasional whispered *on-dits* that she had taken one or another of her admirers as her lover, but it had never been true, and she believed that she had not allowed herself to love for fear that she would fall into adultery, which was abhorrent to her.

But now that she was a widow, as long as she was appropriately discreet, she might have followed her heart with greater impunity. And yet it had never happened. No matter how attracted or enthralled with her latest flirt, she had never succumbed to love, either sublime or passionate. It had gained her the further reputation as a care-for-nobody who collected hearts foolish enough to be worn on a would-be lover's sleeve. She concluded, not without a degree of regret, that she was simply not the sort to fall in love.

Since this was the case, she had supposed she would never remarry, but after three years of her brother's quarter-day complaints and condemnation, three years of the struggle to maintain herself without compromising her style or independence, and three years of returning each night, in a manner of speaking, to an empty house and bed, Julia had begun to think that she might again be willing to exchange her freedom for the silken bonds of matrimony. That it would be another marriage of convenience, she had no doubt. Of the fact that Sir Royden would suit every particular of what she wished for in a second husband, she was equally sure. The only difficulty was that, despite his patent interest, he had yet to come up to scratch.

"Letty means well, of course," Julia said at the end of her recital, "but I could throttle her when she tries to pour balm on every wound. I know that Hal wants what he thinks is best for me, but what he thinks is best is usually vastly different from what I think best."

"And you don't need to be reminded of his good intentions when you are in a passion with him," Tallboys said, turning to her with a quick, understanding smile. "I certainly agree that you were right to tell him to go to the devil when he suggested that you rusticate. Your admirers would be devastated if you abandoned town at the height of the Season."

"Oh, hardly that," she said, casting him a flirtatious sidelong glance. There was something in his voice that made her think he would particularly dislike it if she were to absent herself from town. Perhaps it was wishful thinking, but the maxim "Absence makes the heart grow fonder" suddenly occurred to her. "You should not encourage me to such vanity, Royden. With so many lovely young girls presented this Season, I doubt anyone would even notice that I had gone."

"I should certainly notice."

Julia lowered her eyes, not in coyness, but for fear she would give her thoughts away. For the first time she seriously entertained her brother's suggestion that she visit their sister in Wiltshire. "Should you? You are sweet to say so, but I don't believe you, you know." Julia was well aware that "Out of sight, out of mind" might apply as easily as "Absence makes the heart grow fonder," but if it were the latter, her absence might make him discover that she was more necessary to his happiness than he had realized; it might just provide the push he needed to make her an offer of marriage.

Sir Royden Tallboys was a man of taste and fashion who had just reached his forty-fifth year. He moved in the most exalted of circles; a member of the Carlton House set, without the reputation some had for vulgarity and excess. He had inherited a substantial fortune not long after attaining his majority and lived in the highest kick of style without ever seeming to deplete it. He had never married and most matchmaking mamas had long since given up hope of snaring him for their daughters. But many men of means and independent spirit married later in life and it was still not impossible that he might decide to take a wife.

By the time he set her down again in Half Moon Street, Julia had not only regained her usual equanimity, but was even in spirits. Speculative thoughts chased about in her head and she began to seriously wonder if Royden could be induced to make her an offer. If she could believe the sincerity she thought she heard in his voice when he had said he would miss her, it might be more than wishful thinking. She found she was quite pleased at the prospect that it could be so, and perhaps even more, she was excited by the challenge of the chase.

In her earlier bad temper Julia had almost settled against going to Lady Jeffers' rout, but she wished to see her brother, whom she knew would also be present, to speak to him about going to Dumphree without actually seeming to seek him out. It would never do to capitulate too readily to Hal's demands. Even if she told him the truth of her change of heart, which she emphatically would not, he would probably only believe that it was an excuse to save face.

Though Julia was blessed with the sort of well-formed figure that looked good in almost anything she chose to wear, she took particular pains with her dress and toilette, for she had two men she was determined to charm. She decided on an ivory silk gown of daring cut with a silver gauze overdress that was designed to dazzle Sir Royden without overly offending her more conservative brother. Her only concession to the chill of a February night and rooms that were certain to be underheated was a matching gauze shawl, which she draped over her arms with studied carelessness.

That she had succeeded in dressing to advantage was obvious from the appreciative looks cast her way the moment she entered the room. The first man to approach her, though, took no particular notice of her appearance. He was an exceptionally handsome young man with softly curling black hair, dark-brown eyes that one hopeful beauty had described as smoldering, and features that were perfect enough to be struck on a coin. Only this evening his beauty was marred by a petulant frown.

Julia, seeing him approach her in a determined way, suppressed a sigh. She was quite fond of Viscount Linton, her eldest nephew, in the usual way. Because of the disparity in age between Julia and Hal, only eight years separated Julia from her nephew, but she was often thrust into the role of mother-confidante to Harry because he found her far easier and more sympathetic to talk to than either of his parents.

Unfortunately, he was of an impetuous nature, which had led him into a number of scrapes and near scandals since he had been on the town, and which had resulted in a number of tearful scenes with his mother and furious dressing-downs from his father. But Julia he could always count on to listen to him without censure. She would simply tell him plainly that he was a damned fool, or if she thought him wronged, she would take his part.

This evening, though, Julia had her own purposes to accomplish and was in no humor for the role of confidante, and judging by the viscount's unhappy expression, she had no doubt that he wished to unburden himself of whatever it was that had resulted in his distemper.

"Just the person I wished to see," Harry said without any other greeting. He hooked his hand under her elbow and led her into a corner of the room. "I need you to speak to Father for me, Aunt Jule. He's being dashed unreasonable about my allowance just because . . . Well, never mind the reason, but he said he won't pay my bills for me unless I do what he wants. I don't see what's funny about it," he added crossly as Julia's bubbling laugher rose to the surface.

"My dear Linton, I am the last person to talk to your father about this. I am under a similar command. Did you tell him to go to the devil? I did."

The viscount's brow cleared and he grinned appreciatively. "Did you, by God? I'd have given a monkey to have seen his face."

"He was a trifle upset," Julia acknowledged. "I wonder what on earth has come over Hal? He does like to keep his hands on the reins, but he is usually not despotic."

Linton gave vent to a snort. "You don't live with him, Aunt Jule. He'd live all of our lives for us if he could, but you're independent and can tell him to go to the devil. Jenny and I are forced to live with it."

Julia patted his arm affectionately. "You know I am no champion of your father, but you really can't blame him completely for his concern about your opera dancer," she said, betraying that her knowledge of his present difficulties was greater than he had guessed. "You have been making yourself the talk of the town with her of late, and Ballentree told me the other day that the betting is five to four that you'll make her an offer."

The viscount's jaw dropped and his frown returned. "Dash it, Aunt Jule, you shouldn't even know things like that, let alone say them to me and discuss them with someone like that court card Ballentree."

Julia laughed. "There is more of your father in you than you know," she said with a faint tartness. "Freddy Ballentree is very elegant and wouldn't thank you for that animadversion.

You should know by now that I have no patience with missishness.''

''Is that why you are in father's black books?'' Linton asked, curious. ''Have you done something outrageous again, Aunt?''

Julia shook her head. Sir Royden came into the room and she caught his eye and smiled. She had the satisfaction of seeing him come directly toward her. ''No,'' she said to her nephew. ''I bought a new dress for Jenny's presentation and had a lecture on extravagance read to me. I am to be rusticated so that I may ponder the virtues of frugality.''

''Not really?'' he said, surprised, and after a moment added with a puzzled expression, ''I thought you told Father to go to the devil?''

''I did,'' Julia said with another smile for Royden, who was only a few yards away. ''But I since have decided that a visit to Wiltshire may suit me, after all.''

''Why?''

''Because I am a dutiful sister,'' she said evenly. ''Go away, you tiresome boy. You ask far too many questions.''

''You are up to something, Aunt Julia.''

''What might that be?'' Tallboys asked as he bowed over Julia's hand with a warm smile in his eyes that Julia found quite gratifying.

''I have decided to do as Hal wishes and pay a visit to our sister, Lady Dumphrees,'' she replied readily. ''Harry mistrusts my motive for being so meek.''

''So do I,'' the baronet said at once. ''You can't mean it, Julia. Why should you wish to go now, of all times, at the height of the Season?''

''Perhaps I have finally reached the age where I am beginning to find the constant round of parties and gatherings a bit wearing,'' she responded evasively. ''One is forever stumbling over the same people wherever one goes.''

Her nephew's expression told her what he thought of that excuse while Royden said he thought it a very good thing to always find oneself among friends. Julia, however, reasserted her intention to travel to Wiltshire and made it a definite thing when she sought out her brother later in the evening and informed him of her decision to visit their sister.

Morland was both surprised and gratified and completely forgot that he was out of temper with her. Though he did not offer to immediately pay her creditors, he did say that he hoped that she would spend time meditating on habits of economy so that she could start out the following quarter on a better footing, which Julia took as tacit agreement that he would pay her bills and allow her to begin the next quarter with a clean slate.

2

The majority of Julia's friends expressed surprise when they heard the news that she meant to bury herself in the country for a month or more, not only as the Season was getting under way, but at a time of year when rustic pleasures were at their least attractive. One who flatly refused to believe Julia's excuse that she was weary of the frivolities of town and the shallowness of society was Lady Frances Boyce.

Lady Fanny was an attractive widow who was similarly circumstanced to Julia. She was three-and-thirty and had been married by her family to a man considerably her senior who had been carried off by an inflammation of the lungs about five years previously. Unlike Julia, she had neither the means nor the inclination to set up her own establishment. Since her union was also childless, her husband's title and estates had gone to a nephew, and Fanny had returned to live with her mother and father, the Earl and Countess of Cirland.

She and Julia had been friends since schoolroom days and she was the one person in all of the world whom Julia permitted to tell her she was a fool and to whose advice she listened, at least for the most part. When Julia finally admitted to Fanny that she had an ulterior motive for agreeing to her brother's demands, Fanny was plainly skeptical.

"But, my dear," Fanny said as they sat at tea in Fanny's sitting room at Cirland House, "I don't see that rusticating is in the least necessary. I have been telling you this past month that Royden is on the verge of casting his cap over the windmill. If you will just be patient, I think we shall see you wed before the Little Season without any need for you to take such a drastic measure. Besides, are you really sure that this is what you want? I can remember you saying after Tony died that you doubted you would ever wish to change your estate again."

Julia shrugged. "What I have changed is my mind. I have

given it considerable thought and I do think that Royden and I would suit admirably. We have so very much in common and think so much alike that we are always in harmony and what else can one reasonably ask for in a lifetime companion? You know what I think of people like my excessively romantic nephew, who is always imagining himself to be desperately in love. He hasn't the least judgment in matters of the heart and will likely choose a mate based on the strength of his attraction to her rather than the likelihood that the love he feels for her will endure when the attraction finally fades, which of course it always does."

Fanny shook her head and sighed. "Julia, you are a hopeless unromantic. Did it occur to you that you are an opposite extreme?"

Julia shrugged, unconcerned. "I shall pit my philosophies against the romantics anytime when it comes to endurance."

"Shall you?" Fanny said, leaning forward to pour more tea for herself and Julia. "I hope you may be right."

"So do I," Julia concurred with a laugh. "But why do you think I may not be?" she asked as she took her filled cup from Fanny.

Fanny sat back and contemplated her friend for a few moments. "Is it an offer from Royden that you want, or the satisfaction of receiving it?" she asked baldly.

Julia's mouth opened in surprise. "What a dreadful thing to suggest."

"Remember whom you are saying that to," Fanny said, unrepentant. "I know you, Julia. What a feather it would be in your cap to be the one woman who has finally brought the elusive Sir Royden Tallboys to heel."

Julia was not smiling. "I don't find that a very attractive reading of my character."

"Oh, I don't mean you would deliberately set out to break his heart; you have said in any case that there is no pretense of grand passion between you. I simply am commenting on the fact that you are always attracted to a challenge. It is the excitement of the chase, I think, more so than the capture or your quarry, that gives you pleasure."

Julia was not precisely mollified. "I think you are unkind, Fanny. This is hardly a chase. I have told you that I have decided that Royden and I should suit through considered thought and a weighing of circumstances."

"How cold-blooded," Fanny said with a laugh. "I am not sure it would not be better if conquest were your motive."

Julia broke into a reluctant smile. "You may be right, but I would rather enter a union based on common sense and common interests than on a fleeting passion. I leave that to my romantic nephew and his ilk."

Grist for her argument was provided by Linton when he called on her at the end of the week, once again clearly seeking to unburden himself of some unhappiness. The high flyer who had so besieged his heart and caused Lord Morland much concern decided to bestow her favor on a marquess, who, though not as beautiful as Linton, was in full possession of his fortune and not dependent on an allowance from his father to buy her whatever expensive trinket took her fancy.

"The devil of it is," the viscount said, having, in his wretchedness, gotten over his squeamishness about discussing his paramour with his aunt, "I was never really certain I was in love with her. So why should I feel so dashed rotten that she's found someone else? I should be glad that I found out she was just a common light-skirt before I did get in over my head."

"Pride, of course," Julia said. "It always stngs when we discover that someone we cared for didn't care for us very much, after all. Just before I became brothed to Tony, I had met the handsomest and most dashing man I had ever seen and I was quite certain that he had formed a *tendre* for me as well. But nothing ever came of it, and it wasn't until after I was married that Mama told me that Papa had warned him off because he was determined that I marry Tony. Even though it had never come to anything, I felt hurt that he had been so easily dissuaded against me."

"Do you think that Father has done the same thing with Danielle?" Harry asked, a shade of eagerness in his voice.

Julia had not meant to give him false hope. "No. Morland would think it beneath him. He would rather manipulate you more directly," she added with an edge of sardonicism. "Why don't you come with me to Dumphrees," she said on impulse. "If you stay in town, you will have to bear the humiliation of seeing her on the arm of her marquess, and a bit of fresh air and exercise might be just the thing to clear your mind and make you realize that she is not worth feeling rotten about."

Linton laughed and in an attempt at lightness declared that if he went at all, it would be to see what mischief Julia intended, since he didn't buy for a moment her claim that she was bored with society. But even though he wasn't serious when he spoke those words, in the end he did escort his aunt to Wiltshire. Julia came very near to regretting her well-intentioned offer, though. Instead of riding beside the carriage as escort as she had supposed he would, Harry, still hurting from the rejection of his opera dancer, rode with her in the chaise for most of the journey, not only bemoaning the end of that romance, but rehashing the whole of his stormy romantic history.

Though the temptation to tell him to take a damper was occasionally strong, Julia understood that with his emotional nature he felt these things very deeply and needed someone to unburden himself to. She listened patiently, only occasionally letting her attention wander, and she consoled herself with the knowledge that Dumphrees would be reached by dinnertime.

Their well-sprung chaise and four pulled into the courtyard of the Hart and Hare in Amesbury for the last change before reaching Dumphrees, and Julia said in the hope of diverting her nephew, "I think I would like to get down and go inside for some lemonade and biscuits. Tony always said they had an excellent home-brewed here if you're feeling thirsty."

The viscount shrugged, uninterested. "Why bother? You know Aunt Alicia keeps country hours. She'll likely be herding us into the dining room the minute we walk through the door."

"Oh, no, Harry," she said as she signaled to the nearest post boy that she wished for the steps to be let down. "You forget that my sister sets a great deal by form. She will insist that we change into proper dinner attire even if we cause her cook to burn the roast while we do so."

Linton said again that he saw no point in the delay when they were so close to their journey's end, but Julia ignored him and went into the inn.

The Hart and Hare was a large and spacious posting inn catering to the quality. Inside, the common room was elegantly furnished with polished wood tables and chairs, most of which were well-filled with an odd assortment of travelers and people from the neighborhood.

Many heads turned when Julia walked into the room. She was a beautiful woman, and she was dressed elegantly in a dark plaid carriage dress unquestionably of the latest fashion. The stares of the men were frankly admiring and those of the women envious. Julia entered the room, apparently oblivious to all regard, but in fact, she noticed several gentlemen who would have caught her eye if they could, and one in particular at a corner table by himself, who did not even appear to notice that she had come into the room.

Why this particular man had caught her interest, she could not say. He was quite attractive, though not in the blatant manner of Viscount Linton. He rose even as she noticed him, and she saw that he was above average height, well-formed, and well-dressed, if not like her, in the first stare of fashion. His hair was the brown of rich sable and his eyes a dark-green hazel that was revealed to her when he passed her and their eyes met for the briefest of moments.

He looked through her rather than at her in the manner of strangers, and yet Julia had the impression that he was not unaware of her. She regarded him with frank appraisal as he walked to the door, ignoring the landlord, who had come up to her to ask her her pleasure. It was only Linton coming in the door exactly as the other man was about to go out of it, that brought Julia out of her contemplation and made her aware of her rudeness.

When they were seated and the waiter had brought them their simple repast, curiosity made Julia ask the servant if he knew who the man was who had been seated at the corner table, which was still empty since he had left it.

Julia was rewarded with an affirmative answer and more information than she had hoped to garner. "Oh, aye," he said readily. "That be Mr. Sales, m'lady. He what studies nature or somethin' like it with old Mr. Carstiars at Longview, which is just north of here. The old man is right famous, I've heard, though I don't know much about plants and insects myself."

Linton gave his aunt a curious look. "What was that about, Aunt Jule? Casting about for flirts already," he said to quiz her.

Julia refused the bait. "I just thought he looked familiar," she said in an offhand way. "I don't know him, of course, and it isn't likely that I'll see him again, in any case."

But Julia was mistaken. By the time they left the inn, it had begun to rain, and shortly after they returned to the road, the rain turned to a downpour. The water came down upon them in sheets, forcing the coachman to slow from a canter to a slow trot. Gradually the rain began to ease again, but the road was a slippery mire, and they continued at this pace to avoid sliding into the ditch.

"At this rate, we shall be fortunate to reach Dumphree before they close the house up for the night," Harry complained. "I knew we shouldn't have stopped at the inn."

"Be glad of it," Julia advised him. "If we arrive after Alicia's cook has gone to bed, it may well be the only meal you will have tonight."

Their ride was becoming increasingly uncomfortable as the carriage wheels slid in and out of ruts brought on by the rain, and for one frightening moment the vehicle seemed to pitch and veer to one side, convincing Julia that they were about to be cast into the ditch. It was, in fact, a near thing. In an effort to pull aside for a faster-moving approaching vehicle, the coachman had maneuvered the chaise a bit near to the edge of the road and had nearly lost control of the carriage.

Linton heard the approach of the other carriage and pulled down the window on his side despite Julia's complaint that they would likely be spattered with mud as it passed. It proved to be a curricule driven by a pair and driven to an inch as the driver passed without any shortening of rein. Julia did not watch in open admiration as Harry did when the carriage passed them, but she glanced toward the window for a moment and in that moment she saw that the driver was the man she had noticed at the inn.

Julia found her interest piqued once again. Sufficiently so that she allowed her imagination to speculate on who he might be for the remainder of the drive; and later, when they had finally arrived at their destination, she decided to make a point of asking her sister if she knew of Mr. Sales.

Alicia Dumphrees was a placid, almost bovine woman who, now that her children were grown and settled, rarely left

Dumphree except for visits to neighbors or excursions into the village of Lesser Ansdown for shopping. Though there was a physical resemblance between her and Julia, the eighteen years that separated the sisters and Alicia's inattention to style prevented many from noting it.

Alicia took it in her stride that her nephew and his valet would also be staying with her, though she had had no notion of it until they arrived. She welcomed Julia with a sort of mellow enthusiasm. "Not, my dear," she said to Julia, "that you shall find as much to occupy you here as you would have in town, but we are not without entertainments entirely. We dine with friends at least once or twice a week, and at the end of the month the weekly assemblies at Amesbury will begin for the spring."

Julia laughed. "Oh, I expect we shall be gay to dissipation. You needn't worry about entertaining me, Allie, I can ride and walk and read, which I never seem to have time to do in town, and if I am bored, I shall have no one to blame but myself."

But the words were said for her sister's benefit. Julia had never spent more than a fortnight at one time in the country since her marriage, and then only at large fashionable house parties. She had very little doubt that she would find herself sunk in ennui before the end of a sennight.

Julia waited until she and Alicia were alone in the drawing room after dinner, while Harry and Lord Dumphree enjoyed their port, before asking her sister about the man she had seen at the inn. She was not certain why she had this unaccustomed curiosity about Mr. Sales, and felt a little foolish for it. Perhaps she was, as Harry had suggested, merely casting about for a flirt to wile away her visit in the country.

"Are you acquainted with a Mr. Sales who appears to be visiting in the neighborhood of Amesbury, Allie?" she asked, her question made less remarkable by the fact that they were in the middle of a discussion of neighbors in the district with whom Julia was acquainted. "Is he anything to the Westmorland Sales?"

"Dominic Sales? Do you know him, Julie?" she asked with surprise. "He is something of a mystery, though he is very well regarded."

Julia avoided her query. "A mystery? Is he? In what fashion?"

"He admits to being related to the Westmorland Sales, but other than that, no one seems to know very much about him, other than Caroline Amberly, and she is being uncharacteristically closemouthed about him. He was born in England and educated here, I gather, but he lived most of his childhood in the West Indies. I do seem to recall something about a cousin of the then Marquess of Sales—that would be poor Robert Sales' father—going west to seek his fortune when I was still in the schoolroom. This is his son, no doubt."

"But where is the mystery?" Julia asked, setting down her teacup and then curling herself comfortably in her chair. "His history may be interesting, but hardly remarkable."

"I merely meant that people are curious about him, and he speaks so little of himself other than in his interest in naturalism that it makes one wonder what there is to hide."

"Probably not the least thing," Julia said with a laugh. "I had almost forgotten how little people have to occupy their minds in the country. Everyone condemns fashionable society for its penchant for gossip, but I declare it is far worse in places like this."

"Oh, far, far worse," Alicia agreed amiably.

"Then tell me the gossip about Mr. Sales," Julia prompted.

Alicia was nothing loath to oblige her. "He is a naturalist, and frankly, I don't think much of anything else interests him. I don't mean to say that he has no conversation, but he is quiet and, though personable enough, he does not go out of his way to be friendly."

"A misanthrope," Julia said, summing him up. She felt a faint stab of disappointment at these words. Her sister's description of his character made her feel that his acquaintance was not worth the trouble of pursuing. She could not imagine anything more deadly dull than conversations about plants and animals and local topography, which she supposed must comprise his interests. "Does one meet him in company often?"

"Fairly often. He leases the old Dower House at Amberly and is often to be found in company when the Amberlys are present. They are our closest neighbors, you know, so we see quite a bit of them. You have not yet told me how you know of him,'' Alicia said, remarking her sister's evasion.

''A chance encounter on the road,'' Julia replied, seeing no reason to dissemble. ''He is an attractive man and I am merely curious.''

''You shall certainly meet him, and soon,'' Alicia promised. ''We dine with the Amberlys at the end of the week.''

''I don't know that I particularly care to meet him,'' Julia said truthfully and with a faint note of regret. ''He sounds a dead bore.''

''Then I have given you the wrong impression. He is hardly that.'' Alicia gave her sister a speculative look. ''I would not dismiss him too readily, Julia. Caro has hinted to me that even though he lives simply, he is a man of considerable substance. I think that if he only had a title, she would be throwing Sophia at his head, but she is determined to snare a title for Sophie if she can manage it. As her aunt and guardian she feels she must make the best possible match for the girl.''

''Why should his circumstances be of any interest to me?'' Julia asked, sitting forward a little. ''I am not on the catch for a rich husband.''

''No? Has Hal changed his nip-farthing ways? I think I would be casting about for a means of escape from his control if I were you. A husband of means would offer a comfortable solution.''

Julia relaxed again. She feared that she had in some way communicated her real motive for coming to Dumphree to Elizabeth and that she had written of it to Alicia, but Alicia appeared to be speaking only in generalities. ''It would. But I rather doubt that an unknown rustic, be he ever so rich, would make me a comfortable husband. Tell me who else I might meet while I'm here. I hope there is someone other than Mr. Sales that I can set up as my flirt to amuse myself.''

Alicia readily complied, but as the week progressed, Julia's hopes of finding some diversion to allay her boredom had yet to be realized. Harry had little difficulty finding amusement. Lord Dumphree was a sporting man and they spent much of their days riding, fishing, and shooting, and even traveled one morning to a neighboring town for a racing meet.

In contrast, Lady Dumphree was perfectly content to spend

her days engaged in no more strenuous activity than writing letters to her numerous correspondents, or embroidering altar cloths and chair covers. Neighbors of course visited, but Mr. Sales was not at Amberly when they called, nor did he come with Lady Amberly and her daughter when they visited Dumphree on Saturday morning to welcome Julia to the neighborhood.

Julia forbore to ask questions about him of Lady Amberly in part because she did not wish to display her interest and also because that interest had waned considerably since her conversation with Alicia the previous day. When he was not at church on Sunday, Julia did make note of it to Alicia, and was told that Mr. Sales frequently was away for a few days at a time in pursuit of his avocation.

On Wednesday she persuaded Harry to forgo the pleasure of a day's fishing to go on an exploratory ride through the countryside with her, but his idea of a comfortable ride was to take a neck-or-nothing pace over the roughest possible country. It was a successful cure for her immediate boredom, but she was exhausted from keeping up with his pace and the challenge of maintaining her seat over barriers that a member of the Quorn would not have scorned.

The next morning, over the protests of her sister, who did not think it proper even in the country for a female to ride unattended, Julia went out on her own to enjoy a good gallop and to familiarize herself further with the neighborhood, which she had not visited in over a year.

On Friday, the day they were to dine at Amberly, Julia deliberately rode in that direction. Though she told herself that she no longer cared whether or not she met the elusive Mr. Sales, she found herself speculating as she rode whether or not he would be at Amberly that evening, and if he were, whether she would find him as tedious as she supposed or as attractive as she remembered.

She had been to Amberly many times and was familiar with the grounds, but she had never really noted the old Dower House. Set quite a distance from the main house, it had been replaced by a new and far more modern structure by the present Lord Amberly's mother, who had flatly refused to live in the

Jacobean structure when her son had taken residence after his succession to the title.

Julia told herself that she rode in that direction from mild curiosity to see the old Dower House, but in fact, she gave it no more than a cursory appraisal before riding on. It was a stone-and-wood structure of rambling design with casement windows and numerous chimneys. It looked at once both charming and probably drafty and uncomfortable. Used herself to her modern Georgian town house, she could not blame the now-deceased dowager viscountess for opting for her comfort.

She had no fear of meeting Mr. Sales again by chance, but she did not particularly wish to be caught out staring at the house in case he was in residence, after all. Julia kept to the edge of the wood, where she could see the house freely without being readily seen from inside.

She was aware of an ambivalent wish both to see him again and to avoid him. She was still convinced that she would have no interest in a man who cared only for spiders and twigs—as she regarded naturalism—but there was little else to occupy her fancy and it was as good as any other way to waste a morning rather than spending it hemming linens.

Except for whisps of smoke rising from one of the chimneys of Dower House, there was no sign of habitation. Not even a dog barked. Having seen her fill of unresponsive stone and glass, Julia turned her horse into the wood and found the path that would take her back to the principal road.

She was aware, from the position of the sun in the sky, that she had been out much longer than was her custom. Fearing that Alicia would be anxious for her welfare, since she had so disliked Julia going out without even a groom for escort, she left the road as soon as she reached the beginning of Dumphree land and began to ride cross-country.

At the place near the home farm where the main road cut through the Dumphree estate, she saw two horsemen standing, speaking with two other men, one of whom Julia recognized as Mr. Brady, her brother-in-law's bailiff.

As she rode by them, the bailiff caught sight of her and saluted her. Julia returned his greeting, and as she did so, one of the two horsemen, whose backs were to the road, turned in the saddle. She recognized Dominic Sales at once. To Julia's surprise, a faint smile of recognition touched his lips and she acknowledged him with an equally faint incline of her head as she rode on.

To her amazement, her heartbeat became a bit faster. She was not a stranger to this reaction toward a man she found attractive, but she could not imagine it stemming from an interest she categorized as tepid at best. Almost involuntarily she turned in the saddle to glance at him again over her shoulder, and saw that he had turned also to watch her. She quickly looked away and spurred her horse to a trot and then to a canter. She felt a warmth in her cheeks and could not but laugh at herself for a response she categorized as that of a schoolroom miss in the first flush of infatuation.

Though she was amused at herself for her odd behavior, which she supposed was the result of her increasing boredom, she nevertheless dressed with particular care for dinner at Amberly that evening, donning a silk gown of a brilliant-rose shade that few could have worn with success but that she knew became her excessively. Demure pearls glowed at her throat to mitigate the boldness of her dress. She had Midden dress her hair *à la grecque*, which she knew accentuated her high cheekbones and finely shaped nose and chin. She blackened her lashes to bring out their great length and curl and rouged her cheeks in just sufficient quantity to mimic a natural, becoming blush. When her toilette was finally complete, she pirouetted before the cheval glass in her bedchamber and smiled with satisfaction, quite confident that she would not escape the notice of Mr. Sales, should he be present.

When they arrived at the Amberlys', Julia, with long practice, managed to scan the room for sight of her quarry without giving the least appearance of doing so. She was disappointed. There were a dozen or so people present, most of whom were familiar to Julia, but Mr. Sales was not among them. Her feeling of letdown was instantaneous, and to her mind ludicrous. She put all thought of him from her mind and allowed her sister to guide her about the room, introducing her to those present with whom she had yet to become acquainted.

The company was pleasant enough and the dinner was excellent, but Julia found she was not in a humor to be pleased.

She responded in her usual friendly and spontaneous manner to everyone she met, but there was a flatness to the evening that she could not really justify. But her breeding was equal to the most tedious of evenings, and there was nothing outward in her manner to suggest that she was counting time until they would leave.

After dinner the ladies retired to the drawing room, which had been set up with several tables for cards and groupings of sofas and chairs for conversation. It was to the latter that the ladies gravitated to enjoy a bit of pleasurable gossip until the gentlemen joined them. Since Julia knew so few people in the neighborhood very well, she had little interest in this and sat instead on a sofa a little apart from the others beside Miss Sophia Sutton, Lady Amberly's niece and ward. Though exceptionally pretty, Sophia was a very shy and retiring girl who appeared to be a bit ill at ease with the other, older women.

Julia had been a superb hostess during her marriage, with the reputation for being able to draw out the most difficult and self-effacing guests, and she proved her talent with Miss Sutton, who, after a few awkward starts at conversation, was soon speaking with her in a fairly free and animated manner. Though the young girl's conversation was of nothing more than her life at Amberly and her visits to friends and shopping expeditions to Amesbury, Julia had a kind heart and she listened attentively and stoically. She might have done so with perfect goodwill for the remainder of the evening if necessary, but she was soon rescued when the men began to straggle into the room.

Linton was among the first of them and he came over to them at once, placing himself in a chair across from them, but nearest to Miss Sutton.

Julia saw from his expression that he felt admiration for Miss Sutton, and smiled to herself. She was not surprised. Sophia Sutton was truly lovely; if Caroline Amberly could cure her of her painful shyness, she would doubtless take very well. She might even snare the title that her aunt wished for her when she made her curtsy to the polite world in May.

Julia feared that the girl's shyness would return when Harry joined them, but he was blessed with the same gift of being able to put people at their ease as she was, and Sophia, whether consciously or unconsciously aware of his admiration, became increasingly easy and animated after he sat down with them. After a few minutes, Julia felt she might safely leave them to their conversation, since they seemed to have forgotten her presence in any case.

She walked over to the pianoforte, which had been moved to a more prominent position in the room as an invitation to anyone who wished to play it. She began sorting through music with half a mind to play, when she was joined by General Watney, who with a ponderous attempt at banter persuaded her to sit at the instrument.

As much for her own amusement as to oblige him, Julia played through several popular airs, which he joined her in singing, though slightly off-pitch. She then began to play a Mozart sonata she had unearthed, hoping that he would be bored by it and find his way over to one of the card tables. But the general continued to stand beside her, still addressing comments to her, oblivious to her need to concentrate on the notes before her. It was in glancing up to return some answer to a question he had posed that Julia's eyes caught the entrance of Mr. Sales.

She had given up expecting him, but it was not only surprise that caused her to miss several notes when his eyes rested briefly on her before he went over to Lady Amberly to bow over her hand. Julia's reaction was similar to what it had been that morning, but this time she took the trouble to ponder it.

There was definitely the pull of a physical attraction; whenever their eyes met, she felt a faint inward shiver, almost a sense of anticipation. He was unquestionably a good-looking man, but not at all the sort of fashionable man of the town toward whom she was usually attracted. Yet there was something about him that intrigued her. She felt a sense of anomaly about him: an inward, tightly leashed intensity overlaid with an unremarkable, civilized exterior.

The words "a wolf in sheep's clothing" came to her, and if she had been alone, she would have laughed at herself for her flight of fancy. A quick survey of the room also told her that he was the only man present—for that matter, the only man she had met since coming to Wiltshire who had at all captured her interest. And, in fact, she had not yet even been introduced to Mr. Sales.

Whatever Sales thought of her, he appeared to make no special effort to seek her out, moving about the room at his ease, falling into conversation with various friends. Yet Julia, without vanity, was certain that he was as aware of her as she was of him, for it had seemed to her that just as she had scanned the room to look for him when she had arrived, he had done the same looking for her. She knew it might be only wishful thinking, but she believed that he would eventually seek her out.

The general made some comment that required a response, but she had not heeded it in the least and he called her to order for inattention. Julia, with her usual grace, managed to soothe him with a laughing reference to her musicianship, and turned away from her contemplation of the attractive Mr. Sales. But he was not far from her thoughts and she was beginning to wonder if the general would not prove a more difficult companion to shake than Miss Sutton had been, when Lady Amberly at last brought Mr. Sales to the pianoforte to introduce him to Julia.

"Dominic has begged me to make him known to the beauty at the pianoforte who plays so angelically," the viscountess said coyly as she presented Mr. Sales to Julia. "He is also quite musical and has entertained our dear Sophia many nights with his skill. Perhaps you may play a duet for us before the evening is out." Lady Amberly then made a remark to the general and bore him away, for which Julia was grateful.

Julia thought she caught a trace of mockery in Dominic Sales eyes as he bowed over her hand, though she could not guess why it should be there.

"We have nearly met before, I think, Lady Julia," he said, and she was pleased to hear that his voice was rich and resonant, with an underlying silken quality that she found particularly attractive.

"At the Hart and Hare," Julia said promptly, having no wish to appear to be a coy or simpering miss.

There was almost a blank look in his eyes for a moment and then he smiled. "Ah yes. I do recall that. But it was another occasion that I am speaking of."

Julia knew he could not mean her passing him on the road that morning, but she had no recollection that she had ever set eyes on him before the day she had arrived in Dumphree, and she frankly said so.

"No. I know you do not." He laughed in a self-deprecating way. "At the time you were a dashing young matron and I was a gauche young man, more inclined to be studious than social, who had had little experience of the town. If you saw me at all, it was to look through me rather than at me."

"What a shocking reading of my character," Julia said, aghast. "I have been guilty of gaucherie myself in my salad days, but I hope I was never ill-bred enough to do such a thing."

"I wasn't commenting on your breeding, Lady Julia," he explained, his eyes lighting with an inner amusement that brought a return of Julia's sensation of pleasurable anticipation. "Rather how unworthy I was of notice. 'Unprepossessing' would be a kind description of myself in my younger days."

Julia thought privately that if he had looked to her as he did now, she could not possibly have failed to notice him as he claimed, but she merely questioned him on the occasion and was told that it was at a ball at Lady Jersey's that he had attended while on holiday from Cambridge in the company of his cousin Robert, who was then Lord Sales.

"Then I am all the more surprised that we did not actually meet," she said. "I was tolerably well-acquainted with Lord Sales. He had the most devilish sense of humor. He had many friends, you know, and was greatly mourned when he fell at Waterloo."

Sales nodded. "We were not close, but not because of differences or dislike. Rather because distance and our interests kept us from spending much time together or coming to know each other very well."

"Are you acquainted with the present Lord Sales?"

A smile played on his lips and in his eyes that might have been described as devilish; it caused Julia to imagine a definite resemblance between Sales and his cousin, whom she had known. "Yes. Most definitely, but I have not had much commune with Lord Sales since his succession. I have been too busy with my other concerns, I fear."

Julia looked at him in surprise. "Do you indeed know him? How very remarkable. I think you are the first person who has said that he does. But then since he is a member of your own family, I suppose I should not call it remarkable at all. He is another cousin, I collect. You must tell me all about him so that I can write to all of my friends in town immediately I return to Dumphree. Speculation about the elusive marquess has been rampant since it was learned that the title was not to go into abeyance, after all, as everyone assumed. But then, I suppose if it were not for your cousin, it might have come to you. You must be in the line for it if you are a Sales."

"Yes, I am. But I shan't satisfy your curiosity for you, Lady Julia," he said on a faint apologetic note. "You see, Lord Sales is an exceptionally private man—many would call him a recluse—and he abhors attention of the sort that his title would bring him. It would be most unfair of me to draw to him the notoriety he so assiduously shuns."

"How very disappointing," Julia complained, folding her music and rising. "But I shan't plague you. I suspect it would do me little good."

"None at all," he agreed amiably.

"Well, that is honest," she said with a soft laugh. "I think directness is held to be refreshing because it is so rare."

"I have little habit of polite evasions and subterfuge, Lady Julia. The manner in which I have conducted my life of late has not required it."

"What manner is that," she asked with real curiosity. She moved away from the bench and they fell into step beside each other. "Do you know that you are regarded as something of a mystery yourself in the neighborhood. Perhaps it is a family charactertistic."

Julia gave no thought to having betrayed the fact that she had known of him before they had met, but it did not escape Dominic.

"That is only the result of overactive imaginations. I live simply and openly. I don't talk a great deal about my recent past because I doubt it would be of great interest to anyone, at least in a drawing room. Is that what people imagine to be mysterious?"

"Do you shun notoriety too, Mr. Sales?" Julia said, casting him an arch look. "Will you tell me about yourself?"

Once again there was amusement in his eyes, though he spoke gravely enough. "I was born in England, raised on an island a bit south of Jamaica in the West Indies, but I was educated in England, as my family felt befitted the son of a gentleman.

I have always been fascinated by the study of nature, and when I came to England to live, I discovered that, to me, the nature to be found here is more beautiful and more fascinating than the lushness that I grew up with." He broke into a quick smile. "Carrying this to an extreme, I lived in the Hebrides for two years before coming to Wiltshire to live. My principal companions before the last few months have been fishermen, birds, and sea otters."

"How alarming! Are you fit for society after such deprivation, Mr. Sales?"

He laughed. "Perhaps not. I think you would be the better judge of that."

"Then you must give me the opportunity to do so."

He glanced quickly down at her and she saw a speculative light flash in his expressive eyes. She supposed he must think her bold. In her circles dalliance was too commonplace to be taken seriously, but to him it might well seem to be more than it was.

Julia altered her tactics slightly and with one or two leading questions encouraged him to speak more of his avocation. Though she had not the smallest interest in naturalism, she was too adept at the art of flirtation not to know that one of the surest captivators was to display curiosity.

To her surprise, she found his answers more interesting than she would have supposed. There was an enthusiasm in his tone that was not excessively avid, but yet managed to be infectious. Her succeeding questions were more from a quite genuine wish to know rather than mere self-interest.

"What on earth, then, brings you to Wiltshire?" she asked him. "I have never heard that this part of the kingdom was a haven for naturalists."

"No," he agreed. "Though it is not without interest in some respects. It is a person rather than nature that brings me here. Dr. Carstairs, who is virtually the founder of modern naturalism, has retired to his estate on the other side of Amesbury. He has graciously consented to be my mentor in interpreting and transcribing the research I have collected in recent years, which I hope to publish eventually."

"Is writing another of your talents?"

He gave her another quick smile, which was reflected in his

eyes. "We shall see. It is the first time I have attempted it."

"I am not surprised you are seldom in company. I wonder that you find the time at all."

"One can choose to make time if there is sufficient inducement to do so." There was just enough suggestion in his voice to cause her gaze to move swiftly to his, but for once his expression gave away none of his thoughts and she could not be certain if he were flirting with her or not.

She had no notion how long she had been in conversation with him until her sister came up to them to inform Julia that she had sent for their carriage. "No doubt it is still early for you, my dear," she said without apology, "but I am used to country hours and I am already thinking of my bed."

Julia knew this was all too true, and she wished she might tell Alicia to leave without her. But it would be unreasonable for her to expect the carriage to be sent back for her at that hour and distance, so she allowed herself to be excused to Mr. Sales without giving any hint of her vexation that their interesting conversation was so summarily brought to an end.

Lord Dumphree was an amiable man who was only too happy to fall in with any wish or suggestion of his wife's and he readily relinquished his hand at the card table to another when she spoke with him. It was not as simple to convince Linton to leave. It was not merely a question of the early hour. He declared that it was really too bad to have to leave when he was just coming to know a few people. Though he mentioned no one specifically, Julia suspected that it was Miss Sutton he had in mind. If it had not been for Lady Amberly's gently but firmly drawing her niece into other groups and away from Linton, he might well have monopolized Sophia's attention for the entire evening.

Though Julia deplored his impulsiveness, which sometimes made him forget the strictures of propriety, she was glad that he was expressing an interest in someone again so soon. If Harry was ready to form a *tendre* for another girl so quickly after he had declared his heart broken by the high flyer who had thrown him over for a greater prize, then it was only his pride rather than his feelings that had been wounded. But on the other hand, Julia felt a little apprehension that, still smarting from his mistress's rejection, he might be sufficiently vulnerable to easily imagine himself in love again if Miss Sutton was at all responsive to him.

When they arrived at Dumphree, Harry begged Julia not to retire at once but to join him in a glass of brandy before going to bed. Though this was the most active day Julia had spent since coming into the country, she was no more ready for sleep than her nephew, and she readily agreed.

It was plain at once that Julia's worst fears were confirmed: Linton was already becoming infatuated with Miss Sutton. But beyond a brief sigh for the folly of youth—and the ironic thought that Hal would be beside himself if he guessed that his suggestion that Harry join Julia in her rustication had not kept his son from forming yet another entanglement—Julia did not pay a great deal of heed to her nephew's romantic ravings. She had her own thoughts to occupy her.

She knew she was certainly not prey to anything so vulgar as infatuation, but Dominic Sales very definitely intrigued her, and she speculated for some time, even after she had gone to her room, on what his feelings for her might be. From the way that he had returned her notice that morning, she thought there was at least some interest there. She would have liked to believe that he had come to Amberly even late as he had because he wanted to see if she would be present, but she knew it was far more likely that he had only done so out of respect for the Amberlys, whose tenant he was. Whatever the truth, Julia was not displeased with the events of the day. For the first time since her arrival at Dumphree, she felt not a trace of boredom, and that was something in and of itself.

3

Julia was not far wrong in her suppositions. Dominic had certainly gone to Amberly that night, in spite of the fact that he had returned late from Amesbury, out of respect for the Amberlys. But he had also wondered if Julia would be present, once he had ascertained from Brady that she was staying with her sister at Dumphree. The attraction that Julia felt toward him was not unreciprocated, though with some reluctance.

Though Julia did not remember him from Lady Jersey's ball so many years ago, he remembered her very well. He could still recall her entrance into the ballroom on Sir Anthony's arm, looking radiant and literally dazzling in a gown of gold-shot gauze. He was not of a nature like Lord Linton to be swept off his feet by the sight of a beautiful woman, but he had thought at the time that he had never seen a lovelier vision of femininity. In different circumstances he might have dared to approach her.

But Julia was more than beautiful and elegant and sophisticated; she was courted. Almost before her husband had left her side to seek the entertainment of the card rooms, she had been surrounded by a court of admirers composed of men who were beautiful and elegant in their own right. Dominic, well aware that she would regard him as little more than a schoolboy, had looked upon her with a wistful sort of longing, as though she were a princess on a glass mountain and everlastingly unapproachable. He was of too practical a nature to pine after the unattainable, and he had not given her another thought until he had seen Julia step into the common room at the Hart and Hare.

To his own surprise, he had recognized her at once, though it was ten years since the night he had last seen her. There had been no gold threads or the light of a thousand candles to catch them and dazzle the eye, yet he had been affected in much the same way as he had the first time he had seen her. Something inside of him had stirred, awakened by a sudden, unexpected brightness. It was not an unrecognizable feeling; there had been women he had desired and even loved after a fashion in his eight-and-twenty years. What was surprising to him was that he should feel it for a woman like Julia, who was the antithesis of his usual taste.

If he had little use for society, he had even less for those people whose very existence seemed to be only to shine within it. One reason that Julia, for all her loveliness, had never been a figure of fantasy for him was that he knew she was one of that ilk. Julia was not only beautiful and elegant, she was well aware of it.

He had seen in a moment that she was an accomplished flirt, the sort who regarded the attention of men as her due. He was not the complete stranger to society that he had allowed Julia to suppose. He had met others like her, both in town and in the country, and he had always gone out of his way to avoid such women when he could. But there was something about Julia that attracted him in spite of himself. It might have been merely physical, as he had told himself at first, but after their conversation at Amberly, he had sufficient self-honesty to suspect it was more.

Though he did not purposely dwell on their meeting, he found that it crept into his mind with increasing frequency the following day. Even while struggling over putting his notes in coherent narrative form, he kept permitting himself to be distracted by the memory. It disturbed him considerably, for he had no illusions about her attempt to strike up a flirtation with him. Women like Julia, he knew, collected flirts like trophies, and he had no intention of allowing himself to be collected.

Julia felt none of Dominic's reluctance about pursuing a flirtation. She allowed herself to hope that he would be present when she and Alicia called at Amberly the following day, and she even gave up her morning ride the day after that in the hope that he would call at Dumphree. But he did not. It was another full day before she saw him again, and it was nothing more than a chance encounter in Lesser Ansdown.

Harry had gone with the ladies when they had visited Amberly on the day after they had dined there, and had concocted an excuse to call there again on the next day. His ingenuity would doubtless have supplied him with yet another reason for going to Amberly on the third day if Alicia had not made a caustic comment on his sudden interest in spending time under that roof.

"Of course I am interested," Harry said without the least attempt to dissemble. "Sophia, Miss Sutton, is an angel."

"And Amberly is heaven?" Julia wondered with mild sarcasm. "For goodness' sake, Harry, must you always pursue your passions at full tilt? Handsomely over the bricks, dear boy. Do you wish to make Miss Sutton conspicuous with your attentions?"

Harry's eyes held a hunted expression as they looked from one aunt to the other. "Damme, no matter what I do I get my hair combed for it," he complained. "If I sport myself with the demimonde, I am told I'm a fool to take up with opera dancers and should look to settling down with a woman of my own caste."

"I doubt your father has said precisely that, Harry," Alicia said dryly. "You are still a babe, and you have a great deal of time to decide which woman you will spend the rest of your life with. His complaint, and mine and your Aunt Julia's as well, is that you are intemperate. By all means you may seek to know Miss Sutton better if you please, but if you behave as though you mean to make her a declaration by the end of the week, you will not only give rise to a great deal of unnecessary gossip, you will also very likely terrify the poor chit. I have always found her a rather timid creature."

"She is very delicate," Harry agreed, but then his brow was marred by a frown. "How the devil am I to know Miss Sutton better if I do not make the effort to do so?"

"The Amberlys will be at the assembly in Amesbury on Friday," Alicia said in a flat voice. "That will be time enough to see her again without making a nuisance of yourself."

Harry's expression became mulish and Julia rose from her chair, saying, "Put a sock in it, Harry. I am driving the gig into Lesser Ansdown in a bit to match embroidery silks for Alicia. Come with me. It will not only be a diversion; there is always the possibility that we shall come upon Lady Amberly and Miss Sutton engaged in a similar errand and then you may meet in an unexceptional way."

But it was not Miss Sutton they met in Lesser Ansdown. It was not at all in Julia's mind that she would see Mr. Sales that morning, but as they were leaving the drapers, he was crossing the street toward them. There was a startled expression in his eyes, for she had come unwittingly into his thoughts again, and just as he was about to banish her image, she appeared before him almost as if she had materialized from his own thoughts.

Julia greeted him at once with her usual impulsive familiarity. "Are you out pursuing your avocation, Mr. Sales," she inquired, "or shopping, as we are?"

"A bit of both. There is a copse near here with a warren that I have been observing, but I took the opportunity of proximity to make a few purchases that I don't like to entrust to the servants."

"I suppose I should disgrace myself if I asked you what a warren is, so I shan't," Julia said with a self-deprecating laugh. "I fear I am a town creature and know nothing at all about naturalism, Mr. Sales. You must teach me something of it so that I may converse with you without seeming to have more hair than wit."

Though she spoke in a conversational tone, her eyes invited him to greater intimacy. In spite of being guarded against it, he could not help the response he felt toward her, but he had no intention of letting it rule him. He knew that her interest was more flirtatious than sincere and he would not allow himself to be taken in by it. "If you prefer town life to life in the country, Lady Julia, I fear I would only bore you," he said in such a flat tone that it was clearly a snub.

Her smile was slow and studied. "No. I don't think you would. Perhaps we could ride together someday and you could give me a lecture in a practical manner."

"Perhaps," he said almost curtly, and then speaking a few words to Linton, he excused himself, pleading an engagement that Julia was convinced he had just made up at that moment.

"Presumptuous sort of fellow," Harry said when they went into the inn to take a bit of refreshment. "Gave you a bit of a set-down just then."

Julia's expression was far from chagrined. "I don't regard it so."

Harry's brows went up. "The devil take it, you are casting

out lures in that direction, aren't you, Aunt Jule? If that don't beat all, when you are forever preaching on at me."

"I don't make a cake of myself," Julia informed him tartly. "That is the difference."

Harry shrugged. With every reason to believe that Miss Sutton returned his interest, he was not to be easily put out of humor. "Well, you should know your own mind, but I would have supposed someone like Sales would be tame prey for you. Besides, I thought you were setting your cap for Tallboys. I've got a monkey riding on his making you an offer before the end of the Season at Watier's."

"Do you?" Julia asked, her eyes narrowing slightly. "It is vulgar to bet on such matters, Harry."

"Mama said it's vulgar to gild your toenails, too," Harry returned without compunction.

"*Touché*," Julia said, laughing. "I do admire Royden and consider him a good friend, but I am not made of stone, Harry, any more than you are. Mr. Sales is an attractive man and not without facets to recommend him. Besides," she added with candor, "what else is there to do here but engage in a bit of flirtation and with whom, if not with Mr. Sales? Every man here is either old enough to be my father or too young to be taken seriously."

"I shouldn't have said that Sales is all that old. A bit older than me, perhaps but not by much."

"Alicia said that Lady Amberly told her he was eight-and-twenty."

"Two years your junior," he said, his mobile brows rising again. "Not your usual style, Aunt Jule."

"No, of course not," Julia said with a hint of impatience. "It is hardly a matter of moment, Harry. I want to enjoy an agreeable flirtation with the man to keep from turning to stone from boredom; I don't mean to marry him."

"If his interest in you is no better than what I saw today," Harry said baldly, "I wouldn't have much hope of even a bit of dalliance. I don't think he even likes you very much."

She gave him a catlike smile. "He will, Harry."

Harry gave a bark of laughter. "Mean to break the poor fellow's heart, do you?"

"Perhaps," Julia said in much the same tone Dominic had

used when he had left them, and she then turned the subject as the landlord brought their food.

It was not until the end of the week at the assembly in Amesbury that Dominic and Julia met again. Harry, however, had met Dominic again during the week when, ignoring his aunt's advice he had called again at Amberly.

At first Harry had been annoyed to find Dominic and Sophia Sutton in close conversation and on terms of obvious intimacy. But the moment she had turned her guileless blue eyes on him and given him a smile that made him feel as if she thought him her whole delight, all jealousy vanished. By the end of the visit, he and Dominic were actually on capital terms, having discovered a mutual passion of fly-casting. An engagement was made with Dominic for the following week for them to fish a particularly fruitful stream on Amberly land at the encouragement of their host.

Harry, who would one day inherit his father's estates, had far greater interest in country pursuits than did Julia, and he found Dominic to be a very agreeable fellow, which he informed her of when he returned to Dumphree. "He's a great gun, Aunt Jule. Not like Tallboys and the usual sort that makes up your court."

"And what, pray, does that mean?" Julia wondered, mildly offended. "I thought you liked Royden."

"I do. I only meant that Sales is a different sort of fellow. Direct and sincere. He doesn't play the game all the time. You know what I mean," he said, frowning because he could not be more articulate.

"Do you know, Harry," she said solicitously, "I think this purified air has sadly affected you. You sound like Alicia rather than a man who has wholeheartedly enjoyed every fashionable pursuit since you have been on the town."

"I'm not a fribble," Harry said, in his turn becoming miffed. "Until now I have just been enjoying myself. But perhaps it's time for me to think about other things that are more important and permanent in life. Can't live like a rakehell forever, after all."

Julia's eyes narrowed slightly. She found his words to be ominous. She could not believe that, on the strength of less than a fortnight's acquaintance, he would already be considering making an offer for Miss Sutton. The girl was unexceptional, but Alicia had hinted to her that Caroline Amberly, who was taking her niece to London in a month's time to present her to the world, did not wish to encourage Harry. Hal, too, would likely take a dim view of such a fevered romance, and he would probably blame Julia in some way for allowing it to come about, though what she might do to prevent it, she had not the least idea.

But Julia was too clever to put up her volatile nephew's back by commenting on his imprudence. "That is very true," she said gravely. "But what has any of this to do with Mr. Sales' character, or Royden's for that matter."

"Not the least thing. I only meant that I hope you do not mean to make him fall in love with you if you don't really want him. If he loved you, you might truly break his heart, and that would be a shame because he is a decent fellow."

Julia was intrigued by his comment because she read into it that Harry might be aware that Dominic was attracted to her, though he had yet to display it to her satisfaction. She laughed. "What has Mr. Sales done to gain for himself such a champion? Never fear, Harry. I am hardly the *femme fatale* of my reputation. You said yourself that Sales did not even seem to like me."

To her disappointment, Harry merely agreed that this was so, and she learned nothing further, but it increased her anticipation for the assembly and her hope that Dominic would be present.

It would perhaps be unfair to suggest that Julia had any fixed intention of breaking Dominic Sales' heart, but she did mean to see if she could make him fall at least a little in love with her. In addition to conquering her boredom, the challenge was irresistible to her.

Dominic was with Lady Amberly and Sophia when Julia, in the company of her sister and nephew, came into the assembly rooms. Harry insisted that they go to greet them at once. This concided with Julia's wishes exactly, and Alicia, indolent as ever, concurred. It followed, very much to the liking of aunt and nephew, that their parties merged and spent the better part of the evening together. But by midevening the hopes of neither had been satisfied.

On his best behavior, Harry did not ask Sophia to stand up

with him for more than two dances. But since he had asked no other young woman to dance and had spent the time Sophia was on the floor with other men watching her with an obvious intensity, his good intentions were nullified. It was obvious from the way that Lady Amberly's features set whenever her eyes rested on the viscount that she was displeased with the attention he was giving to her niece, and she saw to it that, between sets, he was not able to monopolize Sophia as he doubtless would have attempted to do if not prevented.

Alicia, in exasperation at Harry's lack of self-restraint, would have said something to him, but Julia advised her against it. "You will only add petulance to the sins in his dish," she said with the wisdom of previous experience. "When he is head-over-heels like this, he hasn't another thought in his head and only resents any attempts to check him to a steadier course."

"But Caro keeps casting daggers at me," Alicia said unhappily. "As if I were urging the wretched boy to forget his breeding."

"Caroline only makes it worse by showing her dislike of Harry's attentions toward Sophia. She will have them imagining they are star-crossed lovers if she doesn't have a care, and then we might end up chasing them to Gretna Green."

Alicia actually shuddered at the prospect of having her peaceful existence so disturbed. "It is because Caro has never had any children of her own that she is so protective of Sophia. But I don't blame her entirely for it. I shouldn't have wanted one of my girls tied to someone before she had even had the chance to make her entrance in the world and seen what it had to offer."

"Sage advice, Lady Dumphree," Dominic said as he came up to them to collect Julia for the country dance. "And successful as well, since I understand both of your daughters are very well-settled."

"And both of them pudding-faced too," Julia said, darting a teasing glance at her sister.

But Alicia knew her sister well and refused the bait. "It is the greatest pity that both of them took after the Dumphrees instead of the Merchants," she concurred. "If either one of them had been half as lovely as Julia, I would have wed her to a duke."

"It is a greater pity that Mama did not possess your skill as a matchmaker," Julia said with mock chagrin. "I think I should have made a superb duchess."

"Undoubtedly," Dominic agreed, his expression grave but with such a dancing light in his eyes that Julia felt her attraction to him more strongly than ever.

The emphathy between them was short-lived, however. Throughout the country dance, they maintained a steady flow of polite conversation whenever the movement of the dance permitted, but Julia's attempts at light flirtation were met with tactful rebuff.

When the set ended, he relinquished her to her next partner with no sign of reluctance, making her a correct bow and walking away without a second glance. Julia was more intrigued than offended by his determination to keep a distance between them. A woman of less self-confidence would likely have taken his behavior as proof that her interest was not reciprocated, but Julia suspected that it was attributable to something quite other than that.

She had no idea why he should wish to deny an attraction to her, but she felt instinctively that he was the sort of man who, if he felt only indifference, would make it known in a manner that could not be misunderstood. Instead, he seemed to disclaim a mutual interest between them, though for what reason, she could not fathom.

Wherever Julia was, be it London or Amesbury, she always attracted the attentions of men. Even with a limited acquaintance in the neighborhood, she did not sit out a single dance as one gentleman after the other approached to ask her for the pleasure of leading her onto the floor.

It didn't surprise Julia that Dominic asked her to stand up with him for one of the country dances, but it did surprise her that he had also asked her to save him the waltz before supper. Waltzing was so commonplace in town that it was no longer considered at all shocking, but it was still unusual for public assemblies in small towns to include the dance, and Julia had expected him to be too provincial to approve of it. Yet, when the music began, it was immediately obvious that he was no stranger to the steps. He moved with a natural athletic grace and danced superbly. He held her in his arms at exactly the correct distance for propriety, and yet she had the sense of being in his intimate embrace. This illusion of intimacy made the commonplace remarks he addressed to her all the more puzzling.

If directness was to his liking, Julia was quite willing to oblige him. "Why don't you like me, Mr. Sales?" she asked baldly after several minutes of polite nothings passed between them.

"Why would you think that, Lady Julia?" he returned, surprise in his tone but not his expression. "I shouldn't suppose I would be standing up with you if I did not."

"You are well-bred, sir, and our parties are commingled. What else could you do?"

A sudden devil smiled in his eyes. "I might have asked Sophia for the waltz and incurred the wrath of your nephew instead."

Julia gave vent to a rueful laugh. "Oh, dear! Is he that obvious to everyone? I fear Linton perpetually wears his heart on his sleeve. My sister thinks that his suit will not prosper."

"At his age he will probably fall in love a dozen more times before he is ready to make a girl an offer."

"Quoth the graybeard. You cannot be much beyond the age of my nephew."

"I shall be nine-and-twenty in three months' time."

"And I was thirty a month before this."

"A great age," he said solemnly.

"You have entirely avoided my question, Mr. Sales," she admonished. "Why do you dislike me?"

"I thought I did answer that I do not dislike you, Lady Julia. On the contrary, I like you very well."

"That is why you address me as if I were your aunt's spotty youngest daughter, I suppose."

"I only have one aunt and she hasn't any daughters, but if she did, I would not ask the spotty ones to stand up with me for a waltz, I assure you."

Julia laughed at his nonsense and received in response so warm a smile that she felt she had scored a definite victory and overcome at least a bit of his reluctance.

At supper they sat apart, but as she was leaving the supper room with Alicia, she found Dominic beside her again and was bold enough to recall to him her invitation for them to ride together and for him to acquaint her with his avocation. "I usually ride out with Harry, though he considers my company too tame for the sort of riding he enjoys. Most often I ride out alone."

"Without even a groom?"

"You sound like my sister," Julia said with a laugh. "I would not do so in town, of course, but I see no reason to be plagued with a trailing servant advising me against every hazard."

But he did not agree. "It is still unwise to ride alone, Lady Julia. It is not only unsafe, for accidents may occur to the most accomplished riders, but it is frowned upon even within the narrow confines of our limited society."

Julia did not take offense at his correction, but was amused by it. And encouraged as well. If he were indifferent to her, why should it matter to him if she did not strictly observe the proprieties? "Then ride with me, Mr. Sales. If you divert me with lectures on naturalism, I shan't find the company tedious."

At this he did smile again. "I only hope you would not find my lecturing tedious. I might bore you into wishing yourself at home mending linens."

"Why don't we make the attempt and see if it is so?" she said, looking up at him through her lashes.

He smiled slowly, lured by her flirtatiousness in spite of himself. "Very well, Lady Julia. Tomorrow if you like. The best time to view nature at its most pristine is as early as possible in the morning. Preferably before breakfast."

Julia wondered if he expected her to beg off because of the early hour. She was habitually an early riser in spite of often keeping late hours in town. "I should like that. Is seven too late?"

"No. Not if we are ready to leave at that hour."

"Is that a warning, Mr. Sales?" Julia said, placing her hand on his arm in a fleeting, flirtatious touch. "If I am not dressed and mounted, shall you go off without me?"

"I hope I would not be so ill-bred. But the earlier we begin, the better."

Julia promised solemnly to be ready for him when he arrived at Dumphree, and she kept her word. She might have satisfied his notion of punctuality by merely being dressed and ready to receive him when he arrived, but as Dominic trotted down the last stretch of the drive and the house came into view, he saw that Julia was indeed mounted and walking her horse along the carriage sweep.

"I am a woman of my word, as you see, Mr. Sales," Julia greeted him.

Though he did not say so, Dominic was surprised, and pleased as well. He knew that most women of fashion rarely rose before nine and many not until much later. Early rising and punctuality were not attributes he had expected her to possess.

He was also pleasantly surprised during the whole of their ride. He quite deliberately took Julia on a rigorous cross-country ride, expecting her energy to flag before long, but she proved herself to be a first-rate horsewoman. He also spoke freely of his interests and noted that her attention never appeared to wander.

Julia had the gift of listening well and her interest was not feigned, for she had a natural curiosity about most things. Though naturalism was not a subject she would have sought knowledge of on her own, she was fascinated by everything that he told her, and her attention was rewarded as he warmed to his topic and his tone became increasingly enthusiastic and less instructional.

He had not intended to go much farther afield than Amberly land, but caught up in their occupation, neither had noted that they were nearly beyond Amesbury. It was actually Julia who noted a landmark she had passed on a previous ride, and commented on it.

"I had no idea we had wandered so far," Dominic said in mild surprise. "Perhaps we had best turn and head back to Dumphree if you are to return home in time for luncheon. The old Dower House is near and I would offer you luncheon, but it wouldn't do with only my housekeeper for chaperone."

Julia's inclination was to suggest they hang convention, but she glanced up at him through her lashes and decided that it would be a strategic error. This man had a decidedly proper streak. "I suppose it would be," she agreed. "I seldom take luncheon, in any case. Do you think it would be equally improper, though, if we were merely to go into your garden? My sister mentioned that Lord Amberly's grandmother was an avid gardener and had the grounds of the old Dower House laid out by none other that Capability Brown. I should love to see it. My groom may walk behind us if you think it would be more seemly,'' she added to appease any objection he might have on that score.

A faint smile played on his lips. He suspected that Julia usually did not have such a care to the observance of propriety. ''If you wish it, of course. But it is too early in the season for you to see it as it clearly is meant to be seen. If you like, I'll have Mrs. Grisham send us tea on the terrace outside my bookroom to refresh us before we head back to Dumphree.''

''I should like it very much,'' she said with a wholehearted smile that affected him more than she knew.

He turned his horse somewhat abruptly, annoyed at his own easy response to her. He found he could not help liking her, but he had no intention of succumbing to any deeper feeling however strong the physical attraction he might feel toward her.

Julia had more opportunity to admire the old house this time as they approached it together. She had seen the new Dower House, a pretty but unremarkable Georgian brick house, and wondered that Lord Amberly's mother could have preferred it to this. She judged that it dated from the end of the century before last. It was not symmetrical, like the newer house, but it had a lovely mellow charm that Julia found far more attractive. She said this to Dominic.

''I quite agree,'' he said with a faint, approving smile. ''Since there is no dowager viscountess to take up residence in either house, Amberly gave me my pick, but for me the choice was made the moment I set eyes on this one.''

Julia was pleased that their tastes should be agreeable. ''Some other time I shall have to bring Alicia with me to act as chaperone. I should like to see it inside as well. Is it as attractive inside as outside?''

He shook his head. ''Unfortunately not. Most things that were worth taking were transported to the new house, and the attics of Amberly, I suspect, were dredged to supply most of the furnishings for this house. But even so, it is not unattractive, merely eclectic.''

The gardens, even though they were still a week or two away from coming into flower, were really quite lovely. They were the gardens of a manor house in miniature. There was not only the formal garden leading off the terrace he spoke of, there was a box garden, a rose garden, and even a small topiary. Julia was enchanted.

"My goodness," she exclaimed as she looked up at a yew that was trimmed and trained to resemble a dove about to break into flight. "The Lady Amberly who ordered this to be constructed must have been a woman of considerable means or magnificent jointure. I have been to the palaces of dukes who did not have anything half so fine. I'll wager the garden had an influence on your choice of house as well."

He nodded. "Even in late fall when I came here, I knew what the potential would be."

They returned finally to the terrace and a manservant brought them tea and scones. The morning they had shared had been far more pleasant than they would have imagined it could be.

Though on one level there was clearly a greater understanding between them, Julia still felt a determination from him to keep a distance between them. She knew enough, though, to be satisfied with the progress she had already made.

"I think it is time for me to return to Dumphree," she said, placing her cup back in its saucer after finishing the last of her tea. "I suppose Alicia, however little inclined she is to be anxious about things, must be beginning to wonder what has become of me."

She rose and he naturally followed her. She held out her hand to him. "Thank you, Mr. Sales, for a truly delightful morning. You see, I told you I should not be bored. I hope you did not find me too abysmally ignorant."

"On the contrary, Lady Julia, I find you exceptionally clever," he replied in a tone so ambiguous that she opened her eyes at him.

"And I have found you to be exceptionally well-bred," she replied, a quizzing gleam in her eyes. "I practically forced myself on you today, and you have accepted my company with good grace."

"It was my pleasure to ride with you today," he responded but in a sincere, not merely civil, tone.

"You would have had to have been wonderfully rude to have successfully discouraged me."

His lips curved upward just slightly. "I think I could have contrived that if I had really wished it."

She shook her head, smiling. "But would you? Alicia is a great friend of Caroline Amberly, and you would not wish to offend your landlady by being uncivil to her friend's sister. That would be cause enough to bear with my company for a single morning."

He laughed softly. "I like the Amberlys, but I'd consign them both to the devil before I'd let either of them influence my choice of companions."

Julia laughed and began to walk toward where their horses had been left tethered at the edge of the garden. "And yet I cannot but feel a certain reluctance from you. If it is not that you felt forced to endure my company or that you dislike me, as you claim you do not, then perhaps it is that you do not wish to like me."

"Perhaps."

His response surprised her and she stopped abruptly, causing him nearly to walk into her. "Then we have come nearly full circle from my question to you last night. Why do you not wish to like me, Mr. Sales?"

There was not a great difference in their heights, but they were standing so close together that he seemed almost to loom over her. Unaccountably, she felt her heart begin to beat faster. She knew he was going to kiss her before he made any move to do so. When his hand came up to touch her cheek and he bent his head to hers, she moved toward him willingly, wanting to feel his lips on hers.

It did not begin as an embrace between lovers, but the kiss quickly deepened and their bodies molded together. Julia felt a completely unexpected surge of excitement, and she knew in that moment that for the first time since her husband's death, she had met a man she wished to take for her lover.

Dominic had never intended to kiss Julia, and he was shaken both by her response and by his own. "I think that is why," he said, his voice controlled with effort. "There is an attraction, but we would suit too ill to pursue it."

Julia had thought much the same herself, and she had sought him out merely for diversion. But his words made her defensive.

"Why do you say so? The time we have spent together has been very agreeable, at least to me."

"Oh, quite. But then, we are strangers exerting ourselves to be agreeable. You haven't any real interest in nature any more than I have in living in town and going to *ton* parties every night of the week."

"Is that what you think I do?"

"Isn't it?"

There was just an edge of disdain in his tone, or at least Julia imagined she heard it. She shrugged and moved a little away from him. "I enjoy town life very much. I know it is always portrayed as mindless and superficial, but like any other sort of life, it is whatever you choose to make of it. Some people would say that the interests you have are vapid and tedious, but it is not so to you and you have made me see as well that it is not. I have enjoyed today very much."

Dominic was silent for a moment, then he said cautiously, "So have I."

Julia turned back to him and held out her hand. "Then, may we please be friends? You are no doubt right that it would be foolish for us to succumb to a superficial attraction for each other, but since we are aware of it, surely we may avoid it. Why should we deny ourselves the pleasure of knowing each other if we enjoy each other's company?"

He hesitated before taking her hand, but only for a moment. "It may be that I have done you an injustice, Lady Julia," he said with a growing smile. "By all means let us be friends."

By tacit consent they returned to their horses and at last began the ride back to Dumphree. Their conversation was more general as they rode, but also much easier and consequently more intimate.

When Julia returned to Dumphree, she found Linton waiting for her in her sitting room. She would have liked to have changed and washed first, but he was obviously eager to speak with her, so she rang for Madeira to be brought to them and settled into a comfortable chair to hear him out. His glum face made her guess that he had probably had some sort of setback in his pursuit of Miss Sutton.

Julia's own spirits were high and she said in a rallying tone,

"You're looking very low, Harry. It is far too lovely a day to be blue-deviled."

"Lady Amberly is a dashed she-dragon," Linton replied, not mincing words. He accepted the wine Julia poured for him mechanically and sat down in a chair opposite hers. "She all but told me outright today that I wasn't good enough for her precious niece and that my suit was not welcome. The devil of it is, Aunt Jule, I don't understand it. I'm not rich as Croesus and the earldom doesn't date back to the Conqueror, but I'm no mean catch for all that."

"Of course you are not," Julia said soothingly. "But Alicia has said that Lady Amberly has very definite plans for Sophia's future. You are very young, you know, and your reputation is not of the steadiest. Very likely she wishes for a more mature man for Sophia, already in possession of his fortune." He looked so downcast at these words that she added, "If Sophia feels as you do, though, and has a bit of spirit, her aunt's ambitions will come to naught."

"No one would ever accuse you of lacking spirit, Aunt Jule," he said, not at all consoled, "but you married Uncle Tony because your family wished it. You told me so yourself."

Years and experience had gone into making her the woman she was now, and she felt far removed from that biddable child fresh from the schoolroom. "Yes. But I was not in love with anyone else. If I had been, perhaps I would have stood up to them."

"Have you ever been in love, Aunt Jule?" Linton asked.

Julia's immediate inclination was to give him a light response, but she saw that his question was sincere and not idle. "No. I don't think so. Not in the romantic way I think you mean. I loved Anthony because he was kind and very good to me, but I don't believe I was truly in love with him. And I have been infatuated with a dozen others since him, but there has never been anyone necessary to my happiness, which is what I have always taken being in love to mean."

"I think it could be that for me this time," he said quietly and with rare diffidence.

Julia was touched, but she didn't believe him any more than she had before when he had claimed to be in love. "Really,

Harry, how can you say so? You haven't known Miss Sutton much more than a fortnight yet. She is a lovely girl, but scarcely even in your style. You will no doubt be in love a dozen times yet before you find the girl you truly wish to have for your wife."

He put down his wineglass on a table next to his chair and stood abruptly, his expressive countenance puckered into an angry scowl. "Don't patronize me, Aunt Julia. You think I'm just a mooncalf falling in and out of love with every pretty face. I don't know why I thought I could talk to you. You know nothing of love, by your own admission." He turned and went out of the room, closing the door behind him with an angry little snap.

Julia gave vent to an exasperated sigh. She had been glad that Linton had come with her to keep him from sighing for his opera dancer; she certainly hadn't envisioned him imagining himself in love again so quickly, and with a provincial miss with none of the town polish of his usual flirts. Less than a sennight earlier she had wondered how she would manage to remain at Dumphree for the time she had promised her brother without expiring from boredom, but in the fortnight that followed, Julia found little time for boredom or ennui.

She begged her nephew's pardon that night before dinner for her want of feeling, and after a day or two she was restored to the role of confidante. But there was little progress in his suit. He was all but certain that Sophia Sutton was not indifferent to him, but she was undoubtedly more distant to him, for which he unhesitatingly blamed her aunt. Remembering that she herself had not been entirely without ambition when her parents had chosen her husband for her, Julia refrained from comment, merely commiserating with Linton.

Julia had very mixed feelings about her own progress in her pursuit of Dominic. Their morning ride became a daily occurrence by tacit consent. When Julia awoke one morning to find it cold and drizzly, she dressed nevertheless, and was awaiting him mounted as usual. She was not certain he would come, but he did, and he confessed later that he had not really expected her to be waiting for him when he arrived. Though he did not say it in so many words, Julia knew she had passed an important test in his estimation, and was pleased that she had endured the damp ride to prove to him that she was not the frail, comfort-loving society creature he thought her.

There was no repetition of the kiss they had shared in his garden, but their intimacy steadily increased. Julia could not help feeling triumphant. His reluctance toward her had virtually evaporated, and there was an easiness between them as if they had been friends of long standing.

As their friendship grew and deepened, she realized how important their time together was becoming to her. She no longer had any complaint for the early country hours her sister kept, and she herself rose with alacrity each morning, looking forward eagerly to their rides. Whenever Alicia ventured out in the evenings, Julia found the success of the evening for her was directly related to whether or not Dominic was also present.

She was as quick to recognize the signs of infatuation in herself as she had been in her nephew. But she was more amused than troubled. It never occurred to her for a moment that she might not be able to control her feelings for Dominic; all she saw was that the attraction between them was stimulating and her boredom was a thing of the past. She felt no need to look ahead to where it might lead; by the middle of May she would be in London again, among all of her friends, and she assumed that her time at Dumphree and her flirtation with Dominic would be no more than a pleasant memory.

4

Occupied as she was with her growing friendship with Dominic, and Linton's sighings for his unrequited love, she had little opportunity to miss her friends and the dinners and parties and balls she would have been attending if she were in London.

Julia had hoped that her absence would make Sir Ronald Tallboys more appreciative of her, and the letters she received from him, while not demonstrative, for that was not his nature, made it clear, nevertheless, that he did miss her. He even mentioned in a light vein in an early letter that he might just take it in his head to visit his friend Lord Amberly, but in the context in which it was written, she did not take it very seriously. Julia was astonished, then, when on a sunny Sunday morning barely a sennight before she planned to return to town, Sir Royden entered the church with the Amberlys and sat with them in their pew.

He saw her reaction and there was amusement in his eyes as he bowed to her in proper formal fashion, as if they were mere acquaintances. Julia felt a sense of triumph that was in danger of becoming smugness. Whatever reason he might give for coming to Wiltshire, she knew beyond doubt that his principal motive was to see her and that her success had far exceeded her expectations.

Julia did not wait in the usual way to greet Royden outside, but met him in the aisle, confessing her surprise at seeing him. They were in the midst of other worshipers and he did not stop to bow over her hand in the usual way, but carried it to his lips instead, a more intimate gesture, in any case.

"My dearest Julia," he said, looking into her eyes in a speaking way, "London has been a desert without you."

"At the height of the Season?" she said, incredulous. "Hardly that. I feel as if I have been out of the world forever. Do you come directly from town? You must tell me all the latest *on-dits*."

"In church? You must allow me to call on you at Dumphree and we may gossip ourselves to a standstill."

"I should love it," she responded, laughing. In the corner of her eye she caught sight of Dominic, who was coming out of the church just behind them, and she saw that he was watching her and Royden. She suddenly turned a dazzling smile on Royden and said, speaking just a little bit louder than before, "I am glad you have come, Royden. I have missed you."

He seemed a little surprised by this. "Have you? I wasn't sure you would even wish to see me."

"Why ever not?" Julia said, surprised in her turn.

"You left town so precipitously. Without even a mention to me that you intended to do so." He put his hand under her elbow and led her a little to one side from the others chatting in small groups outside the church. "I have begun to wonder if I have been mistaken in the depth to which I thought our friendship had grown."

Julia felt a sudden unexpected mixture of emotions. Her main reasons for agreeing to rusticate was in the hope that she might precipitate an offer from Sir Royden. But now that she sensed that her hope was soon to be realized, she was not sure she was ready to accept him. The only reason she could imagine for her sudden reluctance was her original aversion to remarrying at all. Though many aspects of being her own mistress were burdensome, being married would mean giving up at least some degree of the independence she so prized and she supposed that she had not yet come to terms with that despite an intellectual decision to the contrary.

He held her hand and she removed it gently from his. It was a small gesture of withdrawal, and she saw from the change of expression in his eyes that he had noted it as such. She still wished for a declaration from him, but she did not wish to rush it.

"That is absurd. We are very good friends. It was simply an impulsive decision to visit Alicia and acted upon with equal haste. You know that Hal is forever combing my hair about being too impetuous. I'm not even sure I mentioned to Fanny that I was going, or at least no more than in passing."

He gave a soft, mirthless laugh. "I begin to commiserate with your brother. I wish you had told me of your plans rather than allowing me to discover your absence for myself when I called at Half Moon Street. I was very concerned."

"Why should you be?"

"I feared that I had offended you in some way," he said, his eyes searching hers.

Julia felt just a hint of exasperation at his continuing to press the point, but she said quite gently, "And I have told you that there is no reason to think that. My only thought was to astonish Hal into silence by agreeing to his wish that I live quietly for a time."

He smiled, appearing at least to accept her explanation. "My dear, Julia," he said with mock dismay, "that is not like you. I fear you must be sickening for some infection."

"Only if temperance and maturity may be deemed such," she said, returning his smile, glad of a return to lightness. "But I feel quite lost to the world. Come, let us find Alicia, and she may invite you to luncheon and we may have a wonderful coze together."

Alicia, who had not met Royden in over a year since her last visit to town, was delighted to comply. There was no opportunity for conversation in the carriage on the return to Dumphree with the gentlemen present, but Alicia was clearly anxious for a word with her sister, and Julia followed her to her bedchamber when they reached the house.

"My dear, I could scarcely believe my eyes when I saw Royden come into the church," Alicia said excitedly. "It must be to see you that he is come. Caro told me he is only to be here a few days, but I can manage to put together a little entertainment before then for our friends. Not a ball, of course, but a small rout with a bit of dancing. Mrs. Asquith's companion, Miss Crosby, can play the pianoforte for us, I am sure, for she did so for Lady Bandy. We shall have a buffet supper as well. It may just do the trick."

"The trick?"

"Why, bringing Tallboys up to scratch. Isn't that what you wish? You told me yourself that he has been most attentive in the past few months and that you had reason to hope he might make you an offer. I said to myself the moment I saw him,

We shall have Julia Lady Tallboys before the year is out."

Julia felt tolerably confident that her sister was right. What she could not be certain of was what her answer to him would be should he offer for her. This greatly disturbed her, for she had been quite sure of it before she had left town.

On the following morning when Julia and Dominic met for their ride, he mentioned that he had dined at Amberly the previous night and had met Royden. "He told me that he and Sir Anthony were great friends," Dominic remarked.

"They were near neighbors in Devonshire and knew each other all their lives. They also belonged to the same set in town and were good friends in spite of the fact that Royden was ten years Tony's junior." She laughed in a self-mocking way. "Goodness, I am forgetting that twenty-five years separated Tony and me. Age is not a factor, I suppose, were there is common interest and common thought."

He looked at her in a regardful manner. "I suppose you and Sir Royden must have a great deal in common."

Julia knew that he was seeking to define her relationship with Royden. Now that they were friends, she was long past the conceit of attempting to break his heart, but she could not resist awakening a little jealousy in him if she could. "Yes. We have a great many mutual friends and enjoy doing the same things. Do you know that it was he who taught me to drive my high-perch phaeton? Tony declared that I should upend it in a week's time and refused to be the instrument leading me to my doom. But Royden quite agreed that it would be most dashing to drive myself about the park during the afternoon promenade, and he took pity on me to teach me to drive it."

"Against your husband's wishes?"

Julia heard a note of disapproval in his voice, but she found it amusing. As they had come to know each other better, Julia had discovered that while Dominic was far from being the provincial that she had thought him, he had a streak of propriety in him that was rarely encountered in most of the men of the *ton* she knew. She found it endearing rather than annoying when he objected to the mild expletives she had fallen into the habit of uttering when annoyed or startled, and she meekly acceded to his insistence that they always take a groom with them when they rode for the sake of her reputation.

"Oh, Tony truly didn't mind," she said, laughing. "I suppose if I had turned the carriage over and been hurt, it would have been another matter, but Royden is a first-rate whip and I could not have had a better instructor, which Tony well knew."

Dominic did indeed wonder in what relation Julia stood to Tallboys. Even in the brief encounter he had witnessed at the church it had been apparent to him that there was considerable intimacy between them, and Julia confirmed for him that it was of long standing. What this meant, though, he was uncertain of until he saw Julia and Royden together the following night at a small gathering at Mrs. Carew's.

It would be wrong to say that Sir Royden monopolized Julia; he was too well-bred to single her out in a way that would cause unnecessary gossip. But they played whist as partners early in the evening and later sat down to a game of piquet and the parties from Amberly and Dumphree merged at supper, and Royden sat beside Julia in the most unexceptional manner.

In what way this impressed Dominic she had no idea, but she did note that he was more quiet than usual, and she was well aware that he observed her and Royden together. She wondered if he were feeling a trifle jealous, and was not displeased by it. She looked forward to the next morning's ride, wondering what he would say to her, but when dawn arrived, rain was coming down in sheets outside her window and not even the most intrepid of riders would have dared to venture out in such weather. The following day was equally foul, but it was not the cancellation of their rides that concerned Julia, but rather the fact that he did not even call at the house or send a note of regret. She told herself she was foolish, for it was not as if it were a formal engagement, but she had a sense of foreboding that something was not as it should be.

Harry could not bear the confinement, and on the second afternoon he ventured out when the rain let up a bit, taking the gig over to call at Amberly. Even though his reception remained cool, he did not allow it to prevent him from seeing his Sophia. Lady Amberly might have wished she could forbid him the house, but she could not do so without offending Alicia and so she permitted him to call, though with patent reluctance.

When Harry returned to Dumphree, he brought the news that Dominic had left Amberly to spend a few days with Mr. Carstairs at Longview. Though Julia told herself not to be such a ninny, this information made her anxious. Dominic had said nothing to her about going to Longview, and he had talked to her about his mentor and the progress of their project quite freely. She knew that if this had occurred at some time other than immediately after the arrival of Royden, it would not have disturbed her, but she could not help but feel there was some connection. She didn't know why it should matter to her; it was possible that when she left Dumphree she would never see Dominic again, but she knew she did not want their friendship affected while she was still in Wiltshire.

Days passed and nothing was heard from Dominic. No one seemed to remark on it. Some perverse quirk of pride refused to permit Julia to ask Lady Amberly if she knew when Dominic would be back, and it would not occur to Alicia to do so unless Julia asked it of her, and that she would not do. But Julia was far from spending her time worrying where Dominic might be. Rain or shine, Royden called every day and dined at Dumphree far more than he did with his hostess. Julia was diverted by his light wit and they quickly fell into their old habit of fashionable banter. He was not only a diverting companion but a very comfortable one, and Julia had ample opportunity to recall why she had wished to receive an offer of marriage from him.

Alicia was in daily expectation of an interesting announcement from Julia and quizzed her about it when they were alone, but Julia treated this lightly because she was so uncertain of her own feelings that she could not be comfortable discussing them even with Alicia. Royden had not made her a formal offer, but once or twice when they were left alone for a brief time, he turned the conversation into more intimate channels. Julia thought he might have spoken if she had encouraged him, but she did not. She did not understand how she could wish to marry him and shy away from it at the same time.

Her sister's rout was scheduled for Friday, two days before Sir Royden was scheduled to return to town. Alicia was as indolent as ever, and her wish to have everything planned and carried out in so short a space of time might not have been realized without Julia. Julia readily took over the management of all arrangements both because she enjoyed doing such things and as a means to pass time, for now that her mornings were not occupied riding, it was only Royden's visits in the afternoons that saved her from boredom.

On the night before the party Julia retired early to take the time to sort out her feelings, and by the time she slipped between the sheets she believed she had finally done so. Her sudden doubts about marrying Royden, she felt, forcing herself to be honest, was in some way linked to her feelings for Dominic, but these, she concluded, were nothing more than a physical attraction and a compatible sense of humor. She liked Dominic well enough; he had been a welcome diversion when she had supposed she would expire with boredom without her friends in town. But she did not believe it was more than that. Their interests and the worlds in which they lived were too far apart for there ever to be more between them.

Royden, on the other hand, was exactly the sort of man who would most suit her as a husband. He had never kissed in the way that Dominic had done, and he had never made her pulse race, but she believed he would make her an ideal husband because they were of the same world and their interests were wonderfully compatible. Julia was certain he would give her exactly the sort of life she most wished for. She fell asleep with the notion in her head that it was time she gave Royden the encouragement he sought from her.

Julia dressed that evening with extraordinary care in a silk gown of rich blue that made her azure eyes startling in their sparkling beauty. The gown had been made for her by the celebrated Madame Céleste; it was a daring cut that would not have been out of place in a London drawing room but that was sure to raise a few brows in Wiltshire. On the whole, she had been quite discreet since coming to Dumphree, forgoing gilding her toenails or rouging her cheeks, but tonight she left nothing to chance, even blackening her lashes with kohl to enhance them.

"You look exquisite," Alicia assured her at dinner.

"Bang up to the nines," Harry echoed so enthusiastically that Julia laughed. He had been going about so often with a Friday face of late that it was a pleasure to see him in good spirits for a change.

The Amberlys were among the first guests to arrive and Julia felt a small stab of disappointment that Dominic was not with them. He had been sent an invitation, of course, but she supposed that he had not yet returned, for he had not sent his regrets to Alicia. She was receiving guests with her sister, and Alicia had just suggested to her that she might wish to join the others since most had arrived when Dominic was announced.

Julia could scarcely credit the sudden jump in her pulse when their eyes met. He smiled and all of her anxious thoughts that he was in some way offended with her, and her own determination to set him at a firm distance now that she had made up her mind to encourage Royden again, vanished. She extended her hand to him and returned his smile with equal warmth. "How very bad of you to disappear from the neighborhood, Mr. Sales. You have consigned me to the very tedious company of my groom in the morning, and without even a word of apology."

Dominic, too, was startled by the reaction he felt to seeing Julia again. Though he had left in response to a letter from Carstairs, he had chosen to do so in so precipitate a manner because of what he had seen between Julia and Sir Royden and his own unexpected reaction to it. He knew he was physically attracted to Julia and he had come to like her a great deal in spite of his original prejudice, but he had not supposed she had touched him in a deeper way until then. He had deliberately absented himself to gain perspective about his feelings for her. He had thought he had succeeded. Now he was no longer certain again.

"Have you missed our conversations? How very flattering," he said in a light way. "I would have thought, though, that Sir Royden would have been glad to accompany you."

Julia realized that she had never even thought to ask Royden to take Dominic's place for her morning ride. It was as if the exercise belonged to them exclusively. She did not tell him this, though. "Oh, Royden is a capital sportsman, but driving is more to his taste than riding," she said, consigning Royden's considerable skill as a horseman to perdition. But recalling to herself that it was Royden, not Dominic, whom she wished to encourage, she added, "He has called every day, though, to visit us, and we have had a splendid time gossiping and enjoying long walks in the garden."

Julia thought she saw something flicker in Dominic's eyes, but she could not be certain. He said at his blandest, "Then you were not without entertainment. It is fortuitous that Sir Royden counts Amberly among his friends."

His tone was so without inflection that Julia could not guess at his thoughts, or whether he was merely making a comment or being sardonic. He turned then to Alicia again to speak a few words to her and joined the other assembled guests.

It proved to be a night of mixed humors for Julia, and for others as well. She made a point of being attentive to Royden, but it was he who seemed distant to her this night. Dominic too appeared to be more quiet and thoughtful, and when she asked him about it, he merely smiled and pleaded tiredness since he had returned to Amberly from Longview only in time for dinner.

In the early part of the evening, Harry seemed in high fettle, far more the sweet-natured and good-humored young man she knew him to be than he had been of late. She saw him in conversation with Dominic and joined them.

"What do you call that shade of blue, Aunt Jule?" Harry asked, eyeing her gown with less approval than he had earlier. "I've seen more than one of Alicia's friends look at you and then speak to one another behind their hands. I'll wager they've never seen anything like it in the neighborhood before."

"Envy," Dominic said succinctly. "It is not the gown, Lady Julia, which is clearly the creation of the most fashionable modiste, but rather how ravishing you look in it."

Dominic was not given to extravagant compliments, and Julia was quite pleased. "What pretty manners," she said approvingly. "Spoken like a pink of the *ton*."

He laughed. "I would never aspire to such heights."

Harry nodded sagely. "It never pays to pretend to be what everyone can see for themselves you're not."

"Harry! What atrocious manners," Julia said, aghast at the implied insult. "Mr. Sales, I am sure, might aspire to be anything he wished."

"Don't try to soften it, Lady Julia," Dominic said with his quick smile. "I have no such ambitions, nor do I apologize for it. I choose my style of life and the way I dress for comfort and convenience rather than to impress."

"For a woman, I fear, it is exactly reversed," she responded with a smile of her own. "And I am sure you are far more sensible than the rest of us. Keeping up with the latest fashion makes one a slave to it. Take Linton, for example. He fancies himself a Corinthian, so in addition to the more usual articles of dress, he must wear buckskins so exactly made to fit that they are indecent, a drab driving coat with so many capes it takes his valet and a footman to lift it onto his shoulders, and top boots so perfectly shined that he could use them as shaving mirrors. All at great expense and great inconvenience just to be *à la mode*.''

''As if you don't beggar yourself to be in the fashion,'' Linton said, rising to the bait. ''Papa is always complaining that you spend enough on clothes each quarter to keep up a small estate.''

Julia smiled condescendingly. ''Yes, but you see it is quite expensive when one sets the fashion rather than follows it.''

Dominic laughed, and there was such a warm exchange between them that Julia felt she had only imagined that he was cooler toward her tonight.

Going about the room speaking to her sister's guests, Julia noted about midway through the evening that neither Miss Sutton nor Linton was to be found in either drawing room. She looked quickly to the sofa where she had last seen Lady Amberly conversing with Mrs. Carew, and breathed a little easier when she saw that Lady Amberly appeared unconcerned and had likely not noticed the absence of her niece. Julia made a mental note to speak to Harry about such foolhardiness in a company so small that someone was bound to note them missing.

It was some five minutes later that she saw Sophia enter the main drawing room. Her cheeks were a little flushed and her eyes a bit bright, as if she were holding back tears. Julia feared that a lovers' quarrel had occurred and that a scene was precipitate if the girl was not able to control her emotions. But a few minutes later, while Julia was speaking to Alicia, Caroline Amberly, with Sophia beside her, came up to them and made their apologies for leaving so early.

''You know how it is with my poor Sophie,'' Lady Amberly explained. ''She suffers so from her headaches.''

Alicia was all solicitous understanding, but she said privately to Julia when they were gone that it looked to her more as if Sophia were about to have the vapors than the headache. Julia agreed. It concerned her greatly that Harry had not yet rejoined them, and she wondered if she should go up to his rooms to speak with him. If he simply disappeared in such a way, it could not help give rise to talk, for his name was already linked to Sophia's in the neighborhood and people were bound to recall that he had left the company at the same time that the Amberlys had gone.

As soon as she could do so unobtrusively, she slipped out of the room and headed toward the stairs. But passing a small anteroom adjacent to the drawing room, she was attracted by the sound of voices, one of which she thought was Harry's. Risking embarrassment if she were mistaken, she pushed open the door, which was ajar. She found Harry there and Dominic as well.

Harry was standing with his back to her, one hand leaning against the mantel, staring moodily into the grate. Dominic was speaking when she came into the room and broke off, turning to face her.

"I'm sorry if I interrupt," she apologized, "but I think, Harry, that you should go back into the drawing room with the others. The Amberlys and Miss Sutton have just left, and if you are gone as well, people may suspect there is a connection."

"Let them think what they will, damn them all," Harry said forcefully, and then turned, his attractive features puckered into a scowl. "If you're going to tell me again that I'm a fool and that it's only calf love, I wish you will save your breath," he said miserably. "It doesn't matter what anyone thinks anymore. I'll be going back to town with Tallboys on Monday."

Julia could not believe he would speak in such a way before Dominic, with whom he was not that well-acquainted. "What, are you giving up on Miss Sutton already?" she said in a rallying tone. "You are usually more tenacious when you fancy yourself in love."

But the viscount refused to take the hint and answer in kind. "Laugh if you like," he said bitterly. "I hope you never know what it is to love in vain."

"I hope so too," Julia said cheerfully but looking daggers at her nephew. "Oh, don't be such a nodcock, Harry. Sophia Sutton is the only presentable female in the neighborhood, you will feel differently when you return to your usual flirts. I think you should go with Royden. When you are in town again, you will forget her existence within a sennight."

"Perhaps. If Lady Amberly has her way, Sophia will go to the highest bidder," he said in a desolate tone. "If that happens, I only hope I can forget."

Julia saw the pain in his eyes, and her annoyance at his want of breeding dissipated. She went over to him and put her hand on his shoulder. "I won't tease you. I don't believe you can be in love on such short acquaintance and with so little encouragement, but even just a strong attraction can play havoc with emotions at times."

"Well, I'm not a fool, and I'm damned if I'll make a complete cake of myself. If that she-dragon wants to sell her niece to the highest bidder and Sophia won't make the least push to fight it, I can't prevent it."

"It isn't always as easy to fight as you might think," Julia said quietly. "Affection is a powerful weapon."

"But Sophie's not like you," Linton said miserably. "She's very gentle and sensitive and delicate. If they push her off on some aging libertine with a grand title and fortune, she would never be able to make the best of it like you did."

"I thank you for that," Julia said dryly. "Tony was hardly an aging libertine and I was certainly not forced to marry him."

"But if you had loved someone else, would you have stood up to your family and their expectations for you?" Linton demanded.

She was not sure why, but her eyes sought Dominic, who had effaced himself at the opposite end of the room. Their eyes met, but she looked quickly away. "I might have," she said, "but then again, like Sophia, I was very young and not in the habit of going against the wishes of my parents, who I always believed wanted the best for me."

"When Sophia sent me a note this morning asking if we could find a moment to be private tonight, I thought it was to tell me that she meant to defy her aunt, but it was the reverse," Harry said wretchedly. "She told me that her aunt has made her promise that she will not permit me to show her the least partiality any longer and that if I call at Amberly except in your company or Alicia's I shall not be received."

Julia was angered by Lady Amberly's actions but not surprised. She was privy to information that Harry did not know and that Alicia had told her not to tell him. So she could only say rather lamely, "If Miss Sutton is going to abide by this, Harry, then perhaps you should take the hint. It is clear that she is adamant against a match between you, and unless Miss Sutton has the nerve to defy her, it is likely you shall have to accept that she will be married to someone else."

Harry went white. Even though he had just said much the same himself, hearing it from another's lips made it seem even more possible to him. "I think I should rather put a period to my existence."

Julia knew this remark was only bravado, but it frightened her nevertheless. "Don't be such a damned fool, Harry."

"No. You are right. I've been a fool long enough." He turned abruptly and left the room.

Julia stood quietly for a moment, more upset by their conversation than she had realized. She had almost forgotten Dominic was still with her until he came up behind her and laid a comforting hand on her arm. "Don't be unduly concerned," he said gently. "Young men in the throes of unrequited love frequently say stupid things. Linton, for all his flair for the dramatic—or should I say melodramatic—is not without sense."

Julia turned and looked up at him. She felt comforted that he was with her, and she relaxed a bit. "The thing of it is, I begin to wonder if Harry is not more serious this time than before. I have never seen him in such a state. And it is quite hopeless, I fear. Alicia has told me that it is more than Harry's somewhat wild reputation and Caroline Amberly's ambitions for her niece. It is a personal thing also. Apparently Lady Amberly was in love with Hal during her first Season and made something of a fool of herself over him when he made it clear he did not return her regard. 'Heaven hath no rage . . . nor hell a fury.' "

Dominic nodded in understanding. "I have noted that Lady Amberly is an exceptionally proud woman. If she felt humbled by the experience, it is unlikely she would ever agree to an alliance between Morland's son and her niece. It may be for the best. I believe Miss Sutton needs a more mature and steadier man than Linton. She is something of a cipher at the moment, but I believe that with the proper guidance she might blossom quite nicely."

Julia regarded him curiously. "How is it that you are involved in my nephew's sorry affairs?"

"Is that a set-down?" he asked with a half-smile. "I know it is none of my concern other than a somewhat protective feeling I have toward Miss Sutton for the Amberlys' sake. I was near the door into the hall when Miss Sutton was attempting to slip away unobserved to meet Linton. Her anxiety and watchfulness were so obvious that I readily guessed what she was about. She is a poor conspirator, I fear. When the time they were gone from the drawing room began to extend, I thought I would be doing them a better kindness to intervene rather than allow their absence to become obvious to everyone else."

"I had a similar thought," Julia said. "I begin to wonder if they are not a perfect match. They both seem to have an excess of sensibility to make up for a lack of sense."

Dominic extended his arm for her to take. "We had better return to the others ourselves, or we shall be the ones talked about."

Julia placed her hand on his arm and allowed him to lead her from the room. "It is just the greatest pity that Harry must always wear his heart on his sleeve," she said as they entered the drawing room.

"Where it is all too easily wounded," he said with an understanding smile.

As they entered the room, Tallboys approached them and he heard the last part of their conversation. "If I sound callous, I apologize, but I would save my pity for Linton," he said in a dry manner. "He has been falling in and out of love since he has been out of short coats, but he has never, to my knowledge, received any lasting hurt. He shall probably do so a dozen more times before he is ready to be married."

"That doesn't assuage his present unhappiness," Dominic said quietly.

Royden stood very close to Julia, touching her free arm above her elbow in a possessive gesture. "My dear Julia," he said, according Dominic only the briefest of bows and ignoring his remark, "I have been wondering where you had disappeared to."

"I was consoling Linton."

"My dear, you waste your efforts. Linton is more fickle than any ten schoolroom misses. You may mark my words, he will fall out of love again as soon as he has returned to town." He placed his hand firmly under her arm, as if to draw her away. "Mrs. Carew wished to speak with you. I am sure Mr. Sales will excuse us."

Dominic, without a word, took a step back from them and made them a small, formal bow before assuring them of his understanding.

Perversely, Julia was annoyed by Royden's possessiveness. She smiled at Dominic and said, "Do we begin our rides again, Mr. Sales, now that you are returned?"

Dominic could not help responding to that dazzling smile and her gift for making the person she smiled at seem the most important in the world to her, but neither was he ignorant of her purpose. He had noted Tallboys' possessiveness toward Julia and her dislike of it. In another humor it might have amused him that Julia was using him to punish Tallboys, but he felt a sudden shaft of anger and nearly made some excuse to her. He surprised himself by saying, "Of course, if you wish it. Tomorrow at the usual time?"

"I pledge to be punctual as always. Do you know, Royden, that Mr. Sales, who thinks me a frivolous creature, expected me to keep him cooling his heels the first time that we rode together."

Tallboys' expression was shuttered, and his voice, when he spoke, had lost its previous warmth. "Tardiness has never been one of Julia's affectations," he said in a clipped way. "If you have plans to discuss, I know you will excuse me." He accorded them a stiff bow and walked away.

Julia looked up at Dominic to find him regarding her unsmilingly. "You look so somber. Are you suffering from unrequited love like Linton?" she asked, her tone quizzing.

"Is Tallboys?"

"What do you mean?"

"If you mean to flirt with me, I would prefer it to be for my benefit rather than to arouse jealousy in another man."

He spoke without anger, but Julia recognized that it was underlying his words. She linked her arm in his again. "That is nonsense," she said with a soft, silvery laugh. "Next you will say that I only wished to ride with you tomorrow to make Royden jealous, as if we have not been riding together virtually every morning for the past month."

"To alleviate your boredom," he reminded her, his inflection arid.

Before Julia could reply they were interrupted by Alicia. "Can you come and settle a dispute for us, Mr. Sales? Mr. Crosby insists that the red fox is indigenous to England and Sir Arthur is equally adamant that they were brought here from Ireland for better hunting."

"By all means do so, and at once," Julia said, slipping her arm free of Dominic's. "Mr. Crosby and Sir Arthur will argue over whether the sun rises in the east. If you prevent them from coming to cuffs in Alicia's drawing room you will be the savior of her party."

He smiled thinly. "Actually they are both right. The red fox is indigenous to England, but a number were imported from Ireland in the last century to improve the stock."

"Splendid," Julia said, laughing. "They will both believe they are right and neither will feel he must spend the evening justifying himself."

There was little Dominic could do but acquiesce, and there were no further opportunities to continue their discussion, for which Julia was grateful. Dominic had skated too near the truth for her comfort.

5

The following morning was gray and dismal, with the likelihood of rain, but Julia was waiting for Dominic as usual as he trotted up the drive. Linton was beside her and mounted as well. Harry was speaking to a groom standing beside his stallion, and Julia spurred her horse to meet Dominic before he reached them.

"I hope you don't mind that Linton shall be our chaperone today instead of my groom," she said with a smile that was an apology. "He is still feeling very blue-deviled. He wished to ride this morning, so I asked him to come with us."

"By all means. I thought we would go into Maracat Wood this morning. There is another dovecote there I wished to inspect, and then we may ride along the lake if it does not begin to rain."

"That should be great fun," the viscount said caustically, coming up to them.

"I asked you to come with us because I thought you needed a bit of diversion, Harry," Julia said patiently, "but if you dislike the plan, you needn't come to please me."

Linton shrugged and said in a more mollifying tone, "No, I don't dislike it. But I'm not in very good frame this morning."

"So I gather," Dominic said. "Dovecotes may not cheer you, but perhaps the exercise will."

The viscount's only response was a listless murmur. In another minute or so, Julia, who stopped to adjust her stirrup leather, declared herself ready and they set off down the drive at a comfortable trot. They followed the road until they came to a lane that would take them to the wood more directly. Once away from the traffic of an occasionally passing carriage or farm cart, they loosened rein and broke into a canter, easing into a comfortable gallop until they reached the edge of the wood.

As they slowed to a walk along the path, Julia and Dominic at first attempted to draw Linton into their conversation, but found him so little responsive to their efforts that they finally gave it up. Julia was not precisely annoyed with her sullen nephew, for she understood that it stemmed from unhappiness rather than ill-temper, but he was beginning to exacerbate her patience and she was pleased enough to leave him to his unhappy thoughts if he preferred them.

It was true that she had invited her nephew in the hope of diverting him from the pain she knew he was feeling, but she had had her own motive as well. Royden had been cool toward her after her flirtation with Dominic, but by the end of the evening she was certain that any jealousy she had aroused in him had borne fruit. When he took leave of her, he had not merely bowed over her hand in the usual way, but had again brought it to his lips, his eyes on hers, and informed her that he would call tomorrow in a tone that made her suppose his promise had some special meaning. She was still not certain of wishing to accept an offer from him as she had been before leaving London, but she had made up her mind to do it, and if he meant to offer for her tomorrow, she would be ready to receive him.

Her purpose achieved, she decided that a bit of prudence would not be amiss. Tallboys would not dare to object to her early-morning ride with Dominic, for he knew her well enough to know that he would receive cold comfort for it. But Julia saw no reason to press her point excessively. With Linton along as a more exacting chaperone than merely an indifferent groom, some of the sting of her defiance would be removed. She wanted to whet Royden's appetite, not give him a distaste for her.

But her plans went awry.

Julia had almost forgotten how much she enjoyed not only the rides she and Dominic had shared, but their conversation. The easiness between them was in no way affected by their separation and the words they had had the previous night. They were as comfortable with each other as if they had been friends of long standing instead of barely a month. Julia did not even remember thinking that before the first time they had ridden together she had supposed she would find him boring.

The viscount, however, was heartily bored not only with the conversation, but with the tameness of their ride. He was feeling wretched and restless and he wished he had followed his original intent to ride hell-for-leather to work off his unhappiness. He had resisted their attempts to discuss topics he might be interested in, and to include him in their discussion, but in this foul humor, he resented it when they left him to his own ponderings. When they reached the dovecote, he announced abruptly that he was returning to the house.

Julia's exasperation with his ill humor finally got the better of her. "That is really too bad of you, Linton," she said, allowing her annoyance to be plain. "If you didn't wish to come, you should have said so. If you wish to set yourself apart from us and be blue-deviled, that is one thing, but it is unjust of you to force me to curtail my pleasure just because you are in a black humor."

Harry looked mildly surprised at her attack, and when he spoke, his tone was more defensive than angry. "Please yourself, Aunt Jule. I don't want company in any case. I'll probably go back cross-country and gallop out my fidgets."

"Are you forgetting that we dispensed with my groom?" she asked crossly. "If you go back to Dumphree now, so must I, whether you wish for my company or not."

Linton knew he was behaving badly, but he refused to retreat. "You were not used to have such a fine sense of propriety, Aunt," he said waspishly. "I prefer to be alone."

Julia saw that Dominic was about to speak, and guessed from the sternness she read in his expression that he meant to reprimand the younger man for his churlishness. She laid her fingers on his hand for a brief moment to stay him.

"Perhaps I am overly concerned," she said coolly. "By all means, go alone if that is what you wish."

Without even affording them the courtesy of a farewell, the viscount turned his horse and cantered off in the direction they had come.

"That was remarkably graceless," Dominic said in mild surprise. "I wouldn't have expected it of him, I confess."

"I have no right to apologize for him. He is a grown man, even if he behaves like a spoiled child, and must answer for himself."

"What he does for himself is his own affair, but he might have spared your blushes," Dominic said with more harshness than she had ever heard in his voice before.

Julia cast him a swift glance, but there was nothing in his countenance to give his feelings away. She shrugged. "Oh, well! I have no doubt he will realize what a cake he has made of himself and apologize when he is feeling more the thing. I suppose he is taking this so much to heart because it comes so soon after his unhappy affair with the opera dancer he imagined himself in love with."

If Dominic thought it unseemly for her to know of such things, as her brother did, he gave no indication of it. He merely concurred and allowed the matter to drop. After examining the dovecote, they continued on deeper into the woods until they came to the clearing that led to the lake.

Julia knew full well that she should have gone after Linton. It was improper for her to be riding alone with Dominic in such secluded surroundings. If she had feared that Tallboys would dislike her riding with Dominic with only a groom for chaperone, she knew only too well how much she would set up his back if he ever learned of their solitary ride.

But she remained with Dominic and made no suggestion that they return to Dumphree at once. At the lake they dismounted and lightly tethered their horses. The morning was warming in spite of the absence of sun and they walked along the edge of the lake, deep in conversation and scarcely noting the passing of time. The sky began to darken perceptibly before they realized how far they had gone.

"I fear we may be in for a soaking," Julia said with dismay as she looked down at the full skirts of her riding habit. "If I try to run in this, I shall trip myself every other step."

Dominic's eyes scanned the sky. "It's going to rain, but not, I think, that immediately. I doubt we would make it back to Dumphree, but we are much closer to the old Dower House and might reach that in time. If the rain doesn't let up in a short time, I could drive you back in my curricle, which would offer some protection from the rain with the hood up."

Julia agreed, and if they could not run, they walked as briskly as they could to their horses. It was impossible to move with any speed through the wood. The paths were mostly overgrown with trailing branches and roots, making anything more than a walk or, in some stretches, a slow trot foolhardy.

The rain began before they left the heavy covering of the trees, but only a scattering of drops reached them through the thick overgrowth. It wasn't until they reached the clearing that they realized that the rain was steady and heavy. They exchanged rueful smiles and tacitly set their horses at a gallop down the lane. When they reached the road, they turned left toward Amberly.

They passed through the wide gates at the end of the drive at Amberly and, still at a full gallop, veered to the right at the fork that led to the old Dower House. The house was upon them before they realized it, and they came to a sliding stop on the rain-soaked grass at the front of the house. Dominic was off his horse almost before it came to a halt. Casting the reins over the pommel, he pushed open the door and called for assistance.

In less than a minute, a servant came rushing out of the house. He held Julia's mount while she slid to the ground, and then, without receiving any command from Dominic, took the reins of both horses and walked head-down in the rain toward the stables.

"Goodness," said Julia as she entered the house. "What a treasure you have in your servants. If I suggested to any of my indoor servants that they perform the work of a groom, I would be given notice in a trice."

Dominic smiled. He cast his hat and gloves on the table. "It's even more amazing than you think. That was Taret, my valet. He and I have been through a great deal together and understand each other very well. He has been with me on all of my travels, and there were times when he has been groom, footman, cook, and even scullery maid to me. If it had been only myself, I shouldn't have minded leaving my horse at the stables and walking to the house in the rain, but I wished to spare you."

Julia looked down at her wet skirts, which clung to her in heavy folds, and laughed. "From what? A soaking? Though your intent is noble, it comes a bit late."

"A greater soaking, then," he said with a smile. "I wish my housekeeper, Mrs. Grisham, were here, but that can't be helped. She has been given the day off to visit her daughter, who will soon be lying in with her first child. Since she is in my employ, her chaperonage would be given little credit, but she is my only female servant, so there is no one I can send to attend you. You can't go back to Dumphree without drying off a bit. As soon as Taret returns from the stables, I'll have him kindle a fire in one of the bedchambers for you, and he can take your habit down to the kitchen fire and see if it can't be dried out a bit before you leave."

Julia digested his words, wondering what she had gotten herself into. In spite of the unexpectedness of their situation, the impropriety of their circumstances was extreme. Julia might enjoy flouting convention to make the tattlemongers twitch with outrage, but she never did anything that would in any way bring her to ruin. If it were known that she was so completely alone with Dominic, disrobed and unattended, her reputation would be shattered beyond repair. However unlikely it might seem that anyone would ever learn of her visit to the old Dower House, Julia knew from living in the world that it was never impossible.

But she had come with him willingly, and she was already shivering in her wet habit. She followed him upstairs into a bedchamber off a gallerylike hall at the top of the stairs.

He ushered her into the room and then left her, returning in a few moments with a brocade dressing gown over his arm. "It may not fit you very well," he said apologetically, "but it is the only thing I have that will answer while Taret tends to your habit."

Julia accepted the dressing gown, and as soon as he had gone, she stripped off her habit, not without difficulty for the buttons were tiny and she had never before had to deal with them without a maid to undress her. She put on the dressing gown, which was big for her but, as she saw when she went over to the cheval glass at the far end of the room near the windows, not unattractively so.

The curly brimmed beaver hat she had worn during their ride had protected her hair somewhat, but she felt that it was still damp and she removed the pins and let it fall to her shoulders so that it would dry. She was spreading the tendrils of hair with her fingers when there was a discreet knock at the door, followed at her command to enter by the presence of Dominic's valet.

Neither did the servant disdain the work of a chambermaid. He carried hot water in a can for Julia, and while she gratefully washed the dirt of the road from her hands and face, he kindled the fire in the grate and pulled a chair close to it so that she might sit and remove any chill from her soaking. Then, accepting Julia's grateful thanks, he picked up the sodden habit and bowed himself out of the room.

Julia did curl into the chair in front of the fire. For a short time, her mind was occupied with thoughts of Royden and of Dominic, wondering if Royden did intend to make her an offer when he called this afternoon as she surmised. If he ever learned of this morning's adventure, he would surely never do so. At the moment it did not seem to her to be as important as she had thought it only a few hours ago. Lulled by the warmth of the fire and the comfort of the overstuffed chair, she closed her eyes and snuggled against the back of the chair and began to drift into a light sleep.

Dominic tapped lightly at the door and, when he received no response, opened it a bit. At first he didn't see her, but when he did, he felt an unexpected stirring of emotion. Julia, curled up inside the voluminous dressing gown, with her hair on her shoulders and her long lashes fanning her cheeks, looked very young and vulnerable and tantalizingly feminine. He checked at the doorway, almost as if he doubted the prudence of continuing, and then came into the room, closing the door behind him.

He walked quietly over to her, wondering if he should touch her awake, but she opened her eyes as he approached and smiled in a lazy, welcoming way.

"The morning's exercise and the warmth of the fire have been my undoing," she said, stretching a little.

"Are you hungry? Did you break your fast before we met this morning?" he said as he drew a matching chair closer to hers.

Julia nodded. "I had bread and butter and chocolate."

"We should send word to Dumphree. When Linton arrives home without you, Lady Dumphree will be concerned."

"Linton won't be back at Dumphree before dinner," Julia said with confidence. "It is a hallmark of his that when his latest passion is blighted, he goes into a black humor and disappears just long enough for everyone to begin to worry about him and fuss over him when he finally returns."

Dominic's lips turned up in a faint smile as he remembered the excesses of his own salad days. "The attention that engenders is undoubtedly soothing. But this isn't town. Where has he to go here, and in the rain?"

"Trust Linton. He is a charmer, you know, when he chooses. No doubt some farmer's wife or cottager has befriended him and taken him in by now. If anything, Alicia will worry less about us, supposing that I have determined to stay with Harry until he has shaken off his malaise."

"What he needs is to return to the amusements of town. It will affect a wonderful change in him, I have no doubt. I am sure you are right that as soon as he is again among his usual flirts, he will forget Sophia quickly enough."

"He may not have that opportunity," Julia said with a sigh. "Lady Amberly takes her niece to town in a fortnight or so for her first Season. If only she were not so cursed pretty," she said forcefully.

"He is young," Dominic said. "When he is ready to be in love, he'll make his choice based on more than mere physical attraction."

Julia regarded him curiously through her lashes. "Have you ever been in love, Mr. Sales?" His eyes were on hers, but at her question he looked away and Julia knew she had touched on something he would have preferred she had not.

"Love is not always easily defined," he said evasively.

"No, it isn't," she agreed. She was silent for a moment and then said, "I have often wondered if the thunderclap that the poets speak of really exists, or if it is not just a romantic ideal that may even serve to keep one from recognizing love when it does come. I have no doubt that I loved Tony, but I don't think I was ever in love with him. I don't think I have ever been truly in love."

He made no response, but his eyes were on hers. She perceived, or thought she did, something in them that made her feel suddenly restless. She got up, drawing his dressing gown more closely about her. She moved closer to the fire, bending forward a bit, as if for warmth, though it was only an excuse to cover her restiveness. "You have not answered my question, Mr. Sales," she said without turning.

He still made no reply. When Julia finally straightened and turned, she saw that he had gotten up and was standing quite near to her. The snapping of the fire had masked the sound and she was a bit startled, though she did not show it outwardly. Inside, she was aware of an increased pulse, but not, she thought, from surprise.

"I have loved women," he said in a quiet, musing tone. "I have desired women, at times the two together, but if love is a sudden, unexpected thunderclap, then no, I have not been in love either."

He came a step or two nearer her, so that Julia had to lift her chin a bit to meet his eyes. She felt a quick surge of excitement and had no difficulty recognizing it as desire. It was unexpected, but not, she realized, unwelcome.

Though he had never inspired a strong attraction in Julia, Sir Anthony had been a skillful lover and he had taught her the joys of making love with a man. There had certainly been times since her husband's death when she had longed to be in a man's arms again, to feel his lips on hers, but never sufficiently to risk her reputation or abandon her virtue. Until now.

"Perhaps it is something quite different in reality," she said, a faint breathlessness in her voice.

Dominic was as aware as she of the sudden physical tension between them. He had not intended to act upon it, but the lure was irresistible. "Perhaps it is," he said, and closed the short space between them.

Julia knew he was going to kiss her and she moved toward him to meet his embrace. She was taut with the anticipation of pleasure. She felt the hardness and curve of every muscle in his body pressed against hers; the strength of his arms around her made her long for the ultimate lovers' embrace.

Dominic undid the sash that bound the dressing gown, and drew back from her a little to slide the garment off her shoulders. She lowered her arms and let the dressing gown fall to the floor. She stood before him in only her chemise, the soft swell of her breasts just visible above the lace at the low neckline. He gently traced the curves of her breasts with one finger. They both watched the slow, deliberate progress of his caress, palpable excitement mounting between them. Then he looked up at her face, compelling her eyes to his.

Julia felt a warm flush that spread from her cheeks to her shoulders and chest, not from shyness or shame, but from arousal. He said nothing, but his eyes questioned her. Though it was not in her line of vision, she was intensely aware of the large bed that dominated the room. If she did not put an end to their lovemaking now, their passion would be unstoppable and they would share that bed as lovers.

Julia knew the choice was being given to her, and she made it without hesitation. She lifted her arms to his shoulders again and kissed him. His hands came up about her waist and then traveled downward, caressing her and drawing her tight against him.

He drew her over beside the bed and allowed her to undress him with equal deliberation. When they were both naked, he drew her down onto the bed. For all its intensity, their love-making was gentle and unhurried. They explored each other with mutual fascination, their responsiveness heightening with every caress and exploding into pleasure.

Julia lay quietly in his arms and listened to the gradual steadying of his heartbeat. The rain still beat heavily outside, beyond the warmth of the room. She watched the shifting pattern of shadows on the ceiling caused by the flickering light from the hearth, letting thoughts drift in and out of her consciousness, never quite focusing on what was really uppermost in her mind.

She didn't really understand why she had given in to her attraction to Dominic after rejecting the advances of other men who were so much more to her taste, especially now when she was all but certain to be marrying again. Nor did she choose to dwell on her awareness that she had never felt any temptation to abandon herself to passion with Tallboys.

Dominic's breathing was even and she thought he had fallen asleep, but she stirred in his embrace and his eyes opened and he gave her a languorous smile. She raised herself up on one elbow and looked down at him, as if seeking an answer to the questions in her head. But she didn't hold his gaze for long, looking away as she traced random patterns on his chest.

He took her hand in his and brought her fingers to his lips. He sensed her uncertainty. "What is it, Julia? Regret? I hope not."

Julia smiled faintly. "No. Not that. I wonder why this happened, though."

"I think it was probably inevitable," he said without displaying any of her concern. "There was attraction between us before we acknowledged it."

She withdrew her hand from his and sat up, feeling no self-consciousness for her nakedness. "I have been attracted to any number of men since leaving the schoolroom," she said with a slight note of acid in her voice, "but the only man I have ever made love with before was my husband."

"There is more between us than physical attraction."

His words discomfited her. She moved a little away from him. "We have become friends," she agreed.

"It's more than that," he said levelly. "At least it is for me."

"What do you mean?" she said with more sharpness than she intended.

"I have been falling in love with you, Julia. I think you know that. Frankly, I didn't want to. I thought we were too ill-suited even for friends. But I was mistaken and you have cut up my peace and now it is irreversible."

Her discomfort was strong now. She swung to the side of the bed and reached down to the floor for her discarded chemise. "Nothing is ever completely irreversible," she said with an unsuccessful attempt at lightness as she pulled the chemise over her head.

He sat up and took her arm, drawing her to face him. "This is," he said with a quiet intensity. "I have made you mine, and nothing can ever change that now. Marry me, Julia."

He kissed her very gently. Julia permitted the embrace, she even responded to it, but inside she felt a clutching dismay. She had not for a moment expected him to offer her marriage, and she wished he had not. And yet something stirred inside of her, some faint response that made her want to return to his arms and know that she would be there forever. She firmly shook off the feeling and withdrew from him.

"You know you don't mean that," she said with a soft, false laugh. She slipped out of his arms and off the bed. "It would serve you right if I accepted your offer."

"Why would I say such a thing if I didn't mean it?"

Julia shrugged, her back to him as she pulled on her stockings. "The passion of the moment. Fortunately, one of us has a cool head, or we should find ourselves in the suds as soon as we realized what we have committed ourselves to."

"Julia, don't pretend that you don't understand me. And don't pretend that you are indifferent to me. After what has passed between us, I would know it for a lie."

"Because we have made love?" she said with amazement. "My dear Dominic, I know you don't live in the fashionable world as I do, but you can't be so naïve to suppose that love-making occurs only between people who are in love."

"Are you saying that you feel nothing for me at all?" His voice was devoid of inflection.

Julia finished tying a garter in place before answering. "No, of course not. But I am certainly not in love with you, or anyone else, for that matter. I think it would be no good thing for either of us if we did love each other. You are right, we should certainly never suit."

"Why not?" Though he still spoke in a flat way, there was a hardness creeping into his tone.

Julia's laugh was not forced this time. "You know we are creatures of completely different worlds," she said, her tone clearly expressing her wonder that he should even question this. "How could we ever join our lives together? I admit I have enjoyed our rides and talks very much; I like you very well. But a few weeks of communing with nature and country pursuits is one thing, I should shudder with horror at the prospect of spending my life in such a manner. And it would be the same for you. How on earth would you conduct yourself at *ton* parties, which I suspect would interest you no more than the life you prefer interests me. You would be out of place and quite miserable, I am certain."

"I might perhaps contrive to conduct myself with some address," he said aridly. He got out of bed and began dressing in silence.

There was nothing in his movements to indicate his anger, but Julia sensed that he was in a rage and that it was barely contained. In her own way she was a bit angry as well. She had certainly never meant for them to become more than friends, and now that they were lovers, she feared that the friendship would be lost. An emotional element, to which she had no wish to respond, had come between them and they would never again enjoy the easy, comfortable, uncomplicated relationship she had grown to value.

In her surprise at his unexpected offer, she had answered with no thought for his feelings. For the first time it occurred to her that perhaps he meant what he said about falling in love with her and that she had wounded him more than she guessed. It was not her intent.

"I did not mean to imply that you lack breeding or address," she said. "I only meant that you would likely feel out of place in such a setting, which you yourself have condemned as superficial and uninteresting." She picked up the dressing gown again and looked at it in a helpless way as if she could will it to turn into her riding habit, which his valet had not yet returned to her. Even sopping wet, she would have donned it at once to be away from this uncomfortable interview.

He turned and faced her, dressed again in breeches and shirt, the high collar of which sloped gently to his shoulders without the starched neckcloth to keep it erect. His hair was slightly tousled and Julia thought he looked young and vulnerable; she wished with all her heart that her surprise at his offer and dismay at her own behavior had not betrayed her into speaking so abruptly.

He smiled without humor. "You can't put the bark back on the tree now, my love," he said bitingly. "If I were Tallboys, I fancy your answer to me would be quite different. And I don't think you're any more in love with him than you are with me."

There was such a sneering contempt in his voice that Julia felt as if she had been slapped. "Perhaps it would have been," she retorted, stung once again into speaking without thinking. She put on his dressing gown again because she was now excessively uncomfortable standing before him in only her chemise. The irony that she should feel this way when only a few minutes earlier she had lain naked in his arms did not escape her, but she pushed it aside. She would have give up another two months of town life if she could have had the option of leaving this room and this house at once.

"You needn't reproach yourself for this afternoon's work," he said coldly. "The mistake was entirely mine. I judged you as something quite other than you are."

There was no mistaking his meaning, and Julia, to her chagrin, flushed. "If that is what you think of me," she said hotly, "I wonder that you would offer me marriage."

"I acquit you of being a whore," he said with a deliberately nasty smile. "I think you are merely an opportunist. It is one thing for you to share my bed, but quite another my name. Then, it is title and fortune that matter. I have found it usually is, which is why I have no use for it. To me a man is judged not by what he is called but by what he is."

Julia knew that she had wounded him and that some of his anger was just, but she was stung by the nearness of the truth of his words and her temper got the better of her. "What do you know of life in the world?" she demanded bitterly. "You live out of it by choice, perfectly content with your plants and your writings. I could never find contentment in such a life, and without money or position, a woman is nothing in the world, reduced to a dependent begging for bread crusts from more fortunate relatives. My own companion is just such a creature, and try as I might to regard her as my equal, I find her a poor pitiful creature. It is very easy, is it not, to condemn position and fortune when you are yourself well-born and far from a pauper?"

He appeared struck by this and was silent for a moment. He picked up his jacket and ruined neckcloth. "Point to you, Julia," he said evenly. "Let us cry quits, then. What difference does it make what I think? You have made your feelings plain, and there is an end to it. I'll see if Taret has your habit ready and send for the carriage. You may send a groom for your horse whenever it is convenient. Or if you prefer, I'll have Taret bring the horse to you." His eyes held hers for no more than a moment and then he made her the briefest of bows and left.

When he was gone, Julia became suddenly aware that her heart was beating rapidly. She sat down abruptly on the nearest chair as a sick feeling came over her in an unexpected wave. She felt badly shaken, and in her heart she knew why.

Her rejection of him had been almost deliberately cruel, and though she did not wish to acknowledge it, she knew it was because he had touched something inside of her and she had no wish to acknowledge it. It was not that she believed she had been foolish enough to fall in love with him, but she knew she was dangerously close to feeling more for him than she dared. She did not want to be in love with him and had no intention of allowing it to happen. She had been brutal because she wanted no risk of any continuance between them.

What she had said to him was true; she had enjoyed their time together, but she could not conceive of spending her life in such a fashion. She had never known any life but the fashionable one, and she flourished in it. Not even for love would she consider giving it up.

In spite of the fact that she had not married Sir Anthony by choice, she knew that it was only a man like him—rich, fashionable, who would pamper and indulge her—would suit her and the style of life to which she was accustomed. She was completely convinced of this and yet she could not help the strong emotions that now assailed her. She was grateful when Taret finally arrived with her habit, which was still damp but wearable.

Dominic was waiting outside in his curricle. The rain had slowed considerable, but even with this and the hood up, it was an uncomfortable and wet drive home. But the principal discomfort had nothing to do with the weather. Conversation was desultory and no mention was made by either of what had passed between them. Julia watched the passing landmarks along the road back to Dumphree to avoid looking at him. She had never felt more gauche and awkward in the whole of her life.

It seemed an endless drive to them both, and when he at last drew the curricle to rest in front of the house, she did not even wait for the footman to come down to assist her from the carriage. But the voluminous skirts of her habit were nearly her undoing. She caught her heel in the hem and might have fallen if Dominic had not quickly leaned over and caught her arm. She regained her balance and turned to him. Their eyes met and she saw that his were carefully unexpressive.

"Thank you, Mr. Sales," she said very quietly, and turned and went into the house without looking back.

It was as she had predicted: Harry was still not at home and Alicia had not yet begun to feel concern. Her sister listened to the story of their being caught in the rain and of her going to the old Dower House with Dominic without any comment other than to say that it was fortunate they had been near some sort of shelter.

The rain continued without abatement for the remainder of the day and even kept Royden away. He sent a note to Julia with his regrets, promising to call the next day. In her current frame of mind, Julia was inclined to think she had only imagined that he had meant to make her an offer today. He hardly behaved like an eager lover. But her sense told her her expectations were unreasonable; there was no pretense of passion between them. His offer could as easily wait for another day without causing concern to either of them.

With many thoughts to disturb her, Julia spent a restless night and awoke the next morning without her usual spirits. There was no question of riding, both because of what had occurred between her and Dominic and because the bad weather continued and there was a steady downpour that lasted most of the morning.

Julia's inclination would have been to forgo church on Sunday, but she knew that if she begged off, her sister would likely press for a reason that satisfied her and Julia had no wish to have to explain herself. It was simply easier to dress and go with her sister and brother-in-law. Harry had come home late afternoon and had once again taken to his room. Alicia did not press him to go because, she told Julia, she was frankly weary of his mopes.

"I cannot believe that foolish boy actually went to speak to Amberly about Sophia," Alicia said, annoyed. She had had a note from Caroline Amberly concerning this presumption and her expressed wish that Linton would not continue to force his attentions on Sophia, who, the viscountess claimed, found them undesirable. "He must take after Eliza's side of the family," she continued. "He certainly has none of his father's caution or sense."

"He is in love," Julia said, wondering why she was defending him when she felt much as Alicia did that he was a fool to have braved such obvious opposition to his suit.

"That is still no excuse to behave like a ninnyhammer and then go into a black dudgeon when matters go predictably awry."

Julia refrained from further comment. She had been too little in control of her own emotions of late to feel comfortable criticizing this fault in her nephew.

Though the Amberlys were in their usual pew, Dominic was not with them, for which Julia was grateful. It was not that she feared a meeting, but it made matters less complicated if they didn't have to see each other again before she left Dumphree at the end of the week.

Royden was present, however, and was invited to take luncheon with the Dumphrees. Julia was glad enough for his company, for he was in excellent humor and made her laugh. He was even more attentive toward her than usual, and when their eyes met, his held a warmth that was unmistakable. She knew a declaration from him was imminent and she should be glad of it. But there was no real joy in her heart.

After luncheon, Lord and Lady Dumphree tactfully excused themselves, and since it had finally cleared and the sun come out, Julia and Royden went outside to the garden to enjoy the unexpected sunshine. She felt a faint wave of dismay when the Dumphrees left them; she tried to dismiss it but could not. Her uppermost emotion was self-anger; she wanted to want to marry Royden. She felt as if her own feelings were betraying her.

She put him off for a bit, continuing to discuss mutual friends in town, but eventually she could not forestall the inevitable and she composed herself as best she could to hear his proposal, wondering almost fearfully what her answer would be.

Julia sat on a stone bench already dry from the warmth of the sun, looking out over the formal gardens. He came over to her and sat very close beside her. Julia turned to him, and he took her hand in his, his smile a bit grave. "We have had the pleasure of knowing each other for more than ten years, Julia," he began. "When Tony first introduced you to me as his betrothed, I confess, I envied him."

Julia gave a soft, spontaneous laugh. "For my sophisticated beauty?" she said, quizzing him. "That's doing it too brown, Royden. I was a gauche schoolgirl until Tony took me in hand. I am entirely his creation, I admit it freely."

"You are your own woman, Julia. You always have been, and that is much of your attraction. Half the men in London are in love with you, you know, and now I am the one, because of our friendship, who is envied. But unlike Tony, I haven't the security of knowing that you are mine." He took both of her hands in his and bestowed a gentle kiss on each before saying, "Will you give me the right to name you my own, Julia? Will you be my wife?"

At last the words that Julia had waited and hoped to hear were spoken. Her design to bring him up to scratch was successful. But what triumph she felt, if any, was faint. She knew neither how nor why her doubts had begun, but there was no question that they existed and that she could not give him the unqualified answer to his proposal that she had intended. It was absurd. She told herself that it was absurd, but she could not deny her feelings.

She would not allow herself to be craven; her eyes met his as she spoke. "You do me great honor, Royden. I know that it is a trite thing to say, but it is true. Most any woman would feel herself fortunate to be singled out by you in such a manner."

"But you cannot accept my flattering offer," he interpolated in an arid tone. "What is it, Julia? I thought you felt as I do. Surely I cannot be guilty of so great a conceit without some encouragement from you."

Julia would not allow them to sink into melodrama. She gave him a teasing smile. "Am I accused of leading you to believe I felt as you do, or to conceit?"

He smiled thinly. "Julia, your levity is much of your charm, but this is most serious—at least to me."

Julia looked down at her hands held in his and gently withdrew them. "It is serious. I beg your pardon, Royden. I am not playing with your affections, I promise you that. You are not mistaken. I have encouraged you to believe that I am not indifferent to you, but the truth is that I find I am not certain I wish to be married again. Not to anyone."

"A not unnatural reaction," he said reasonably. "I know how attached you were to Tony. To lose him so unexpectedly and at such a tender age has doubtless left its scars."

"I suppose it has," she agreed, "but it isn't that. At least, I don't think that it is. I thought that this was what I wanted, but . . . but now it is not." She smiled in a rueful way. "I'm sorry, Royden. Shall you be able to forgive me so that we can at least remain friends?"

He was looking beyond her, obviously in consternation. He did not respond at once and Julia had the unhappy feeling that she had indeed offended him irreparably. She was sorry for it, but she found it did not disturb her quite as much as she thought it would have.

He turned and walked a little away from her. "I see this is not false modesty, Julia. You really have had a change of heart toward me. I wish I knew the cause of it, which you so gently elude. Is it Sales?"

A surprised laugh escaped Julia, so great was her astonishment. She put out her hand against the stone bench almost as if to steady herself. "Mr. Sales? Whatever has made you think that?"

Tallboys gave a faint shrug and turned to her. "Perhaps it is the way that he looks at you across a room. He is in love with you, I think. Is it reciprocated? I would rather the truth, Julia, than a false concern to spare my feelings."

"Don't be absurd," Julia said sharply. Her unresolved feelings toward Dominic made this a spot too tender for touch, especially after what had happened between them yesterday. In the narrow society of a country neighborhood, she supposed there was some talk about the time they spent together. In spite of the fact that she had delighted in creating gossip and sensation in town, she found she thoroughly disliked the idea that anyone should guess, however obliquely, that she and Dominic were any more intimate than casual friends. And this was not for the sake of her reputation.

More temperately she said, "Mr. Sales is a very interesting man and I have enjoyed his company. In fact," she said, her quick smile returning, "if he had not taken pity on me and deigned to instruct me on all the interesting flora and fauna in the neighborhood on our rides, I think I should have been ready for Bedlam by now. The country life, I fear, shall never be for me."

"Then neither shall Sales be for you. He is a provincial, hardly the sort of man who would fit into the world you and I flourish in," Tallboys said in a dismissive way.

Julia could not disagree. "I have said he is not the reason I have refused your offer," she said calmly.

"Then, what is?"

"I don't know." She saw the disbelief in his eyes. "Truly I don't."

He gave vent to a sigh that turned into a short laugh. "It is unlike you not to know your mind, Julia, but I shall accept your answer. At least for now." He took her hands again. "Must this be final between us? Will you give me permission to approach you again when we have both had time to understand our feelings better?"

Julia could not object to this; in fact, she honestly hoped that, once back in her own environment, she would better understand what had come over her to make her behave so out of character. She also hoped she would come to her senses, for it seemed to her that at times she was quite out of them.

6

Linton left Dumphree to return to town on Monday with Sir Royden, but Julia elected to remain until Friday as originally planned to avoid any awkwardness between her and Royden during the journey. Just as she and Dominic had tacitly met each day for their ride, by the same means the activity was abandoned. She spent most of the remaining week at Dumphree, venturing out only occasionally, and she did not see Dominic again before she left for London, nor even have word if he was in the neighborhood.

Solitude proved not to be her friend, though, as her thoughts plagued her not only during the week but for the two days it took to reach London as well. She contrasted this journey ironically with her trip to Dumphree and wondered what had become of her well-ordered life. She had been so sure of herself and so certain she knew what she wished for her future then, and now it was another matter entirely. She amused herself with the thought that it was caused by an excess of country air and that the noisesomeness of the city would soon see her to rights again.

When she arrived home, she found Lettice all atwitter. "My dearest Julia," she said, hugging her with such force that Julia had to steady herself to keep from being swept off her feet. "How tedious it has been since you were gone. More than once I nearly overcame my dislike of travel and joined you at Dumphree. Without your vibrancy town has been a dull place indeed."

Julia smiled and gently disengaged Lettice. She was quite used to her excesses. "Well, it certainly couldn't have been duller than Dumphree," she replied untruthfully, but she had no intention of discussing any but the impersonal aspects of her visit with her companion, who was an inveterate gossip and not to be trusted to be discreet. "These were the longest two months I can remember since I was waiting to be graduated from Miss Seilberg's Academy for Young Ladies of Distinction in Bath when I was fifteen."

A knowing look came into the companion's eyes. "It can't have been so very dull for the last fortnight at least. Lady Morland confided in me that Sir Royden told her he would be visiting friends in the neighborhood of Dumphree. Surely he called on you there."

"Yes. He did."

"Oh, my dear," Lettice said in a gushing way, "you must tell me everything, and at once. I shall help you unpack." She turned and started up the stair in the wake of the footman carrying a portion of Julia's baggage.

Julia groaned inwardly. Two months' separation from her voluble companion had caused her not precisely to forget how tiresome Letty could be, but to remember her foibles with less annoyance. Lettice's offer to help was merely figurative, for that would be Julia's dresser's duty, but Lettice was already in Julia's bedchamber sitting on the edge of the bed with a look of pregnant anticipation on her countenance.

Julia responded monosyllabically to her companion's queries about Sir Royden and what had passed between them, but Lettice would not take the hint. Finally, Julia's patience began to wear thin. "I am really quite worn out, Letty," she said as she shrugged off the bodice of her traveling dress and pushed the skirt off her hips, letting it fall in folds about her feet. "Would you mind very much if we talked about my stay with Alicia after dinner tonight?"

Lettice's disappointment was plain in her expression. "We are to dine tonight with dear Lord and Lady Morland. There will be no opportunity for private conversation."

Julia's brows rose. "I had no invitation to Morland House."

"Oh, I am so forgetful," Lettice said, her brow crumpling in consternation. "I quite forgot that Lady Morland herself stopped by not an hour before you arrived in the hope of finding you already home. She said we were not to think of housekeeping ourselves tonight but must come to her for dinner. I said we should be delighted, and sent instructions to the kitchen that we would not require dinner. I knew it would be what you would wish. It will be a very comfortable evening for you after your long journey."

Julia unfastened her petticoats and stepped out of them as well. She bit at her lip to keep back the angry interjection that rose to her lips. She knew she would have felt quite guilty later if she allowed herself to be drawn to deliver a set-down to Letty so soon after her return. She was excessively vexed that her companion had taken it upon herself to accept Eliza's invitation, for the last thing in the world she wished for tonight was a quizzing from Hal, which was inevitable if she dined at Morland House.

"I wish you had not given Elizabeth a firm answer, Letty, without waiting to consult me," she said, her voice deliberately controlled. "But I suppose it hardly matters, for Eliza's curiosity would likely have driven her to call tonight in any case."

"Is there some reason you do not wish to speak with Lady Morland?" Lettice asked, puzzled.

"No, of course not," Julia said, not quite able to keep a faint edge out of her voice. She turned to make a comment to her dresser about one of the gowns she was lifting from her trunk.

Lettice subsided into silence while the unpacking continued. Julia, now clad only in her chemise, washed the dirt of the road from her hands and face and then, donning a dressing gown, made herself comfortable on the chaise longue near the hearth. She closed her eyes as if she intended to sleep and hoped that her companion would leave, but Lettice waited until the dresser had put the last undergarment into the armoire and herself went out of the room before she rose from the bed and went over to the chaise.

She sat beside Julia, uninvited, and said in a low, vibrant voice, "Have you suffered a disappointment, my love?"

Julia did not bother to suppress an exasperated sigh. "I am not out of spirits, Letty, merely tired."

Lettice patted her hand in a manner to show her understanding. "Of course you are," she said in the rallying tone of a nurse speaking to a patient. "I quite understand."

"I knew you would," Julia said dulcetly, and closed her eyes again until Lettice at last crept out of the room.

But Julia's escape was only temporary. Lettice was almost as annoying in her consolation of what she supposed were Julia's blighted hopes as she had been in her sly hints and innuendo. Julia saw her say something privately to Lady Frances, whom Elizabeth had invited to dinner to welcome Julia home, shortly after they were shown into the saloon before dinner, and from the speculative look that Fanny bent on her, Julia knew her punishment for subterfuge was likely to be a determined cross-examination from her friend.

Linton was also at home for dinner that evening and appeared to be in far better spirits than when she had taken leave of him on Monday. Julia was pleased, but also dubious. He had been so in the throes of despair after Lord Amberly had rejected his suit for Miss Sutton that she might have been frightened for his welfare if he had not been in Royden's company. Yet now, when he addressed her, he smiled broadly and there was nothing in his demeanor to suggest that his heart had received a devastating blow.

"Dashed good to be back in town. Likely think so yourself, Aunt Jule, since you were never much for the country life," he said as he dutifully kissed Julia's cheek. "That sort of thing is all good and well for a spell, but it's cursed wearing after a bit."

"It is a pity you think so," his father remarked in a caustic manner. "Since you shall one day inherit two considerably large estates and several minor holdings in the country, which you affect to despise, it is to be hoped that you eventually overcome your prejudice."

Julia suppressed a sigh. Eve if she had missed the gaiety of town, there were other aspects of returning that made her already recall her recent stay at Dumphree with idylic nostalgia. "Actually Harry was very well-occupied, Hal," she said to avert any possible altercation between father and son. "In addition to the usual pleasures of fishing and riding and the like, Harry spent quite a bit of time with Thomas going about the estate, and Thomas told me himself that he was impressed both with Harry's knowledge of how a well-run estate is organized and his desire to learn those aspects he was ignorant of."

Lord Morland made no comment to this, but Julia had not expected it any more than it was likely Harry did. But she knew her brother would digest it and be pleased by Lord Dumphree's ecomiums. It did serve the intended purpose, however.

Hal turned his attention to her. "Well, Jule, you don't look worse for the experience, though you seemed to think you would sink into a decline in a fortnight, if I recall correctly. I confess myself pleased. I thought we should have you back in town before a month was out. You're a Marchant, I'll give you that. All Marchants are stayers."

From her brother this was high praise, and Julia duly acknowledged it as such. It was so unique to receive compliments instead of criticism from that source that Julia's spirits lifted. Perhaps it would be a more pleasurable evening than she had anticipated.

There was further cause for her brother's good humor. Only two days previously Lady Jennifer Morland had announced her betrothal to the Earl of Cannabray, a gentleman not only comely of appearance but the possessor of a title of ancient creation, connection with royalty, and a fortune said to put the nose of Golden Ball out of joint.

"He has been one of her admirers since her come-out," Elizabeth said, her pride barely held in check to prevent smugness, "but I admit I did not think he was so serious. I saw no point in writing the news to you when I knew you would be back today."

"And Lady Morland made me promise to say nothing until she had told you herself," Letty interjected, obviously quite proud of herself for her discretion.

"This is splendid," Julia said with delight. "Do you see, Hal? The court dress was not such a poor investment, for Cannabray is one of the King's Gentlemen and it was at court that he and Jenny were introduced."

The earl merely made a comment that was something between acknowledgment and a grunt, but Julia had scored her point and was content with the minor victory. Dinner was announced, and as she accepted her nephew's arm, she asked after her niece and was told that she dined with Cannabray and two of his maiden aunts who lived near Richmond.

"Do you give a betrothal ball, Eliza?" Julia asked as the footman drew her chair for her. "The whole world will expect you to celebrate in considerable style so signal a conquest."

The pleasant atmosphere remained throughout dinner. Fanny and Elizabeth regaled Julia with all the *on-dits*, and the earl added his might with the occasional telling comment. Harry spoke of his activities since he had returned to town, and offered an occasional comment about the time they had spent at Dumphree, but Julia found that his failure to make any mention of Miss Sutton somewhat disturbing. She could not believe that her nephew was so fickle that he could have been so in love one minute and all but forgotten his beloved a few days after leaving her. She waited also for him to make some comment about her and Royden, but he did not, and she supposed that Royden had given him no hint of what had passed between them.

Morland was clearly exerting himself to be pleasing to his sister. He consistently addressed her in a hearty way that she supposed he imagined to be brotherly. "I've never seen you looking better, Jule," he said to her during dinner. "Don't you think, my love," he added, addressing his wife, "that a bit of rustication has done Julia a world of good?"

"Julia is as lovely now as before she went to Dumphree," Elizabeth said, her tone intended to somewhat dampen her husband's unaccustomed heartiness, which she thought fit him poorly. "However, I suppose her admirers will agree that there is improvement simply because they have been deprived of her company. Although there is at least one who cannot put forth that complaint." She cast a quick searching glance at Julia.

"It was an unexpected and very pleasant diversion to have Sir Royden staying with the Amberlys for a few days," Julia said in a noncommittal tone. "Linton was glad of it too, for it gave him an excuse to come back to town a bit early when Royden offered him a seat in his chaise."

"Harry has told us that you had another admirer in the neighborhood," Fanny said archly. "I declare, Julia, you cannot go anywhere without breaking hearts."

"Hardly that," Julia said dryly, but felt discomfited knowing that she had caused Dominic pain, however unintentionally. "Mr. Sales is a very pleasant and interesting man and we formed the habit of riding together frequently. He is a naturalist studying in the area and writing a treatise of previous studies with the assistance of a man in the neighborhood who is renowned in the field."

"You're doing it a bit too brown, Aunt Jule," Linton

declared. "Never knew you to give a tinker's hoot for plants and weeds before."

"And I don't now," Julia admitted freely. "You know how Alicia feels about horses," she said to Elizabeth, "and Harry was always off on his own pursuits, so I might have expired with tedium spending every day hemming altar cloths, putting up spices in the stillroom, and visiting every old tabby in the neighborhood. I was quite grateful to Mr. Sales for taking pity on me and offering to ride out with me most mornings. We did not, after all, discuss plants and weeds the entire time."

The viscount gave a bark of laughter. "I daresay you didn't," he said with a lascivious smile. "By the time I left you were leading the poor fellow about by the nose. They don't call you the Fatal Widow for nothing, Aunt Jule."

His mother admonished him for his vulgarity, but Linton, unrepentant, cast his aunt a quizzing smile and finally subsided. But not before he had succeeded in touching an exposed nerve in Julia.

"I am surprised you had time to note anything at all about me or Mr. Sales, Harry," she said in quick retaliation. "You were so occupied making a cake of yourself over Miss Sutton." She saw the stricken look come into his eyes and instantly wished the words unsaid. It was obvious that his good humor was fragile and that his pain was still very real to him.

"Oh, for God's sake, Harry," his father said in exasperation. "I sent you to Dumphree to keep you away from the petticoats for a time. Can't you go anywhere without making a damned fool of yourself over some female?"

It was not an untypical expostulation from the earl to his son, but the viscount did not this time take it in part. The stricken look was replaced by sparks of instantly kindled anger, and the conviviality of the evening was shattered. "You needn't worry this time that I'll disgrace you with my choice. Miss Sutton's guardians liked me for a suitor less than you would be likely to regard her as an acceptable daughter-in-law," he said with bitter vehemence. "But if you think I'll let you do to me what you and Grandfather did to Aunt Julia, you're fair and far out. The damned succession can go into abeyance when I die without issue for all it matters to me." So saying, Linton abruptly pushed back his chair, cast his napkin on his plate, and left the room, heedless of his father's command to mind his manners and remain at table.

"It would appear that your time at Dumphree was not quite so tedious as you would lead us to believe, Julia," said the countess with a dry inflection. She too pushed back her chair, though in a more genteel manner than her son had done. "I think we are finished, are we not, ladies? Hal has an engagement with friends at the Daffy Club, so I doubt he will be joining us in the drawing room." This last was said with a meaningful look to her husband, who paid her no heed, his features set as if stone in stern lines.

Elizabeth walked up the stair to the drawing room beside Julia with Fanny and Lettice behind.

"I appear to have set the cat among the pigeons," Julia said ruefully. "Poor Harry. I truly didn't mean to open a fresh wound or call Hal's wrath down upon him. He was so full of Miss Sutton when he left Dumphree that I simply assumed he would tell everyone about her when he returned home."

"Not a word, my dear," Elizabeth assured her. "And that is most unusual. Harry can never resist talking endlessly about his latest flirt. Unless, of course, she is not quite respectable?"

This last was clearly an inquiry, and Julia hastened to assure her that Sophia Sutton was quite respectable. When they were comfortably settled in the drawing room, Elizabeth commanded her sister-in-law to tell her all about Miss Sutton and her son, and Julia complied as far as she was able. "The worst part of it," she concluded, "was that in spite of every hint that the Amberlys would not countenance his suit, Harry went to Amberly to make a formal offer for Miss Sutton. He was completely wretched, but I could have shaken him for his obtuseness. The best plan would have been to bide his time until Sophia's aunt brings her to town. Perhaps then something would have occurred —or not occurred, if the offers Caroline Amberly expects for her niece are not forthcoming—to make his suit more acceptable to the Amberlys."

Elizabeth laughed without humor. "Never. My dear, don't you know that Caroline Amberly detests the Marchants? She made a complete fool of herself over Hal in her first Season— in fact, it was common belief that that was the reason she didn't receive an acceptable offer until the following year. If Harry were suddenly elevated to a dukedom and the king opened his coffers to him, I doubt she would find him a suitable match for her niece.''

''Alicia told me of it. Poor Harry.''

Lady Morland rolled her eyes heavenward. ''Oh, well. It has been a quiet two months without either you or Linton to set up Hal's back. I am sufficiently rested to endure the excitement.''

''Harry is a dear boy,'' Lady Fanny said, ''but we have been enduring tales of his unhappy *amours* since he was out of short coats. Tell us of your adventures in the wilds of Wiltshire, Julia.''

''I had none,'' Julia said repressively. ''The only thing that made me endure one day to the next in such dullness was the knowledge that at the end of my rustication Hal would keep his promise and pay all my debts.''

''Now, why, I wonder,'' Fanny said thoughtfully, ''would you not regard Tallboy's visit as diversion? I thought it was what you hoped for.''

''My dear Lady Frances, perhaps it would be best if we did not ask Lady Julia to discuss that,'' Lettice said with gentle admonishment. ''I fear she has had a disappointment.''

''What? Do you mean he did not offer for you, after all?'' said the countess, outraged. ''I think that is the shabbiest thing imaginable after seeking you out in Wiltshire in such a particular way. What else would you suppose but that he meant to come up to scratch?''

''Actually, he did,'' Julia said calmly.

The countess was silenced by these words and even Fanny had no comment to make, but Lettice gave a surprised titter. ''Have you been hoaxing us, Julia? It is really too bad of you not to tell us at once that we might wish you happy.''

''You may certainly wish me happy if you like, Letty, but not because I am to marry Sir Royden. He did ask me to marry him, but I declined the offer.''

This time it was Lettice who was bereft of words and the countess who spoke. ''But why, Julia? Have you taken leave of your senses? I thought you agreed to Hal's absurd demand in the first place because you wanted Tallboys to realize what he might stand to lose.''

''I did.'' Julia shrugged. ''I don't even know myself for

certain why I turned him down. Perhaps it was too much like Tony again, after all."

"Or perhaps it was the mysterious Mr. Sales, after all," Fanny said shrewdly. She really didn't think it, she was only casting, but she saw something flash in Julia's eyes an expression that was gone almost as soon as it appeared.

"Oh, it could not be," Lettice said firmly. "Julia said he was a botanist or some such thing, and spends all his time in the country studying plants or insects or the like. What could there be in such a man to interest our dear Julia?"

What, indeed? wondered both Julia's sister-in-law and friend. But neither pursued that avenue for reasons of her own. Lady Fanny knew her friend too well to suppose she would receive information from Julia that she did not care to reveal, and Elizabeth was too finely bred to push a topic that might give someone else discomfort. And it was very obvious that whatever had occurred at Dumphree to cause Julia to reject the offer of a man that she had deliberately cast out lures to to that end, she did not wish to share it with anyone—at least for now. The countess had a remedy for this: she intended to draft a letter to Alicia first thing in the morning and discover what she could of the unknown Mr. Sales.

Morland's good humor toward Julia for her obedience to remain in Wiltshire for the time he had decreed did not outlast a sennight after she had returned to town. Elizabeth had insisted that he come with her and their daughter, Jennifer, to Almack's the Friday after Julia's return, and he had not been there ten minutes when he spotted his sister wearing a daringly cut gown with a diaphanous silver gauze overdress and sporting a diamond collar that he had never cast eyes on before. He asked her plainly if it were new and Julia acknowledged that it was.

"The gift of an admirer?" he said hopefully.

"I hope I am not so lost to propriety, Hal. It is far too expensive a gift to accept from a man who is not my husband or at the very least my betrothed," she said, casting him a taunting sidelong glance. She fingered the collar caressingly. "I was bored on Thursday and needed something to lift my spirits."

"I warn you, Julia, if you mean to outrun the bailiff again—"

"Will you rusticate me again, Hal?" she wondered.

"I'll let you cool your heels in the Fleet this time," he said furiously.

"Poor Hal. Do you know your face has gone quite red? If you do not have a care, you shall be carried off in an apoplexy one day." She gave him her most dazzling smile and drifted off in a cloud of gauze.

It was a small revenge but Julia quite enjoyed it. It would never do to let her brother think she had come to heel. But beyond the diamond collar, she did not indulge in any great extravagance. She found her former satisfaction in confounding her brother was waning. In fact, in many ways she felt differently than she had before she had gone to Dumphree. She was delighted to be back in all of her favorite haunts, but the routs and balls that had amused her at the beginning of the Season failed to please her as much as she had expected them to when she had been longing for them in Wiltshire. The trouble was not that her tastes had changed but an inner dissatisfaction that nothing seemed to distract her from.

Sir Royden, not put off by her rejection of his suit, was as attentive to Julia as he had been before. She felt grateful for this, for she told herself that she was just suffering from some oddity of humor that would surely pass. Yet thoughts tormented her in her quiet hours that would not pass however much she tried to put them from her mind.

It would perhaps be overstatement to say that Dominic and that last afternoon they had spent together haunted her, but in any unguarded moment she would find herself slipping back to memories of their lovemaking, of his telling her that he loved her, and of her own unexpected and much-unwanted feelings. She had given up telling herself that she felt nothing at all for Dominic—that was patently not the case—but she would not believe that it was any lasting attachment. In a few weeks or so the memories were bound to fade, and her feelings with them. Out of sight, out of mind.

With this intent she filled her waking hours as much as she could accepting every invitation to Venetian breakfasts, al-fresco lunches, dinners, routs, card parties, and any other entertainment an ingenious hostess could devise. When invitations were thin, Julia went with friends to Vauxhall, to the theater and the opera; anything was preferable to a quiet evening at home, where she could indulge her thoughts.

Julia loved music, and the opera was a particular favorite. It was a warm evening for the season when she attended a production of Mozart's *Die Zauberflöte* in the company of Royden, Fanny, and Mr. Montgomery, who was assiduously courting Fanny.

The opera house was a sea of pale, floating colors, the ladies having exchanged their usual evening silks and satins for gauzes and muslins to combat the legendary heat of the opera house, which on an unnaturally warm evening was nothing short of stifling. As they entered, they exchanged greetings with various friends in nearby boxes. All the ladies were applying their fans, and Julia glanced about her, noting that a number of gentlemen, who did not have the advantage of being able to dress so lightly, were already looking a bit wilted.

It was shortly before the production was about to begin that Fanny called Julia's attention to a box across the theater from them. "That is Lady Amberly come in, is it not?" she asked. "I suppose that striking girl next to her is the infamous Miss Sutton who has captured Linton's fickle heart. Now that I have seen her, I don't wonder at it; she should take very well if she has the fortune you claim and a bit of conversation."

Julia obligingly lifted her opera glass and peered across the way. "Yes, that is Miss Sutton. Unfortunately," she added with a sigh. "I knew they planned to come to town before the Season was out even though Sophia is only seventeen and will not be formally presented until next year, but I have been dreading it. The tiresome boy is sure to cause *on-dit* if he wears his heart on his sleeve for all the world to see, and that means that Hal will be impossible."

"Perhaps concern is premature," Fanny said hopefully. "Even if she only goes out in a quiet way, she is so pretty she is bound to gather a court about her, and if she does not reciprocate his feelings and pays no great attention to Harry, he may well tire of of playing the aggrieved lover. He won't want for eager young women to console him. I saw him only yesterday when I was on my way to the lending library with a pretty little Cyprian on his arm."

"I can't guess how deeply his feelings go," Julia admitted. "In Wiltshire I had come to believe that he had truly fallen in love with her, so great was his wretchedness when he was rejected, but at times he seems to be quite himself again. It remains to be seen how he will react when he sees Miss Sutton in town. The important thing is to prevent Harry from feeling that he is a victim of blighted love, for that is an attraction he may not be able to resist."

Julia had looked away from the other box but a glance in that direction again a few moments later nearly made her catch her breath. Two gentlemen had joined Lady Amberly and her niece. Julia had no need to raise her glass again. One of these men was certainly Lord Amberly, and even at that distance she had no doubt that the other was Dominic, even though he remained at the back of the box in the shadows. She looked to Royden to see if he had recognized their friends from Wiltshire, but he was in conversation with Andrew Montgomery and never even glanced in that direction.

She felt no schoolgirl flush or palpitations at seeing Dominic again, only a rather queer feeling deep in her stomach, as if it were suddenly very empty. She looked away, afraid that if she stared, she would draw his gaze.

The opera was a favorite of hers, and she turned her mind to following it, listening with pleasure to the superb singers portraying the parts. She was sorry when the interval came not only because she would have to wait for the next act, but because she knew that the others in her party would wish to join the fashionable promenade in the corridor and she did not relish a public meeting with Dominic in front of her friends. It was not that she expected him to allude in any way to the last time they had been together, but she feared there might be some awkwardness between them and she preferred it not to be witnessed by Royden or Fanny.

Fanny did suggest that they leave their box during the interval and Mr. Montgomery and Sir Royden were pleased to agree, but Julia surprised them by insisting that she preferred to remain in her seat.

"But why?" Fanny persisted, unaware that Julia could have throttled her for pressing her. "These chairs are not the most comfortable and you must be feeling as cramped as I am."

"But not as cramped as I am tired," Julia replied untruthfully. "Jenny and I went shopping for her bride clothes this afternoon and then I attended Mrs. Kramer's waltz party and nearly danced myself to a standstill."

Fanny started to disdain this excuse, for Julia never tired easily, but something in Julia's expression warned her and she said instead, "Come along, then, Andrew. Do you join us, Royden?"

"No. I shall stay with Julia," he replied without hesitation.

"No, please don't." Julia had glanced over at the opposite box and she saw that though the Amberlys and Miss Sutton had yet to leave it, Dominic was gone and she feared that he also had seen her and was coming to her. If a meeting was unavoidable, then at the least she wished it might be private. "A little solitude would suit me very well."

Royden's eyes questioned hers. He heard plainly that she did not wish him to be with her, and it troubled him. But she smiled warmly at him and he let it pass. Thus it was that Dominic found her quite alone in the box when he entered and sat down beside her as if she were expecting him, which, of course, she was.

She turned and regarded him with a long, appraising look. The man beside her was doubtless the same she had known in Wiltshire, yet outwardly he appeared very different. The Dominic she had known had been quite attractive, if in an unremarkable way. The man whom she regarded now was unquestionably striking. His naturally curling black hair had been cut and styled in a way to give it a fashionable, tousled look that was enhancing to his features. He was dressed in a black silk evening coat and smalls that were in the latest mode; his linen was snowy white and of the finest quality, and his cravat was tied in an intricate style that a Bond Street beau would not have scorned. There sat beside her a man of fashion and distinction.

Julia was surprised and inwardly gratified; she could not help thinking that this transformation was to convince her that she had been mistaken when she had claimed he would never fit into her world. She was both anxious and curious to know what his manner toward her would be, given the last cold words they had said to each other in Wiltshire. She even wondered if he had come to try to persuade her to change her mind.

"I had not thought to see you in town, Mr. Sales," she said with deliberate formality.

He gave her one of his quick smiles that had yet to fail to stir her. "No. I know you did not. You made that clear the last time we met." His smile became caustic. "There is no need to look dismayed, Julia," he said, not taking her lead in formality. "I haven't come to berate you for rejecting my offer—nor to renew it, for that matter."

The bubble of her vanity pricked, Julia scarcely knew whether to be amused or chagrined. His manner was so easy, she could not believe it concealed a broken heart. She knew perfectly well that Dominic was not like Linton and would not wear the willow for all to see, but she had supposed that if they were ever to meet again, he would have treated her at the least with reserve to mark the blow she had delivered to his hopes.

"Well," she said with an uncertain laugh, "I am glad to see I have dealt you no lasting wound."

His eyes became serious again for a moment. "Would you have wished to?"

"No, of course not."

He smiled again. "I thought for a moment that you sounded disappointed. After I had left you at Dumphree, I thought a good deal about what you had said to me, and I came to agree. There exists an attraction between us—that is hardly arguable—but I was doubtless carried away by the passion of the moment, as you yourself suggested. I suppose I should thank you for being so sensible, Julia. Very likely we both should be in high dudgeon now if you had accepted my impulsive offer."

Julia was not sure what she thought of his words or whether or not she believed them. She did not think he was at all the sort of man to declare himself in love one day and out of it the next. Her own thoughts and feelings had been disturbed since he had asked her to marry him, and it was hard for her to be convinced that he had resolved his so readily. Or at least her vanity made it difficult for her to credit. She was too honest not to realize she had flattered herself to believe that her rejection had caused him considerable pain.

But whatever the truth, if he wished to resume their acquaintance and treat what had happened between them as having little consequence, Julia was only too willing to comply. She did not wish for a renewal of his offer to her, but she found she had missed him more than she had thought she would and it pleased her to think they might be friends again. "Very likely," she agreed with a dry laugh.

He looked at her in an appraising way, much as she had done when he came into the box. "You look remarkably well, Julia," he said in a level voice. "Returning to your natural environment obviously suits you."

"I must say this environment suits you as well, sir," Julia said, returning his smile. "I don't believe I have ever seen you quite so fine before."

There was a brightness in his eyes that Julia knew was sardonic amusement. "Protective coloration," he said quite gravely. "It is always wise to blend into one's habitat."

Julia laughed. "And who should know better than a naturalist. What manner of plant or animal can you be studying here, Mr. Galco?"

"The most enigmatic of creatures."

"Man?"

"And woman."

"If that is all, you might have remained in Wiltshire. There are sufficient examples there of the species."

She expected him to return a flirtatious answer, but he said only conversationally, "True. But I have finished the first draft of my writings and I thought it was time I attended to a number of matters that I have neglected for some time and that require my presence in town. The observation of selected specimens is merely for diversion."

Julia cast him a glance from beneath her lashes. "And I suppose you have select specimens already in mind."

His smile was bland. "No. Not yet. I have only been in town a bit over a sennight and have been attending largely to my wardrobe. Both you and Linton did imply that I was not fit for polite society in the comfortable raiment I affected in Wiltshire."

"It was merely jest," Julia said, but mechanically. She felt an unexpected sense of rejection. He had been in town for days and had made not the smallest effort to contact her. Her eyes searched his, but his gave none of his thoughts away.

"I know," he said pleasantly. "But it was not without truth. It is, perhaps, a sad thing to be nearing thirty years without acquiring the sort of town polish that is considered essential to a gentleman's education. I would not be a disgrace to my forebears."

Julia knew he spoke lightly, but she responded in a more serious vein. "You would never be that. You have excellent address, Mr. Sales, and your breeding is impeccable."

"I seem to recall that you said something quite different last time we met, Julia," he reminded her, but with no trace of anger or accusation.

Julia recalled only too vividly the things that her surprise and discomfiture had caused her to say. She felt warmth steal into her cheeks. "Spare my blushes, please. I said a number of stupid things that morning."

"So did I," he responded levelly, though Julia saw a light of inner amusement come into his eyes.

She was only too glad to gloss over that last conversation at the old Dower House. "A fair hit! I am totally disarmed," she said, laughing and raising her hand in the gesture of a fencer. "I am glad you have come to town, Dominic," she said, finally abandoning the formality that he ignored in any case. "And I am glad that you do not hate me, though I think I feared you would. I wish we might be friends again."

His expression as she spoke was not somber, but neither was it expressive.

She felt suddenly uncertain and said, "If you wish it. I do."

He did not make an immediate response and then it was not possible, for the door opened and Royden came into the box. Julia was actually relieved, though she would have preferred it if he had not found her *tête-à-tête* with Dominic. Royden was smiling as he entered, and though he continued to do so when he saw Dominic, there was a subtle change in his expression that Julia recognized as displeasure.

Dominic rose and the men exchanged greetings. "I understand, Sales," Royden said, "that a new form of address is in order for you. I met Lady Amberly and her niece in the corridor and they told me of your change in status. I know it is not good ton to felicitate a man on his succession, but since it is merely a revelation of it and not the actual event, I hope I may do so without giving offense."

Julia had not the least idea what Royden meant by his words, but she saw at once that Dominic did and that he was not pleased.

"Not the least offense," Dominic said, his tone civil and nothing more. "My cousin and I were not particularly close, and though I certainly regretted and even mourned his loss, it is, as you say, not a present tragedy."

Royden turned to Julia, who was regarding them both in open puzzlement, and smiled with just a hint of malice. "My dear, has Lord Sales still not told you of his succession to the marquessate? He is the elusive fifth marquess that has had the whole world for the past year guessing who he might be."

"No," Julia said, forcing herself to disguise her complete astonishment. "Perhaps he was saving it for a surprise," she added dulcetly.

Dominic's slight smile was apologetic. "It could not be otherwise. I apologize to all my friends and acquaintance in Wiltshire for saying nothing; it was not meant for the purpose of deception. I came into the neighborhood as 'mister' because I wanted quiet and anonymity for my work. But I have allowed myself to be persuaded by the Amberlys to acknowledge my title now that I am in town. It was inevitable that I should be known as such in any case, for I have reopened Sales House and am presently deciding whether it is worth refurbishing. It is an immense house for one man to live in and by my estimate not an extra groat has been spent on its upkeep in the past twenty or thirty years."

"Perhaps you will marry, now that you have taken your place in the *ton*," Royden suggested politely. "There are quite a number of delightful beauties on display in the marriage mart this Season. You must have Lady Amberly introduce you to Sally Jersey or Maria Sefton, either of whom would be only too happy to supply you with vouchers to Almack's."

"Perhaps I shall," Dominic replied with equal politeness, though to which suggestion remained ambiguous. He then bowed over Julia's hand and excused himself.

"Did you know Sales was in town," Royden asked Julia perhaps a bit too casually as he took the chair beside her that Dominic had sat in.

"No," Julia said rather tersely. "I only knew of it tonight, as you did."

"I had thought there was some friendship between you,"

Royden continued, refusing to heed Julia's obvious disinclination to discuss Dominic. "It surprises me that he would not have confided the truth about his title to you, if the Amberlys were already aware of it."

It surprised Julia as well and disturbed her far more than she knew it should have. She was not at all certain what she believed about his subterfuge, but in addition to her amazement, she felt hurt that he had not trusted her with the truth. She recalled that she had asked him directly if he were acquainted with Lord Sales, and she remembered his smile and the way he had looked down at her with amusement and knew that he had enjoyed his private jest at her expense. She could forgive him for that when they had first met, but she could not understand his continued imposture as the intimacy between them had grown.

Lady Frances and Mr. Montgomery returned to the box and Royden finally allowed the subject to drop. Though she was deeply disturbed by her meeting with Dominic, Julia did not allow it to interfere with her pleasure in the opera, but she did beg off going with the others to a ball being given in honor of a friend's daughter's betrothal.

"My dear, whatever is the matter with you tonight?" Fanny demanded. "You are behaving so strangely that I would suppose you had the headache, but you never do."

"It isn't the headache," Julia confirmed, "but I am feeling out of sorts. Please don't let me dampen your pleasure in any way. I think I just wish to return home for an early evening."

"With a glass of milk and a good book?" Fanny suggested astringently.

Julia laughed. "Well, perhaps a glass of wine instead. But I think I shall retire early."

"Fanny and Andrew can take the carriage," Tallboys suggested, "and I'll find a hack to take us to Half Moon Street."

"You are kind, Royden, but you needn't come with me," she insisted, frankly not wanting his company. "I am not only out of sorts, I am out of temper as well and would really prefer my own company."

Tallboys was hardly pleased with her refusal of his escort and she saw that plainly in his eyes along with something else, a searching look. Instinctively, she guessed that he was linking her sudden megrim with her meeting with Dominic, and she knew that if she were not to give him grist for that mill, she would have to be more circumspect in the future. But at the moment she wanted only the time and solitude to reclaim her disordered thoughts.

When Dominic left Julia at the box, he was thinking similarly that he needed to sort out his thoughts and evaluate his feelings. As he came out of the box, he saw Lady Frances, whom he knew by sight, coming toward him and he deliberately turned in the opposite direction to avoid a meeting. He was not certain what Julia had told her friends of him and what they had been to each other, and since he was so uncertain of what, if any, their relationship would be now, he thought it best to be least in sight.

He had sought Julia out with the intention of making it clear to her that he bore her no ill-will for her rejection of him. Though she had in fact hurt him deeply, he thought he had recovered sufficiently for a meeting to have no great effect on him; he was mistaken. His pride had carried him through the interview, but he was unquestionably shaken. He did not think he was still in love with her; he felt himself cured of that, since he had realized he had so mistaken her feelings for him. But to be near Julia was to want her. The attraction was as powerful as ever.

It was true that he had not come to town solely to show Julia that he was not the provincial she thought him, but after the drumming his pride had received at her hands, it mattered to him that she see that he could, if he chose, take his place in the *ton* with elegance and style. It was not his specific intention to make her regret her refusal of his offer, but he was human enough to want her to realize that she had turned down far more than she had supposed.

He was absorbed in his thoughts when he returned to the Amberlys, but the opera began soon afterward and his abstraction was not remarked upon. He would have begged off from the ball also if he could have thought of a graceful excuse. But Lady Amberly was so excited about presenting the elusive Lord Sales to all of her friends that he could not bring himself to disappoint her.

Unlike Julia, he scarcely heard the music being performed

during the second act. Julia had stated plainly that she wanted their relationship, at least as friends, to continue. He was not certain that he wanted that. He was not afraid of falling in love with her again—he would not be a fool a second time. But he was concerned that friendship, now that they had been lovers, was impossible, and a warmer alliance, he feared, might prove dangerous to his peace.

When the opera ended, he was forced to abandon his introspection, but feeling that he had made no great progress toward resolution, he did so readily enough. For the remainder of the evening, he conducted himself in the manner of a man with nothing in the least to trouble him. It was only in solitude that he admitted that peace had eluded him since the afternoon he first had seen Julia at the Hart and Hare.

7

Julia did not expect to see her sister-in-law the following day, but Elizabeth called shortly after ten, the usual hour that Julia, in town, took her breakfast after a night of revels. But Julia, having sought her bed early, had risen equally early and gone out to ride with a groom for escort. There was no outward thought in her head that she might meet him during her exercise, but when she returned to Half Moon Street, having met no one at all of her acquaintance, she was conscious of a feeling of disappointment. It was likely that their next meeting would not be as friendly as the last, but she was eager for the confrontation.

Julia had already broken her fast and was tending her correspondence when Elizabeth was announced. Not bothering to observe the usual pleasantries, Elizabeth launched into her tale as soon as the footman who had escorted her upstairs closed the door. "You were so very wise to decide against the Wistons' ball, Julia. It was the most wretched party imaginable."

"I am sure Lady Wiston would be horrified to hear you say so," Julia said, dimpling. "Was the wine watered or did she neglect to offer her guests lobster patties and oysters?"

"It is not a subject for levity," Elizabeth chided. "I swear that boy hasn't the sense he was born with. There have never been any imbeciles on either Morland's side or mine that I am aware of, but Linton can play the fool worse than the village idiot."

Julia broke into a peal of laughter, causing her sister-in-law to reproach her again. "I take it that Miss Sutton was present. Did poor Harry clutch at his heart and stagger out of the room when he set eyes on her?"

"Very nearly," said the viscount's aggrieved mother tartly. "I was not actually present at the encounter, but I am reliably informed that he broke off his conversation with Lady Jersey—

Silence, of all people—turned perfectly white, and called out her name in a choked whisper. If that were not enough, the silly chit, who obviously has no more wit than he, responded by fainting into her mother's arms. Lady Amberly claimed it was the heat of the room—which was excessive, in truth—but the *on-dits* are now rampant."

Julia commiserated with her sister-in-law. Her remark about Linton had been made only in jest, for she had thought that he had adjusted to his disappointment with Sophia Sutton. She felt sorry for her nephew, but she was also very annoyed with him, for he was not likely to recommend himself to either of the Amberlys by his behavior. In fact, it would only make matters worse, if that were possible. Short of an elopement, which she did not believe Harry would ever be foolish enough to attempt, it was not likely that he would ever realize his dream of wedding his beloved Sophia.

Elizabeth had had a wretched evening. Not only had she had to deal with Harry's indiscretion, her husband had blamed her for what had happened, accusing her of spoiling their son and even her usually gentle Jennifer had demanded that her mother "do something about Harry" before her betrothed began to suspect there was insanity in the family and cried off. Julia dutifully listened with apparent attentiveness and sympathy, but a part of her mind was occupied with a number of things she needed to see to before the day was out. Her attention was suddenly caught, though, when she heard Elizabeth mention Dominic's name.

"Was Lord Sales at the ball?" she interrupted without compunction.

"Yes, he came with the Amberlys," Elizabeth said, unaware that she had sparked any special interest in Julia. "He is finally come among us. I spent a bit of time in conversation with him and he informed me that he has opened Sales House and means to remain with us at least until the end of the Season. He is still living amid dustcovers and cobwebs while a virtual army of servants attempt to make the place habitable again. I gather he has been long acquainted with the Amberlys and spends a great deal of his time at Amberly House or going about with them to escape the disorder. He won't want for invitations in his own right now that people know he has come to town. There is a great deal of curiosity about him, but he is an attractive and very pleasant-looking man and will no doubt be popular for his own sake. Have you met him yet, Julia? He must be connected to the Mr. Sales that you knew at Dumphree if he, too, is known to the Amberlys. It would be too great a coincidence otherwise."

Julia agreed. "No doubt that is the case," she said without expression.

But Elizabeth had no more than a passing interest in Lord Sales. She was understandably far more concerned with the behavior of her son and his father's subsequent ravings and threats and the commotion it was causing in her own household. She continued to bemoan her plight, but Julia was not as attentive as before. Elizabeth had to repeat a question to her twice and call her to order for her inattention. "Wherever have you gone, Julia?" she said, annoyed. "I don't think you care in the least that we may all be cast into a wretched scandal if Harry does not stop making such a damned fool of himself. I shudder to think what will occur if what Sally Hennessey told me is true."

"What is that?" Julia asked in an appropriately repentant tone.

"She says that Caroline Amberly told her that she has hopes that Sales may make her niece an offer before the end of the Season. One certainly can't blame Lady Amberly for throwing the chit in his way. A marquessate and a handsome fortune into the bargain."

Julia thought ironically that Lady Amberly had told Alicia she intended to produce a title for her ward, but no one at Dumphree had guessed that she had her choice already to hand.

Julia's ambiguous feelings toward Dominic continued. If they were to remain friends—and she was not certain of this—he would have to provide her with an adequate reason for not telling her the truth about himself. She was not sure why she was disturbed by this, but she was.

As it happened, it was several days before she had speech with him. She expected him to call the morning after they had met at the opera, but he did not. They both attended another ball two days afterward, but it was the sort of party destined to be described the following day as a shocking squeeze and pronounced a great success because it was virtually impossible to make one's way entirely around the ballroom, so great was the crush of people attending.

Julia saw him—not in company with the Amberlys this time—across the room when an unexpected parting in the company revealed him. He acknowledged her, if such was the case, with a faint smile of recognition, and Julia fully expected that he would eventually make his way to her side to speak with her or perhaps even to ask her to stand up with him, but he did not. She saw him again a bit later standing up with a young woman who was unknown to her, but that was her last glimpse of him and she had no idea if he even left before or after her.

All of this reminded her of their first introduction when she had had her interest in him piqued and yet a more formal and proper meeting between them remained tantalizingly elusive. As an unmarried woman, she could not call on him and she would not stoop to asking her brother to leave his card at Sales House, thus mandating a return call at Morland House by Dominic.

She did, of course, visit Amberly House in Berkeley Square, but Dominic was not among Lady Amberly's callers, nor Sophia's admirers that morning, so the courtesy was singularly unproductive and resulted in a kindling of anger toward Dominic when Lady Amberly admitted that he had told her and Lord Amberly the truth about himself from the beginning.

"What else could I do, Lady Julia?" she confided. "When he came to the old Dower House, he begged us not to relate his true identity to anyone, and both Arthur and I felt obliged to give our word on the matter, though of course we hated to deceive our friends."

Julia did not deign to ask why Dominic had so adjured them, and she had not a moment's doubt that so far from hating the deception, the viscountess had enjoyed duping her friends.

A meeting between them finally came on Friday in the sacred precincts of Almack's. Julia had come with her niece to give Elizabeth a respite from chaperoning Jennifer. Jennifer quickly discovered several of her particular friends, and Julia was left to the part of chaperone, remaining at the perimeter of the room in conversation with Lady Fanny, who was also there as a chaperone to her own niece.

They were discussing the merits of Mr. Wilke, who Lady

Fanny felt was on the verge of offering for her charge, when Dominic, in company with Lady Amberly and Miss Sutton, came into the assembly room. They were no more than a few feet apart; if Julia had put out her arm and stretched only a little, she might have touched him.

Their eyes met and he smiled in response. Lady Amberly greeted Julia and Lady Fanny with a show of enthusiasm. "What sacrifices we go through for the sake of society," she said. "Almack's is the most tiresome place but quite, quite necessary if one is to have any position at all in the world. Sophia hates it, poor thing, for you know she is still a bit shy and she is so pretty that she is made much by her admirers, is she not, Lord Sales?"

"Oh, deservedly so. The exquisite Sophia is an indisputable diamond," Dominic responded.

Julia was astonished at his tone. His voice was drawling and he spoke with great ennui and with a slight but discernible cynicism, the hallmark of a man of fashion. Even the quality of his voice seemed different to her, and his air of polite indifference was quite alien to his usual manner.

Dominic was outfitted with such elegance that Julia doubted any other man in the assembly room might be found to be better dressed than he. Once again his black silk evening coat and breeches were clearly cut by the hand of a master tailor—Weston, most likely; his cravat was tied in the impossible mathematical; and the points of his shirt collar were fashionably high without making movement of his head virtually impossible. In short, before her stood a man of fashion and elegance beyond even what she had observed at the opera.

There was a coolness in his manner toward her that had not been present then, and Julia wondered at it. But there would be no opportunity for private discourse in such a place and in such company. Their eyes met again and Julia, supposing that this earnest portrayal of a man of the town was for self-amusement, expected to see humor there, but his expression was carefully neutral. She was not certain what she thought of this but that did not surprise her; none of her feelings concerning Dominic was understandable to her of late. He bowed over her hand, asked politely after Lord Linton, and then turned his attention to Lady Fanny. His manner toward Julia's friend was mildly flirtatious in contrast to his correctness toward Julia. Lady Fanny, unaware that Lord Sales and the man Julia had met in Wiltshire were the same, was delighted to be so singled out by an attractive man and responded in kind.

Julia, turning away from Dominic and Fanny, spoke with Sophia, inquiring about her impressions of her first Season in town. The girl admitted that she felt a bit overwhelmed by it all. "Not that everyone has not been very kind," she hastened to add, "but it is so very different from Lesser Ansdown or even Amesbury, where one knows everyone and is always comfortable."

"Come now, Sophia," Lady Amberly chided. "It is not as if you had no acquaintance in town. We have counted Lord Sales among our friends since he first came to us in Wiltshire."

"And there is Lord Linton as well with whom you are acquainted," Julia said with an air of innocence.

Lady Amberly stiffened and was clearly displeased, which was Julia's intent. But Sophia's reaction made Julia regret the barb. The girl became quite pale and looked almost as if she would be sick, and Julia was sorry she had spoken.

Julia glanced to her right to see that Dominic had ended his conversation with Lady Fanny and was watching her; she imagined she read censure in his expression. One or two young gentlemen were hovering nearby, obviously hoping to speak with Sophia and ask for the honor of standing up with her. Julia smiled warmly at the girl and said, "I am sure you are making many new friends now that you are here, Sophia. We shall not keep you from them. Come along, Fanny. We had best find a spot in a corner among the other chaperones and ape-leaders."

"Oh, you would never be that, Lady Julia," Sophia blurted ingenuously. "You are so very beautiful. Is she not, my lord?"

With poetic justice, it was Julia's turn to be put out of countenance by Sophia, however much the girl had meant her words as a compliment. Julia felt her cheeks grow warm, but she saw that Dominic was more disturbed than she by the innocent comment.

He responded with aplomb, though. "Lady Julia is well-known as an incomparable," he said in accents purely of civility.

Julia acknowledged the compliment, though she could not feel that it was meant as such. Insincere sentiments were expressed by Lady Amberly that they would meet again later in the evening, and they parted, Julia and Fanny seeking to find two chairs by the wall to rest and watch the younger people dance.

"I didn't know you were acquainted with Lord Sales. Andrew and I met him at the Wistons' on Saturday," Fanny said when they had made themselves comfortable. "Is he a connection of Dominic Sales?"

Julia could not give her friend the vague answer she had given her sister-in law. "He is Dominic Sales."

"Julia, you wretch," Fanny said with outrage. "But you have known him since you went to Wiltshire. How could you keep such a thing from your best friend?"

Julia gave her a wry smile. "I didn't know it myself until Saturday when he came to our box at the opera during the interval."

Fanny regarded her in surprised silence for a moment. "He never told you? I had the impression that you were friends. I think that is quite shabby."

"So do I," Julia agreed, but with none of her friend's indignation. "I daresay he had his reasons."

"You mean he has made no explanation to you?"

"None," Julia admitted. "Dominic and I rode together and I enjoyed our conversations and his instruction on naturalism. Don't build it into more than that, Fanny. He is under no obligation to tell me anything that he does not wish me to know, nor am I in a habit of confiding in him."

Julia's tone was kept too deliberately modulated to fool Lady France, who knew her well. She let the subject drop temporarily but after a time said, "I had heard that Lord Sales was in town again, who has not? But I had not heard that he was such an attractive man. I can give credence to the rumors I have heard that Caro Amberly is on the catch for him for her niece. Did you think there was any interest there? I can't say that I noticed any on either side, but then it was only a brief encounter."

If she hoped for any interesting reaction from Julia, she was disappointed. Julia knew that Sophia regarded Dominic in the light of an older brother and that her heart appeared to be as given to Linton as his was to her. What Dominic felt she had no idea. In Wiltshire she had not seen Dominic display any partiality toward Sophia beyond an avuncular affection, but she was not certain that the Dominic who was now addressed as Lord Sales was the same man she had known in Wiltshire. "I suppose it is possible," she replied noncommittally. "Even men of learning are often attracted to a pretty face over a pretty wit."

But in spite of her unconcerned response, Julia did take note of Dominic and Sophia when she saw them together again later in the evening, and she could honestly say to herself that she saw no special attentiveness toward Sophia on Dominic's part. At least not more than there had been in Wiltshire.

Again Dominic came to speak with her or asked her to stand up with him, and Julia could not help wondering at it. If he had not wanted to see her again, he need not have sought her out at the opera; she would not have liked it, but she would have understood if he had wanted to terminate their friendship completely. She had supposed that they might never meet again when she left Wiltshire, but now that they had, she knew she wanted to continue to see him. Since he had come to her first, she had assumed that he wanted that also. It surprised and disappointed her that he appeared not to want to resume their friendship, after all.

The following afternoon she drove herself in the park in her high-perch phaeton during the hour when all the world was to be found on the strut, to see and be seen. There were a number of others driving smart carriages in the park, many people on horseback, and still more strolling in the company of friends. Dominic was one of the latter. He was with Mr. Hervey and Lord Castledon, both of whom were well-known to Julia, so it was not at all remarkable that she should pull her horses up to speak with them when the latter gentlemen hailed her.

The usual sort of elegant banter that borders on flirtation was exchanged among Julia and Mr. Hervey and Lord Castledon, but Dominic remained a little apart from them and did not participate. Castledon became aware of this and said, "Are you acquainted with Lady Julia Halston, Sales? If not, I must certainly make you known to the Fatal Widow," he added with a roguish smile for Julia. "She has earned her sobriquet, I promise you. If you don't have a care, she will break your heart as she has done to all of us."

Julia could have cheerfully choked Castledon for that remark, though he could not have known that it would have any special meaning to Dominic, but Dominic did not seem to regard it. He flashed one of his sudden smiles that lit his eyes and made them quite beautiful. "Yes. Lady Julia and I are acquaintances of long standing."

Julia saw both men look at her with some surprise. If Dominic had meant his comment to be deliberately provocative, she would give him no satisfaction for it. "Oh, surely more than acquaintances, my lord. When we were in Wiltshire communing with the birds and the trees, we used to regard ourselves as friends."

Castledon made Julia a bow. "My dear Julia," he said in some awe, "my compliments. Dust never settles on you, does it? How like you to meet Sales before any of us and steal a march on us all."

Julia laughed, understanding him perfectly. "I am never behind the fashion, Charles."

"And always a little ahead of it," Mr. Hervey said.

Julia inclined her head in acknowledgment of the compliment.

"Then you have likely had the unique experience of driving with Lady Julia, Sales," Castledon commented. "She is a capital whip, you know, but her style is not for the faint at heart."

"No. I have not had that pleasure," Dominic admitted.

His eyes twinkling with merriment, Castledon said, "Then you must persuade Lady Julia to take you up, Sales. She must test your mettle as she has tested ours."

Castledon's tone was expressive of deeper meaning and Julia looked to Dominic to see his reaction. His expression remained serious, but there was a sardonic smile in his eyes as they looked into hers. "I would be most honored."

"Then, by all means," she said. "Will you join me, my lord?"

Dominic replied that he would, and when her groom jumped down from the high, precarious seat above the enormous wheels, he adroitly climbed the side of the carriage and took his place beside Julia.

When they had exchanged a laughing good-bye with the other two men, Julia applied her whip to the leader with an expert touch and they began again along the road.

"Did you truly wish to come?" Julia asked baldly as soon as they were out of earshot of the others.

"Yes."

Julia looked at him, waiting for him to say more, but he merely advised her to mind her horses before she ran down a group of pedestrians who stood half in the road talking to friends. Julia took the chastisement in good part and did exactly as he suggested until they were clear of most traffic at the end of the area set apart for promenade. She then turned down a narrower road and gradually let her horses out. High-perch phaetons were built for lightness and speed, and pulled by two dun geldings bred for swiftness and perfectly matched in gait, this purpose was achieved.

There were many who disliked the sporting vehicle, claiming that it was dangerous, and it was true that in inexperienced or inexpert hands a high-perch phaeton was rather easily overset, but Julia was neither. They sped along the road, which was far from straight, at an easy gallop, and Julia so skillfully feathered each turn that the carriage clung to the road without even swaying precariously. If Dominic felt the least danger that Julia would overturn them, he gave no sign of it.

The road gradually dwindled into a lane and finally Julia slowed her team. When they reached a clearing, she turned her horses with the ease of great skill and headed back in the direction they had come, though this time at no more than a brisk trot.

"My compliments, Julia," Dominic said when she had turned the carriage. "You are as superb a whip as you are a horsewoman."

"High praise indeed. I thank you, my lord," she responded. "But it is I who give my compliments to you." Julia quite deliberately allowed her eyes to travel over him appraisingly. "Your transformation from provincial scholar to man of the town is complete, even to the acquisition of a title."

Dominic heard her sarcasm, but did not take offense at her words. He understood her annoyance at his dissemblance, however much duplicity had not been his intent. He smiled. "It has proven useful."

"As it was useful to claim no title in Wiltshire?"

"Quite."

"So now you may be a pink of the *ton*, after all."

"You know I aspire to no such heights." He paused and

added, "Why do I have the impression that you disapprove, Julia? I should have thought that I would rise considerably in your estimation. When we last met, you condemned me for a hopeless provincial."

Her brows rose. "Is that what this is about? Have you come to town to prove to me that you are not?"

He laughed with genuine amusement. "It would be excessively rag-mannered of me to suggest that you flatter yourself, but the truth is that I am here as I had planned to be nearly a year ago. I had to see to my inheritance eventually, but I wanted to wait until my writings were complete so that I would not be distracted in any way. Since we have established a policy of plain speaking between us, I shan't hesitate to tell you, Julia, that you had nothing to do with my decision to come to town."

Julia felt stung by his words, though he spoke lightly. She attributed this to a bruised vanity, for in spite of telling herself not to be absurd, she had not been able entirely to resist regarding herself as the reason for his transformation. "I should not be surprised," she said acerbically. "You certainly didn't think enough of me to tell me the truth in Wiltshire."

"I nearly did," he said after a moment. "Once we had gone beyond being merely acquaintances, I knew that I should tell you, but I was afraid to do so. I thought it might make a difference in how you felt about me." He saw that Julia turned on him a look of pure puzzlement, and sighed. It had been a difficult decision to make at the time and he had always felt that he would be damned if he did and damned if he didn't. "In the beginning I felt that there was no need to tell you, and once I realized that my feelings for you were deeper than friendship, I was concerned that the truth would color your feelings for me."

Julia had thought he would have no greater power to astonish her or dismay her, but he did so yet again. It was not easy to hear that he thought her so shallow. She raised her hands and pulled her team to a stop. She turned to him and his dark hazel eyes remained steady on hers. After a moment she laughed in a mirthless, self-mocking way. "I suppose I am well-served for that. Account paid in full, my lord. I rejected you because you were too provincial, and you thought me so superficial that it would matter to me that you had a title. Did you suppose I would set my cap at you if I knew I might be Lady Sales one day?''

''No.''

''Then what did you think?'' she demanded coolly.

''I preferred that you accept me for myself exactly as you found me,'' he said, gently eluding a direct answer to her question. ''You told me often enough that you are a creature of the world and that the things of the world matter to you.''

''But I do not choose my friends by how they are styled. If I had accepted your flattering offer, would you have told me then?'' she wondered with a touch of acid.

''Well, I must have done, then,'' he said with an infuriating smile and no hint of apology.

Curiously, Julia found she liked him the better for not trying to fob her off with a whitewashed excuse. It was difficult for her to accept that this had been his opinion of her character, but in the beginning, she reminded herself, she had labeled him in similar ways. She even wondered herself if it would have made a difference in her answer to him, but she knew it would not have. It was not because she had thought that he lacked position that she had refused him.

She lowered her hands and her horses started again at a walk. Silence continued between them, which neither attempted to breach. Julia knew she had to come to a decision. Either she could nurse her injured sensibilities, or she could accept that they were now tit for tat. Because she wanted them to begin again as friends, she chose the latter course.

''Do you think there is any hope for us as friends?'' she asked him plainly. ''I think you must have your own doubts, for you have not even called since the night we met at the opera.''

''I have reservations,'' he admitted.

''Even now that we have spoken so plainly to each other?''

Dominic was not prepared to tell her the true cause of his hesitation. He said instead, ''I saw the way that Tallboys looked at me when he came into the box. I think he would have liked to plant me a facer. I thought it might be best if I did not make difficulties for you in that quarter.''

''Royden does not choose my friends for me,'' Julia informed him. "I have missed our rides and conversations. Perhaps we can meet again in the mornings as we used to."

"While keeping town hours?" he said skeptically. "I have it on good faith that a man of fashion never leaves his rooms before ten, and then only to pay morning calls."

"Is that what you wish to be?" Julia said doubtfully.

His expression became pained. "You wound me, dear lady. I thought I was in a fair way to attaining that goal."

"Oh, a very fair way," she assured him. "You have all the proper airs and graces. And the wonder of it is that you came by them so quickly."

"Dormant traits, no doubt," he said blandly. "Neither did you expire of boredom in Wiltshire as Linton told me you had thought you would. We are wonderfully adaptable creatures, you know."

"Any circumstance may be endured if one knows it is not forever," she said caustically. "Do you mean to make a long stay in town?"

"Until the end of June, in any case."

Julia was pleased to hear this, for she meant to remain until after the fete at Carlton House that would mark the end of the Season, when the Prince Regent moved his court to Brighton. "And then you will return to Wiltshire?"

"No. I'll likely go on to Sussex, to Briarwood Abbey. I made a brief visit there before I went to Wiltshire and discovered that my cousin did little to keep up the estate other than what was needed to keep it from actually becoming a liability. Not only the house, but the entire estate will need considerable undertaking to restore it to what it doubtless once was."

"Your inheritance has not proven a great boon to you, it would seem," Julia remarked.

He laughed. "Hardly that. It is a good thing that I sold all of my assets in the Indies before I went to the Hebrides. I might be sorely tempted to wish it all to the devil and return to the simpler life in the islands."

"I suppose you might do so in any case if you truly wished it," Julia said, glancing away from the road for a moment. "Do you?"

"No," he said, and fell silent.

There was an even greater abundance of people abroad than there had been when she had taken him up in her carriage, and Julia's attention was absorbed by the need to maneuver her high-spirited cattle through the traffic without incident.

She offered to return him to Sales House, but he declined and suggested that she let him down at the end of the promenade. When he descended and was beside the carriage again, he reached up for her hand in a gesture of leavetaking. "I was pleased to drive with you, Julia," he said. "You are a truly fine whip."

Julia smiled. She felt that he had rebuffed her overture of friendship, but she was determined not to let him see that it mattered to her, though she was very disappointed. "Perhaps I should have tested your mettle and given the reins to you for a time, my lord."

"I would not have acquitted myself half so well," he replied with a self-deprecating smile in return. "Will you ride with me in the morning?"

This was so unexpected that Julia didn't answer him for a moment. Everything about Dominic seemed to throw her off-balance. But there was no hesitation in her answer once she recovered from her surprise. "Yes. I should like that above all things."

"Tomorrow, then," Dominic said, and released her hand and walked away from the carriage.

Julia sat where she was for a long moment until the wheeler, objecting to the inactivity, began to toss its head for a better feel of the bit. Julia applied the whip in a mechanical manner to the leader and set her pair at an easy trot to return to Half Moon Street.

Julia could not deny that she felt a sense of excitement at the prospect of meeting Dominic again for their morning ride. She had not realized just how much she looked forward to being with him again. Feelings that she had barely acknowledged as existing in Wiltshire and that she had pushed firmly aside since her return to London were again surfacing, and it caused her considerable disquiet. The thought occurred to her that she cared more deeply for him than she was willing to admit, but was instantly dismissed. Yet even fleetingly acknowledged, it was an unwelcome revelation that she could not ignore.

Julia did not disappoint him and in the morning was awaiting him at seven just as she would have been at Dumphree. Considering that since the last time they had ridden together they had become both lovers and strangers, Julia found it remarkable that they fell back into their easy habit of conversation and banter as if nothing out of the ordinary had occurred between them.

And they continued that way. They met not only in the morning to ride, but frequently during the day and at evening as Dominic accepted invitations with greater frequency from hostesses eager to lionize. The rapport between them grew, and Julia was pleased to observe that they still possessed the trick of exchanging glances in absurd or amusing circumstances and knowing that they shared a single thought.

Dominic still had doubts about the wisdom of beginning again with Julia, but after much consideration during the sennight he had avoided her, he had concluded that his own emotions were sufficiently in hand that he need not deny himself the pleasure of her company. And yet there were other feelings that were not so easily put aside.

In spite of the fact that she had shared his bed at the old Dower House, Dominic believed that Julia was a respectable woman who had succumbed to the powerful attraction between them, as he had. But in town he heard the whispers that speculated that she had had lovers before him, and he saw himself the affectations that had caused her to be labeled a bit fast. He began to wonder if it was only his naïveté that caused him to believe she was better than she was. She was flirtatious not only toward him but toward other men who formed her court of admirers, and at times it seemed to him that she openly encouraged him to renew his advances toward her.

His desire to make love to her again remained unabated, and he began to seriously consider making her an offer different from the one he had made her at the old Dower House. He found it ironic that Julia would not have him as a husband but would take him as a lover. He supposed, with a growing cynicism that was not affectation, that he was too provincial, after all. He had values that were not esteemed in this world. The members of the *ton* might whisper scandal behind their hands, but as long as lovers were discreet, such liaisons were not only tolerated, they were almost as accepted as a marriage blessed in church.

Julia did not really wish to examine her feelings for Dominic; they were too disturbing. But she knew that she had never been happier or felt more alive in her life. She was still not certain that this was love, but she knew that being with Dominic mattered to her—too much. In spite of the renewal of their friendship, Dominic gave her no hint that he intended to repeat his offer of marriage, and even if he did, she was no more certain that she did wish to marry Dominic than that she didn't wish to marry Royden.

No doubt spurred by the return of Dominic in Julia's life, Royden became increasingly attentive and she realized only too well that ultimately a resolution was soon going to be forced upon her one way or the other. The practical Lady Julia Halston, who had ruled her heart for so many years, still believed that she and Dominic were unsuited by nature; she wanted to give Royden the answer he sought, but another softer, more romantic facet of her personality was beginning to emerge and take control. In quiet moments she remembered the taste of Dominic's mouth, the scent of his skin, and the feel of his warm flesh against hers, and she wondered if she could bear never to know the nearness of him again.

It had been a remarkably dry spring and one beautiful day passed on to the next. The Season was slowly dwindling to an end and soon Dominic would retire to his estate in Sussex, and Julia, the Morlands, and Royden would set up residence in Brighton. Julia enjoyed each day for itself and cravenly avoided the decision she did not want to have to make.

She considered it a blessing that Jennifer had attached Lord Cannabray. Hal was so caught up in his delight that his daughter had made such a superb match and Elizabeth was so immersed in all the myriad details to be seen to before the wedding, which was to take place at Morland at the end of the summer, that neither one seemed to take a great deal of notice of the affairs of Julia's or of their son's.

Linton was not encouraged to call at Amberly House, but he still managed to spend some part of an evening with Sophia whenever they were in company together. Lady Amberly might not wish for the connection, but she could not refuse to allow her ward to know the viscount, for Harry, in spite of his scapegrace reputation, was received everywhere. One of the schemes he thought of to spend more time with Sophia was to arrange for a picnic at Cannabray Court, which was near to Richmond and nearly rivaled the famed royal estate for the beauty of its gardens. His suggestion that they drive out with his sister and Lord Cannabray was unexceptionable, but Lady Amberly refused to regard another unmarried couple as suitable chaperones for her niece and withheld her permission and only relented when Harry abandoned his hope for an intimate foursome and suggested a larger party.

Harry asked Julia to come because he knew she would cast a tolerant eye on his flirtation with Sophia, and he added to this Lady Frances to keep Julia company, and finally Letty, who had heard of the party and clearly wished to be asked, though in general she disliked driving out beyond the bounds of the city. He thought this would be sufficient, and was dismayed when Lady Amberly intimated that she too intended to come, and it was Lady Amberly who without a blush invited Dominic and several other friends to join the expedition. The viscount watched in dismay as his cozy picnic grew to the proportions of an organized event. He called at Half Moon Street the morning before the picnic was to take place and was bemoaning the plans that had gone awry when Royden was announced.

"It is just as well that you are to have company, Harry," Julia was saying as she idly sipped tea. "Lady Amberly would have insinuated herself into the party in any case, and think how dreadful it would have been if there were only the four of you and that she-dragon."

Royden seated himself across from Julia without ceremony, like the comfortable friend he was to her. "Is this the infamous picnic that Fanny told me about last night at the theater?" he said, smiling. "She seems to think it has all the elements to make it either a melodrama or a capital farce."

"No point in your being left out," Linton said moodily. "Come see for yourself which it is to be. You might want to bring Prinny with you as well; it wants only that to make it a royal progression."

"What the devil is he in such dudgeon about?" Tallboys asked when Linton took leave of them a few minutes later. "Was his invitation to me sincere, do you think?"

Julia hesitated, but only for a fraction of a second, so it was not discernible. "I imagine so. Do you really wish to join us? We go only to Cannabray, to picnic and stroll about the gardens. Hardly an enticing invitation."

"But you are going along, aren't you?"

Julia said she was. She wished that Harry had held his tongue. Though Harry complained about the size of their party, it was still small enough to have the potential for awkwardness with both Dominic and Royden present. There was nothing Julia could say to discourage Royden from accepting Harry's impulsive invitation without giving offense, so she accepted it with good grace and only hoped that her pleasure in the outing would not be quite destroyed.

8

When all the members of the riding party assembled the following morning at Morland House, Julia felt that Linton's complaints were not unjustified. Their company consisted of two curricles, one barouche, and nine members on horseback. Sophia, who was an indifferent rider, and her aunt accepted the offer of a seat in the barouche, and Harry was reduced to jogging along beside the carriage, flirtation virtually impossible.

Julia rode beside Royden for much of the way but did not allow him to monopolize her. She rode beside and spoke with several other friends and eventually found herself next to Dominic.

"This is not your usual pace, Julia," he said, smiling as she joined him.

"Nor yours," she rejoined. "Poor Harry's nose is quite out of joint, but he is impervious to all hints and insult and will simply not give up. I must say I am coming to admire his tenacity. He will wear down Lady Amberly's resistance, after all."

Dominic shook his head sadly. "I would not encourage him to think that. Lady Amberly is adamant against his suit and has convinced Amberly to her thinking. Sophia is infatuated with Linton, but not sufficiently to defy her guardians."

"I would not encourage him to abandon hope, either," Julia argued. "If he is truly in love with Sophia, how could he give her up without a fight?"

Dominic's eyes dropped away from hers and he looked again to the road ahead of them. "If it is hopeless, then he only prolongs his unhappiness."

"But if love is strong enough, is it ever truly hopeless?"

Dominic turned to her and he was smiling again. Whatever emotion her words had engendered in him, he had himself in hand again. "You are turned suddenly romantic, Julia. This is a new start for you; I thought you ever pragmatic."

"I hope I have more than one side to my character," Julia said lightly. She had meant more by her words than their surface meaning, but she saw that he did not mean to reveal his thoughts to her, so she gave it up. In a few more minutes they were joined by Mr. Hervey, and a little after that Julia left them and rode beside Fanny for the remainder of the journey.

Linton had predicted a disastrous party with so many people, but the journey was accomplished with high spirits and everyone in perfect charity with one another. When they reached their destination, Lord Cannabray rode ahead to personally conduct his guests into the garden, and his mother, who lived year 'round on the estate, was a charming hostess. She invited everyone to roam about the gardens and house as they pleased before partaking of the picnic luncheon near the lake at the edge of the park.

The sky had been slightly overcast when they had started out, but the clouds had cleared on the way and the day was as bright and perfect as anyone could have wished for. Flowers abounded and the air was fragrant with their perfume as they strolled about the many paths in couples and larger groupings.

Royden attached himself to Julia's side as soon as they dismounted. They admired the formal garden and the rose arbor together and enjoyed a comfortable but impersonal conversation. Julia, who had visited Cannabray a number of times before and was familiar with the gardens, gently steered him away from the more secluded paths to prevent any more intimate discussion. With considerable grace she finally disengaged herself from Royden when they met up with Cannabray and his betrothed. As Julia passed a fantastical yew cut into the shape of a crowing rooster in the topiary, she was startled when an arm appeared from behind the bush and caught at her wrist. She gasped and turned in astonishment to see her nephew.

"For heaven's sake, Harry," she said crossly. "Couldn't you have spoken my name first so that I wouldn't have been startled half out of my wits."

"If I had, you would have probably been even more frightened," he said unrepentantly. "You might have thought it was the bush come to life."

"If it did, I should rather have it speak to me than clutch at my arm," she said in an acid tone.

"I need you to do something for me, Aunt Jule."

There was an urgency in his tone that made Julia cautious. "We shall see. What is it?"

"Sophia has been walking with Sales for the last half-hour. If I were to join them, it might be deuced awkward if I asked for a private word with Sophia, but if we met with them together and you managed to draw Sales off, it would be quite another matter."

Julia smiled to herself. It was in hope that she might find Dominic, whom she had not seen for a bit, that she had separated from Royden. "I don't know what good it may do you, Harry. Caroline Amberly is dead against you, and even if the girl is willing to listen to you, she doesn't strike me as the sort with enough spirit to defy her guardians and wait until she is of age if they refuse their consent."

"Sophia doesn't lack spirit," he returned quickly, stung by this animadversion on his beloved. "She is just such a gentle soul that she wishes to please everyone."

It occurred to Julia that Sophia would hardly be pleasing Harry if she married someone else at her guardian's bidding, but she didn't speak the words. Harry was a young man in love, and thwarted in love at that. He didn't wish to hear anything that ran contrary to the perfect image of his dear Sophia that he had created.

"Do you know where they are to be found?" she asked instead.

"They were headed toward the maze when I saw them last," he said, drawing her arm into his and already walking in that direction, pulling Julia along with him. "If we are quick, we shall catch them up before they go into the maze, for then we might have the devil's own time finding them."

Julia refused to be literally dragged into his scheme and she forced him to slow his pace. "We might as well announce our intention if we are going to come up to them in a hurly-burly manner all out of breath."

His fears were not realized, in any case. They found Dominic and Sophia in the small clearing beyond the maze. They stood at the edge of the ha-ha overlooking the larger park, where tame deer grazed in a placid pastoral setting. Dominic looked up as they approached, and a warm smile came into his eyes that made Julia feel almost as if he had embraced her.

"Have you ever been into the maze, Lady Julia?" Sophia asked when Julia came up beside her. "Lord Sales assures me that we should not lose our way and need to be rescued, but Miss Bryce told me that exactly that happened to her; it was quite an hour before they were able to find her and lead her safely out. I would be quite frightened if that happened to me, but I did so wish to go in, for I have never been in a maze before."

Linton dismissed the intrepid Miss Bryce with a wave of his hand. "We've all heard Penny Bryce's story of the maze a dozen times. It is the only exciting thing that has ever happened to her and she embellishes it with each telling. There's not the least danger of being trapped inside for any space of time."

"In any case," Julia put in dutifully, "Miss Bryce, I believe, went in quite alone. I have been through it a number of times and know the turnings well, as does Linton."

"Will you come with us, Lady Julia?" Sophia said hopefully. "I should feel quite comfortable if we were all together."

Julia, no more than Harry, had any intention of remaining all together, but a tactful separation could easily be engineered once they were inside the high hedge walls. "Of course. Do you come too, my lord?" she said, looking up through her lashes at Dominic.

He smiled down on her, his expression lazily amused. "Like Sophia, I have never been inside a maze before, but shall brave it with you and Lord Linton as such competent guides."

Julia interpreted his words and look as flirtatious and returned it with an encouraging smile of her own. "What an onus of responsibility," she said with mock chagrin. "We must take great care, Harry, not to make any false turns."

As they walked to the entrance of the maze, they were still coupled as they had been at the ha-ha, but as they passed between the narrow lane of hedges, Harry moved forward a bit to speak with Sophia and Julia fell backward in step beside Dominic.

They chatted of commonplaces as they made their way through the first part of the maze, making an occasional false turn to a dead end and retracing their way to go on again. But gradually more distance was placed between Harry and Sophia and Dominic and Julia, and eventually, by Harry leading Sophia in one turning and Julia gently guiding Dominic in another, they were at last separated.

Dominic and Julia followed one path and found themselves at a dead end. They retraced their steps to the last intersection and took the other turning, only to find that it too led only to a blank wall of green. Julia laughed. "It would appear that I am not as familiar with this maze as I have claimed to be."

There was a small marble bench just wide enough for two to sit at the end of the passage and Dominic suggested that they rest there for a while. There was a smell of fresh green foliage and earth and Julia felt a sense of *déjâ vu* from the many times they had dismounted during their rides in Wiltshire to walk along the banks of a lake or to enjoy some other prospect while their horses grazed peacefully behind them.

"It seems a very long time since we were last together like this," she said, a little turned toward him.

"In what way?"

"In such solitude and peace." She took in a breath of the fragrant air. "I have enjoyed our rides in the parks in town, but it has not been the same as it was in Wiltshire."

"No," he said with a terse inflection, and Julia knew what his thoughts were. "I am surprised to hear you say so, Julia," he said, turning away from any deeper interpretation of her words. "I thought you disdained such things."

Julia laughed softly. "Country life was not as dreadful as I imagined," she admitted. "Do you find town life to be as unpalatable as you had supposed?"

"No. I have no desire to exchange it for the life that I prefer, but it is far more tolerable to me than I would have supposed."

"Then your friends may hope to see you in town with greater frequency," she said lightly, but she was in fact eager for his answer. She wanted to hear that the differences between them were not as great as she had supposed. Increasingly she feared she could not give him up, that marriage to Royden and the ideal life she supposed she would have with him were not sufficient compensation for the loss.

"I suppose so," he replied, but in an absent way. Neither said anything as moments passed, but it was not an uncomfortable silence. They sat close beside each other, almost touching. Julia was intensely aware of his physical presence. She didn't need to wonder at his thoughts now; she knew they were both remembering the last time they had been together at the old Dower House. Other than the comments he had made to her the first night she had spoken with him at the opera, they had never discussed the morning that Julia had spent at the old Dower House. But their shared memory of their lovemaking and the aftermath of it was almost a tangible barrier between them, and Julia knew that the time would come when they would have to speak of it.

As if his thoughts were identical, he slowly turned to her. His eyes held hers, gently questioning, and then he bent his head to hers and kissed her in a gentle but unromantic way. A bittersweet echo of the passion they had shared.

"I'm sorry for the wretched way we parted in Wiltshire, Dominic," Julia said with quiet sincerity.

"So am I," he replied in an equal tone.

Julia shook her head. She could not permit him to share the blame for her insensitivity and, she had begun to think, stupidity. "The regret must all be mine. I have thought many times of the things that I said to you that afternoon. Sometimes it almost seems as if some other woman spoke them; I wish it had been. I was so . . . cold, so unfeeling. I never meant to be, or at least I did not mean to hurt you."

There was neither grimness nor sadness in his expression; his tone implied acceptance. "It is over and done. I, too, often ask myself why I said the things I did that day."

Julia smiled. "I told you you would regret such an impulsive proposal." She saw that her words were not felicitous, for something flickered in his eyes that was far from tranquil. But then he smiled, and in the fraction of a moment it was gone and she almost wondered if she had imagined it.

"That was not precisely what I meant, but you were quite right. Who manages to pass through life without at least an occasional ruing?"

"Certainly not I," Julia said with feeling. She pressed her hands in her lap, looking away from him for the first time, finding words were becoming more rather than less difficult.

"It was not just the way that I spoke to you that day, it was what I said. All of it was so . . . unexpected."

"It was inevitable, perhaps," he said without discernible emotion. "I have thought that if we had acknowledged the attraction between us more openly, it might not have erupted with such intensity when the circumstances between us became unexpectedly intimate."

"Well, that was quite your fault," she chided, but in a teasing way. "I attempted to flirt with you but you would have none of it."

Amusement danced in his eyes. "There were not a great number of presentable men in the neighborhood. I thought you wanted to set me up as your flirt to alleviate your boredom and perhaps for the sake of the conquest."

With a soft laugh, Julia admitted that this was so, but only at the beginning. "We became truly friends, I think."

"We are friends, Julia."

"Even after the dreadful things I said to you? Could you ever forget them?"

He saw that she wanted his absolution, but he could not give it unconditionally: the wound she had delivered to him had been deep and the healing over was not yet entirely complete. "I won't forget that morning, Julia, any more than I think you will, but I don't mean to let it come between us. We are very good together, Julia. We understand each other and laugh at the same things. It would be a pity to ignore that and recall only the hurt."

Julia looked away from him and down at her hands in her lap. It was rare that she could not find the words to express her feelings, but she knew suddenly and beyond doubt that her regret was far deeper than that. She could not trust herself to speak without a catch in her voice, and she needed a moment to compose herself.

Dominic took her chin in his hand and raised it to force her to look at him. "I was not at all what you wanted, was I?" he said softly as if to himself. "I thought you meant to marry Tallboys."

Julia shook her head within the constraint of his grasp. "I refused him as well."

Dominic's brows rose. He was genuinely surprised. "Now, why, I wonder?"

"I am not as acquainted with my own mind as I had supposed," Julia said, meeting his steady, searching gaze.

Dominic was genuinely mystified by this. He had thought he understood her and her motives, but she had managed to shake him yet again. It was a point in her favor, but it made no great difference, after all. She had used and discarded him as heartlessly as any hardened libertine might have done to a member of her own sex. What did it matter to his feelings that she had shattered Tallboys' hopes as well as his own? All that mattered now was that he wanted her again. They were already so close that it required little motion to gather her into his arms.

Julia offered no resistance. The remembered feel of his lips on hers was at last real again, and far too sweet to resist. But as the kiss deepened and became more demanding, she was aware of a difference from the last time they had been together. There was an urgency in his manner that was not perhaps surprising, but she knew instinctively that it was derived from desire, not love. He wanted her very much, she had no doubt of it, her own need for him was strong, but this time if they made love, it would be purely carnal.

If she heeded her own desire, she might have taken this half-loaf from him, but her pride forbade it. She pushed him away from her with a sudden force that clearly startled him. Julia's breath was shallow and rapid. "Not like this," she said in a breathless voice.

"What, then?" he asked in a voice that was oddly cold for the passion that he had just displayed. "We have not the convenience of the old Dower House here. If we are to be lovers, we must find our pleasure where we may."

"We are not to be lovers," she said savagely, her anger spurred by a pain she barely understood.

He moved back from her a little. His eyes, usually so warm and expressive, were steel-cold and hard. "I see. You still don't know what you want, do you, Julia? Or is it just that all things must be on your terms?"

Julia heard the unconcealed contempt in his tone, and a small, sick feeling replaced the hope she had felt for a few brief moments when she knew he was going to kiss her. She understood his bitterness, but that didn't prevent her from feeling angry and hurt that he would use her in such a way. "Is this what you have wanted from the beginning?" she said coldly. "The opportunity to insult me to pay me out for refusing your offer?"

"How have I done that?" he demanded, his own anger surfacing. "You are a beautiful woman, Julia. I've desired you from virtually the moment we met. That hasn't changed. It was you who made it plain that you had no interest in marrying me, though you had no objection to sleeping with me."

Julia felt as if he had slapped her. She stood to put distance between them. "Why don't you just call me a whore and be done with it?"

"That is never what I have thought of you, Julia," he responded more temperately. "But I do think you hedge your bets to your advantage. We should never suit, I believe you said, because our worlds were so divergent. You will forgive me, I am sure, if I fail to find your sudden interest less than flattering, now that you know I am not the hopelessly countrified nobody you thought me."

This was certainly not true in entirety, but just enough for his words to sting. "I suppose you think I deserve that," she said furiously. She walked about the cul-de-sac because she could not contain her agitation.

His smile was slow. "What did you imagine, Julia? That you could pick me up and put me down again at your choosing? You can't have believed I was stupid or foolish enough not to guess the cause of your sudden change of heart."

Julia turned to him abruptly, her eyes flashing with unconcealed rage. She started to deny his scurrilous attack but stopped. What was the point? From the very beginning his opinion of her had been even less flattering than hers of him. She supposed it said something for the strength of his physical attraction to her that he had overcome his dislike of her character to regard her in a warmer light, however briefly. "You, at least, my lord, are more consistent. You have never ceased to think poorly of me. I can only suppose that your flattering offer of marriage was made out of a misguided sense of honor after the intimacy we had shared."

"No. It was not that."

"Whatever it was, it was apparently short-lived," she said with a sardonic smile. "Do you think you could contrive to find your way out of this maze without me? I cannot imagine us making inconsequential conversation for the next quarter-hour if we did so in company."

"I shall manage." His voice was indifferent.

He had called Julia a cold fish, but she felt chilled by his disinterested response. Their eyes met for a final moment and then Julia turned and walked away without a backward glance. She could not ever recall feeling as she did now. Not even when she discovered that her father had paid Mr. Battersby to dispense with his flattering attentions toward her. It was a sensation that defied description. It was an emptiness, and yet she felt an overwhelming sensation of burden.

This time she made not a single wrong turning and came out at the place where they had entered it a scant half-hour earlier. Her sense of irony engaged and she thought it incredible that such a short period of time could make such a difference in her life. She had not even guessed when she had entered between the walled hedges that what would occur there would affect her so profoundly.

Whatever had been between Julia and Dominic, whatever their different perceptions of it, it was at an end. She would not continue to tease herself with the fantasy that in some way they could overcome their differences and yet be together. She had always known it was hopeless; she had been as gulled by his presence in her world as he had been by hers in his. She had allowed her emotions to get the better of her sense. As she stepped out of the shadow of the hedges, she told herself that it was for the best and even believed that she would feel relieved as soon as she had managed to salve her wounded pride.

She saw Royden approach her from the topiary. She had not meant to go in that direction, but rather to return to the house. But she turned her steps and met him, her smile warm and nothing in her expression to indicate that there was anything at all to upset her. Julia prided herself on her cool, serene demeanor and she would let no one, especially not Royden, know the extent of her inner turmoil.

"Have you been in the maze by yourself?" he asked with surprise. "I have been searching for you this quarter-hour. If we are to be back at dinnertime as we planned, we had best begin to find our stragglers and begin the picnic."

Julia was in perfect harmony with this suggestion. The time for them to leave this place could not come soon enough for her now. She avoided telling him that she had been with Dominic, saying, "Harry is in the maze with Miss Sutton. I have no idea where anyone else is to be found."

A frown gathered on Royden's brow. "If they are alone together, was it wise to leave them?" he questioned.

"For heaven's sake, Royden," she said with a short laugh, "I hope I am not yet relegated to the class of duenna. Harry is not a libertine; he'll take no unfair advantage of Sophia."

"I didn't mean that. I think it unwise to encourage them when it is so well-known that the Amberlys will not countenance a match between them." A thought occurred to him. "Do you wish for it?"

"I have no particular interest one way or another in my nephew's affairs," she said with languid disinterest. "I see nothing to object to in the match, but if the Amberlys do not think it fine enough and Sophia will allow herself to be led, it is no concern of mine beyond wishing that Harry were not so foolish as to pursue something that is likely to lead only to his unhappiness."

Sir Royden was silent for a few moments as they walked through the topiary. "There is surely no path more treacherous than the one leading to matrimony," he said tentatively, glancing down at Julia to see her response, but there was none. She appeared to be attending to him, but he thought he detected a faint air of preoccupation.

"It is a bit hypocritical of me to condemn Linton for his unwise pursuit of Miss Sutton, I think," he continued. "I had always supposed that when the time came for me to choose a wife, it would be a simple matter of mutual attraction and interest, with the outcome in little doubt. But reality, as is so often the case, has not lived up to my expectations."

"It rarely does," Julia said in agreement, but it was not really in response to his comments but to the thoughts still running rampant in her own head. She had never imagined that she would fall in love at all, and certainly not unsuitably.

"In some instances it is clearly a matter of *mésalliance*,"

Royden said, "but in others the reason that love does not meet our expectations is more difficult to define."

Julia's head came up sharply. For a moment she almost imagined that he had read her thoughts. "It certainly is in the case of Harry and Sophia," she said, to pull her own thoughts away from Dominic.

"It was not Linton's unfortunate *amours* that I was thinking of," Royden said quietly. "I know I promised you I would not importune you with repeated offers you did not wish to receive, but you did give me reason to hope that your answer to me at Dumphree was not final. Have you given any thought at all to my proposal since then, Julia?"

"Of course I have," she said.

He waited for her to elaborate, but once again she was silent and he was forced to delve for a greater response. "What have you thought, Julia? I think you must agree that we should suit very well. We are companion spirits, our interests and pursuits are not just compatible but virtually identical. We should complement each other exceptionally well."

"I quite agree," Julia said without hesitation. "But we are hardly crossed in love. What you have enumerated has little to do with that emotion."

"I think there is a sort of love between us. Not romantic love, perhaps, of the sort that is causing poor Linton to make such a cake of himself, but surely we are both too sensible to be searching for an emotion that has better validity in one's salad days than when one has reached the age of maturity and sense."

"Only fools fall in love?" Julia smiled, but there was a flickering of wistfulness in her eyes as she did so.

"Only fools believe the world well-lost to love. Mutual affection, understanding, and companionship are the ingredients of a lasting attachment."

Intellectually, Julia agreed, but her heart denied that truth. She stopped and turned to Royden. "Are you asking me to marry you again?" she said plainly.

He seemed a bit surprised by her directness, but he answered without hesitation. "I don't know that I would have pushed for an answer again today, but since you ask, yes. I still want you to be my wife, Julia. Will you?"

"Yes." She spoke the word simply, not trusting herself

to say more for fear she would qualify it in some manner.

He looked at her for such a long moment before reacting that Julia wondered if he had expected a different response, but in fact, he was only surprised by the quickness of it. In spite of the fact that they had spent much time together since returning to town, he had felt that Julia was placing a distance between them, a line beyond which she did not wish him to cross. It was not that he felt there was no hope, only that she might not yet be ready to hear him.

He had been puzzled by her original refusal of his offer of marriage, for he had been certain that she reciprocated his feelings. He was now almost equally puzzled by her unexpected turnabout. Yet he was content enough that she had given him a favorable answer to question it too far. "Dearest Julia," he murmured, drawing her into his arms.

Julia accepted his embrace and permitted him to kiss her, but she was very much aware that she did not really wish to encourage him to make love to her, not after what had just passed between her and Dominic. She told herself that when she succeeded in putting Dominic from her mind, she would feel very differently about Royden and would be eager for his embrace. But she knew in her heart that no other man had ever made her feel the desire that rose within her with Dominic.

Royden would have kissed her again, but Julia gently pushed him away. "We are not young and foolish lovers," she said, smiling. "It would never do for us to be caught kissing in the shrubbery."

"Now that you are to be my wife, it doesn't matter who might see us."

"It matters to me," Julia said, a coolness coming into her voice. "We are not even formally betrothed yet."

Sir Royden laughed. "My dear Julia, is this a new come-out? When has it ever mattered to you if you set the world on its ear?"

"It is one thing for them to whisper," she said with unaccustomed primness. "It is quite another for anyone to witness me behaving in an improper fashion."

Taliboys was not put off, but rather pleased by her wish for propriety. Her reputation as a care-for-nobody and the knowledge that she was considered at least by the high sticklers as somewhat fast had troubled him some. It was less the opinion of the world that concerned him than his own fear that there was justification to the gossip.

"You are right, of course," he said, releasing her. "There is ample time for that sort of thing. We shall be together for the rest of our lives."

His words should have been reassuring, or at at the least, she should have felt gratified that she was so secure of him. Instead, she was aware of a sense of discontent. She knew it was not what she should feel at the prospect of her marriage to Royden, but she chose to ignore it. This was the life she wanted, and her other choice, if she would have made it at all, was lost to her in any case.

9

Her brother, of course, was delighted. In fairness to the earl, he was genuinely pleased for Julia's sake that she would be happily settled again, but there was certainly self-interest in his approval. He would be only too glad to turn over the management of his sister's affairs to her husband. Julia had been true to her promises and had not been particularly extravagant since her return to London, but she was still expensive, living a style of life that was better suited to a married woman who had command of her husband's fortune rather than a widow living on a jointure, however handsome.

Elizabeth was also very pleased, as were Julia's friends, for Sir Royden was considered an excellent match for her by the standards of the *ton*. The constant good wishes and expressed approbation of her friends and acquaintances did much to confirm for Julia that she had made exactly the right choice, whatever her feelings for Dominic, and these, she was determined, would soon enough fade now that she had made her decision.

She was a little surprised that Dominic made a point of wishing her well, and quite proud of herself for receiving his good wishes with civil cordiality. Neither made any mention of their conversation in the maze at Cannabray, and the only outward effect of her betrothal was the curtailment yet again of their morning rides. They still saw much of each other in company, though, and behaved with outward friendliness, but all intimacy was at an end.

If Julia had any feelings of chagrin that Dominic accepted her betrothal with such complete equanimity, she would not allow them to rise to the surface to plague her. Even in the guise of Lord Sales, Dominic would never have suited her; this she was determined to believe, needed to believe for her peace of mind.

One friend who did not seem particularly overjoyed by the

news of Julia's betrothal was Lady Frances. She said all the appropriate words, at least at first, but Julia knew Fanny too well and felt her lack of approval. On a morning about a sennight after the announcement of Julia's forthcoming nuptials had appeared in the *Morning Post*, Julia and Fanny were taking tea in the sunny morning room that overlooked Julia's small but well-cared-for garden, and the topic was finally discussed frankly between them.

Julia was enumerating the dresses she had ordered from Madame Céleste for her bride clothes, which Harry had offered to pay for as a betrothal gift. "The truly marvelous thing," Julia said as she flipped through the pages of *La Belle Assemblée* in an idle fashion, "is that Hal is so delighted that I am finally to settle into marriage again and cease to be his concern that he has not said a word to me about either the number of gowns I have ordered or the fact that I am having them made by Madame Céleste at a positively ruinous price." She laughed. "I think he feels it is worth a minor fortune to have me off his hands at last."

"I hope it is not to be free of Morland's control that you have accepted Royden's offer," Fanny said as she looked through the fashion plates strewn across the table.

"No, of course not," Julia said, surprised at the suggestion. "I admit that I am very glad myself to know that in a few short months I shan't have to stand in front of Hal's desk like a recalcitrant schoolgirl any longer and have him ring a peal over me for buying a decent champagne for my parties or a Norwich shawl at twenty-five guineas."

"No. Now that shall be the chore of your husband."

Julia closed the magazine. "Do you think that Royden is going to be a pinch-penny like Hal? I would own myself astonished if it were so. The settlement papers are being drawn and Royden has been most generous. The figure I am to receive for my pin money each quarter would positively take your breath away."

"That was not precisely what I had in mind," Fanny said, and then attempted to turn the subject by asking Julia if she intended to have a formal wedding breakfast or merely a family party.

But Julia would have none of it. She answered that it had not yet been decided in a perfunctory way and then said, "What did you mean, then? Do you think I shall have something to regret in marrying Royden?''

''Only you could be the judge of that,'' Fanny said non-committally.

''Fanny,'' Julia said with a laugh that was halfway between amusement and annoyance, ''stop being so exasperating. If there is something you wish to say to me about Royden, please say it. I hope we are dear-enough friends that we may speak our minds to each other on any subject.''

Fanny looked dubious, but like Julia, she was direct by nature and disliked dissembling. ''It is less about Royden than about you. Are you truly certain that you wish to marry him?''

Julia allowed her eyes to widen in an expression of surprise, though it was largely assumed. She had already guessed what it was that Fanny wished to say to her, and wondered if it was wise to encourage her. ''But of course. I admit I was uncertain if I wished to marry at all when I first returned from Alicia's, but I have always believed that Royden would make an excellent husband and that if I were to marry, I could not settle on a better choice.''

''How cool you are,'' Fanny remarked with reproach. ''I begin to pity poor Royden. If I were he, I would want something a bit warmer.''

''There has never been any pretense of a love match between us, Fanny, you know that.''

''Is that what you want?''

Julia's laugh this time was a trifle forced. ''Provoking creature! Are you deliberately trying to make me doubt my decision? You should be encouraging me and congratulating me. You yourself said you thought Roy and I should deal together extremely.''

''That was before you went to Dumphree.''

A hint of distance came into Julia's voice. ''And pray, what has that to say to anything?'' Fanny said nothing but her eyes held Julia's until the latter deliberately looked away and got up to fetch a copy of the *Morning Post* on a nearby table. ''I wish you will stop imagining that there was anything more than a pleasant diversion with Dominic. I assure you it was nothing else. Flirting with him saved me from being bored into perdition.''

"Mmm. But I think you were not as indifferent to him as you wish me to believe," Fanny said with persistence.

"Perhaps I was a bit infatuated for a time," Julia admitted, deciding that she would be better-off taking some of the wind out of her friend's sails.

"I have noted a particular empathy between you."

"Of course there is. We are friends. I won't have you building it into a romance when there is none, Fanny."

The doorbell pealed and there were sounds of arrival as they spoke, followed finally by the announced entrance of Viscount Linton. He dutifully kissed his aunt and Fanny as well, for she was a very pretty woman and he had known her since his cradle days. "Interrupting an exchange of confidences, am I?" he said as he cast himself into a stuffed chair near the French doors. "Who have you set up as your flirt now, Aunt Jule? You're supposed to be all staid and proper now that you are betrothed to Tallboys."

Fanny laughed. "I doubt we shall ever see Julia conforming to either of those virtues. I have merely been questioning where her affections truly lie."

Linton raised his brow. "Have you? What is this, Aunt Jule? Unrequited love gone awry. Are you marrying Tallboys to help you forget Sales?"

Julia felt a stab of alarm. Fanny and Harry between them were skating far too near a truth she did not even acknowledge to herself. She sat down again and dropped the newspaper, unopened, onto the table. "You may both quiz me as much as you wish," she said with deliberate casualness. "I am marrying Royden because it is what I most wish to do, and there is no blighted romance with Lord Sales beyond Fanny's imagination."

"I suppose that must be the case," Linton said practically. "If it were Sales you wanted, there wouldn't be the least reason for you not to marry him."

"It is to be hoped that Julia doesn't have second thoughts," Fanny said, casting Julia a speculative glance. "It is likely too late, in any case."

Even aware that it was bait, Julia could not help rising to it. "Why should it be?" she asked, aware that she should have simply let Fanny's comment pass.

"I have heard rumors that there will be another interesting

announcement in the *Post* soon," she said with a knowing smile.

Julia did not comprehend her statement, but Linton sat suddenly upright, all his attention on Fanny. Julia regarded him curiously for a moment but was more concerned with Fanny's oblique hint. "From whom?"

"The Amberlys."

"About Miss Sutton?" Julia said in mild surprise. "Is she to be married? To whom?"

"Dominic Sales."

Julia was perfectly still, not daring to speak or react in any way lest she betray the tumultuous emotions that had suddenly arisen in her.

The viscount was not so controlled. "No," he said as if the word were torn from him. "Never. Sophia would not have Sales."

Dismay came into Fanny's expression. She momentarily had forgotten Linton's interest in Miss Sutton in her attempt to tease Julia about Dominic. "Well, it is not a settled thing," she said, backtracking quickly. "I only had it from Mary Hatter, whose dresser is the sister of Caro Amberly's butler, that it is expected that Lord Sales will call on Lord Amberly before the week is out."

Harry relaxed visibly. "Servants' gossip," he said scornfully. "They are forever spreading rumors, half of them spiteful."

Julia could not console herself with such hopes. She knew too well Lady Amberly's determined pursuit of Dominic, and recalled comments that Dominic had made to her that convinced her that he might well fall in with that lady's schemes. She did not for a moment believe he had suddenly fallen in love with Sophia Sutton—she could not believe that such a young untutored girl could hold his interest for any length of time—but she believed that he might well deem Sophia a suitable wife and offer for her. "No doubt it is that," she said, though, unwilling to disabuse her nephew of his willful obtuseness.

Fanny thought it was time to retreat from her attempt to discover if Julia was indeed marrying Tallboys to put an unadmitted affair with Dominic from her mind. She rose, mentioning a luncheon engagement as she did so. To her surprise, Harry stood also and, claiming an appointment of his own, offered to walk out with her.

Fanny's fears that he had a motive for doing so were confirmed as soon as they stepped into the street. He grasped her arm above the elbow and said in an urgent undervoice, "It isn't more than servants' gossip about Sophia and Sales, Fanny, is it?"

She wished with all her heart that she had held her tongue. She wanted to tell him that it was nothing more, but she read the need to know the truth in his eyes, and decided she would do him no kindness by prolonging a false hope. She sighed and admitted that it was more. "It was until yesterday, when Caro Amberly told me herself that Sales told her he intends to call on Amberly when he returns from a visit in Horsham."

His expression became so stricken that Fanny almost flinched from the intense emotion she saw written in his countenance. "When?"

"Today. Very likely it has already occurred."

The pain in his eyes became anger. "By God, it shall not be." He released her and abruptly turned and walked in the direction of Amberly House at a quick, determined pace.

Lady Frances stood irresolutely in front of Morland House. She furiously castigated herself for her lack of discretion. Her first thought was to go back in and warn Julia that Linton was in a highly emotional state. But Julia's own involvement in the matter stayed her. She had had no malicious intent, but she clearly had set the cat among the pigeons. Vowing never again to meddle in such a dangerous game, and acknowledging her own cravenness, Fanny turned in the opposite direction and returned home chastened.

Julia's reaction was far from being as violent as Linton's but in her way she was no less upset than he. She had no doubt that Dominic was not attracted to Sophia Sutton in the way that he had been attracted to her, but she also knew that he would doubtless find the gentle, biddable young girl a far more appropriate wife than Julia could ever be for him. Sophia liked the life of the *ton* even less than he; she would doubtless be quite content to spend most if not all of her time buried in the country filling her nursery while her husband pursued his avocation.

Julia was not a woman given to tears, but she felt the only

thing that kept her from abandoning herself to weeping was an inner hollowness that made even negative emotion remote. Lady Frances had been more successful than she could have hoped for: Julia at last admitted the lies she had been forcing aside. She had not accepted Royden's offer because she knew he was the right man to spend the rest of her life with, but because the one man that she wanted to have for her husband had rejected her.

Julia possessed a great deal of inner strength, but at this moment she did not know how she would bear seeing Dominic with Sophia as his wife, knowing that it was Sophia who shared his life and and his bed. It did not bear thinking of, and Julia would not have done so if she could have helped it, but for once in her life, she could not control her feelings or her thoughts.

She did not see her nephew again that day or the following day, and on the third day, as she sat at breakfast listening with only half an ear to Letty chattering on in her usual inconsequential manner, she read the words in the *Post* that she had been dreading: the betrothal between Dominic and Sophia was formally announced.

Julia had plans to go driving with Royden that morning, but knew she could not face him with her usual poise. She sent a footman with a note to his house begging off the engagement, and then, to prevent any possibility of having to receive him if he called on her to assure himself of her welfare, she dressed and went out herself. She kept herself as occupied as she could during the day, even deliberately seeking Letty's company, preferring her companion's incessant chatter to solitude and her own ruminations. She had thought herself resigned to Dominic's betrothal to Sophia, but seeing the announcement in print made it more than just gossip. Now it was fact.

She would have gladly remained at home that night or at least attended some entertainment where she could be reasonably certain neither to see Dominic or Sophia nor to hear the talk of their betrothal, but she knew that was craven and it was pointless to avoid what was inevitable, in any case. She had no idea if it had cost Dominic dearly to wish her well when her betrothal was announced to Royden, but it took every ounce of her considerable will and strength to offer him her congratulations that evening. Her sole satisfaction came from being reasonably certain that she had given Dominic no hint of her true feelings.

Nor did Royden, nor Fanny, nor her many other friends guess that Julia was deeply unhappy. She maintained her usual calm, mildly cynical facade with flawless command of herself. It was only at night, alone in her bed, that she permitted the dejection she felt to manifest itself in tears that were alien to her but that she could not control.

Julia wondered how she, who was so determined to order her life comfortably, had come to such a pass. This should have been a time in her life of perfect contentment. She was to marry the man of her choice and live her life as she most wished, but she knew neither satifaction nor peace.

She went on in this wretched state for two days until on the third morning, shortly after rising, she caught sight of herself in the mirror of her dressing table before her hair had even been combed out, and was horrified at the image reflected back to her. She saw there neither beauty nor vivacity but a countenance that looked drawn weary and eyes that were red and a bit puffy from weeping.

Julia put her hands to her face as if to reassure herself that it was really her own image she saw. She sat abruptly on the stool before the dressing table and stared at herself for several minutes. Then her expression changed and she suddenly laughed aloud—at herself for being so foolish. She wondered how she had allowed herself to come to such a pass.

If she could not help loving Dominic—and it seemed, despite her considerable determination otherwise, she could not—then she knew she needed to do something to resolve her present unhappiness. She knew that what she wanted to do was to go to Dominic and tell him plainly that she loved him, had probably loved him even in Wiltshire, though she had fought against it. If he had made his choice for Sophia, it was likely that he would only reject her again, but at least she would know that she had tried. If there was the least chance she could rekindle any spark of the love he had claimed to feel for her, it was at least worth the trying.

She bathed her face in lavender water and was reasonably pleased with the result. She was not perhaps her usual sparkling self, but at least she did not look haggard. She also donned a cotton walking dress in her favorite cornflower blue, which brought out the beauty of her eyes and gave her confidence a boost.

She was almost ready to leave when Elizabeth was announced. Julia bit back an expletive and told Davies to tell Elizabeth she would be with her in a few minutes. Julia chafed at even a slight delay, for even though she was determined on her course, she feared that her courage might yet fail her. She completed the last touches of her toilette and went down to the morning room.

Elizabeth was looking far from herself as well and, after the most perfunctory greeting, confessed that she had come because of her concern for her son. She began to cry and Julia resigned herself to a lengthy delay; there was no way she could fob Elizabeth off in this condition. She led her sister-in-law to a sofa and sat down beside her.

"I am being stupid, perhaps," Elizabeth said, dabbing at her eyes with an already damp lawn handkerchief. "But I have scarcely gone out in the last few days for fear of leaving Harry alone. I would have sent you a note to come to me, but I didn't know what to say that would sound urgent and yet not alarm you. I had to plead the headache this morning to Jenny and Cannabray when they asked me to visit his aunt with them because I do not like to admit it to anyone else. Do you think me foolish, Julia?"

Julia had not seen Harry since the morning that Fanny had mentioned Dominic's pending betrothal to Sophia. He had seemed to gloss over his concern at the time, but Fanny had later confessed that she had told him it was more certain and that he had been very upset. But Julia had not been overly concerned. Harry was not a fool, however headstrong and emotional he might be. If she thought anything at all, she supposed that he was deliberately avoiding a meeting with Sophia or Dominic to spare himself unnecessary pain.

"Do you think that Harry is in that bad a state?" Julia asked, her own concern deepening.

"I have never seen him so distraught. You know how he is, forever falling in and out of love with quite unsuitable girls. When it has gone badly, he has carried on for a day or two and then shrugged it off and gone on to the next one, but this time it is different. He is almost beside himself with wretchedness.''

When Julia thought of the coil that all of their lives had become involved in, she could scarcely believe that it had happened in so short a space of time. If it were a farce being played out on a stage, it could not be more unbelievable. And in a way she blamed herself. If only she might have known her mind and her heart on that morning at the old Dower House, matters would certainly have fallen out differently, not only for Dominic and her, but possibly for Harry and Sophia and Royden as well.

''Is Harry at home?''

Elizabeth nodded. ''He has not left his bedchamber since yesterday morning. He did not come home at all two nights ago, and sent no word. It was the day that the announcement appeared in the paper and I could not be surprised because I knew he would take it badly. Hal was upset, of course, but not nearly so much as he was when Harry did come in the next afternoon. He was thoroughly castaway. He could not even make it up the stairs without the assistance of one of the footmen and then he was horribly sick most of the day.''

She gave an uneven sigh. ''He finally talked to me, though, and that is what has frightened me. He spoke with that wretched girl on Wednesday and she could not simply give him his congé; I think he might have accepted that. She told him that she loved him but that she felt she had to marry Lord Sales because it was what her aunt wished her to do. And since Lady Amberly would never give their consent to her marrying Harry, she had given into their demands.''

Elizabeth threw up her hands and walked restlessly to the window overlooking the garden. ''It is complete nonsense. Caro Amberly is a wicked woman to blight the happiness of the niece she claims to love. I confess that I do not think a great deal of Sophia—she is pleasant enough but too much of a cipher—but if Harry loves her so much, I would rather see him happy than married to the daughter of a duke.''

''Harry is no bluestocking, Eliza,'' Julia commented. ''She would certainly suit him far better than Lord Sales, but it would seem that Cupid's aim is off of late.''

''Love is blind,'' the countess said caustically. ''Isn't that what they say? Linton chooses only to see that his beloved Sophia is being constrained to marriage, not that with a bit of spirit she might have flatly refused to accept her aunt's choice for her. The way that he spoke last night of his life being blighted and not knowing how he could go on knowing that she was another man's wife was quite wild, and it has scared me to death. Do you think you might speak with him, Julia?'' she said, a pleading note in her voice. ''There is no one in the family whom Harry respects as he does you. If you were to talk to him, he might see that he is reacting excessively.''

Julia had more sympathy for her nephew's excesses than his mother did, for her own feelings were not dissimilar. It was a question of degree; Julia did not give way to her emotions in the manner that Harry did, but that did not mean she did not feel them in equal measure. She did not really want to speak to Harry. Elizabeth could not know the pain that would cause her, but feeling responsible as she did at least in part for the unhappiness that afflicted them all, she could not refuse. She resigned herself to putting off her visit to Dominic and returned with Elizabeth to Morland House.

She found Harry in his darkened bedchamber, in bed in his nightshirt, unshaven and unkempt-looking. He did not want to talk to her either. He told her plainly to go away when she came into the room, but Julia ignored him and went directly to pull back the draperies to let in the sun. She had the thought that if nature were in tune with their feelings, it would have been a wretched wet day to suit, but instead, it was a glorious morning. She opened the windows as well to rid the room of its stale, closed smell.

Julia then went to the bed and pulled back the bed hangings, causing Harry to bury himself deeper beneath the sheets. But Julia ignored his protests and demanded that he sit up to speak with her.

''Whatever are you about, Harry, behaving in such a self-indulgent way?'' she chided, but with gentleness. ''Do you have any idea how much you have upset your mother? She is even afraid to leave the house because she is half-convinced that you mean to put a period to your existence if there is not someone nearby to prevent you.''

Harry turned over on his back and regarded his aunt with a

jaundiced eye. "If that was what I meant to do," he said flatly, "I don't know what she or anyone could do to prevent me."

"Is it what you mean to do?" Julia asked calmly.

He wouldn't meet her eyes. "I have thought about it."

"Stuff and nonsense," Julia said, sitting on the bed beside him. "I understand that you think your life has been ruined by what has happened, but that is now, when the hurt is fresh and very painful. You will not feel the same in a month or even a fortnight."

"You don't understand," Harry said angrily. "No one does."

"Linton, you are two-and-twenty and too old to be talking like a foolish lovesick boy. Do you imagine that I know nothing of your feelings?"

"It isn't the same," he insisted, turning on his side, away from her. "This is not as if I loved Sophia and she did not return my regard. I spoke with her after Lady Fanny told us the gossip about Sophia and Sales. I forced her to admit that she does love me—as much as I love her—but the Amberlys have made her believe that if she does not marry as they wish her to, she will never be permitted to marry as she wishes herself and will likely end her days on the shelf, which she cannot support."

Julia was glad he could not see her expression, for she had no doubt her contempt was clearly displayed. But she knew that speaking poorly of Sophia's understanding would only alienate him, so she said, "That is absurd. Lady Amberly would not want to see Sophia unmarried for the rest of her life. Couldn't you convince Sophia that when she is one-and-twenty she may marry as she pleases? I know four years seems an eternity at your age, but if your love is truly deep and lasting, it would not be insupportable."

Harry sighed deeply. "You don't understand," he repeated. "I know she would wish to wait, but she is not strong like you. If it were not Sales this time, it would be someone else later on and they would hound her mercilessly until she gave in."

"I think you both are allowing your imaginations too much reign," Julia said dryly. "Neither Lord nor Lady Amberly is an ogre. They want what they perceive as best for Sophia because they care for her and are responsible for her welfare, but I can't believe they would force her into a match that is repugnant to her."

"Well, they have."

Julia, who had many times seen Sophia smiling and laughing and clearly content in Dominic's company, could not feel that Sophia was in any way repulsed by him. Exasperation beginning to override her good intentions, she said so. "If she told you that, I think it was merely histrionics. Lord Sales is hardly a man that any woman would find repugnant. She may not be in love with him, but she gives every appearance of liking him, at the least."

"Would you wish to share your life and the bed of a man you merely liked?" he said scornfully.

I did, was Julia's thought, and she felt a sudden sympathy for Sophia. Julia had felt no repulsion toward her husband, but there had been a void in her life that nothing had been able to fill. She had been aware of it without really knowing what it was until she had acknowledged her feelings for Dominic. She hoped that if she had loved someone else, she would have resisted her parents' attempts to push her into a marriage of their choice, but she could not be certain of it. Who would have guessed that she would have made such a botch of her relation ship with Dominic?

"Yet Sophia has accepted Lord Sales' offer freely," Julia pointed out but with greater gentleness, "so it would seem that she has made her choice."

The viscount pushed himself upright. "She felt she had no choice," he reiterated. "I tried to convince her to elope with me, but she believes she would be sunk beneath reproach if she did so, and likely disinherited as well, for she thinks there is something in her father's will that she forfeits her inheritance if she marries without the Amberlys' consent."

"And she is quite right," Julia said severely. "You would bring scandal down on all of our heads."

"But what the devil am I to do?" he said on almost a wail. "I can't let her marry Sales. I have even thought of inventing some excuse to call him out."

"My God, Harry," Julia exclaimed, horrified. "What answer would that be? One of you dead, perhaps, and the other forced to flee the country?"

"I know," Harry said miserably. "I just know I couldn't bear to know that she was his wife. I have considered speaking to him, man to man, and asking him to cry off because it is me Sophia loves, but he would probably laugh in my face."

"I doubt he would be so cruel. Very likely he would tell you that if Sophia feels as you do, it is her place to do so."

"She cannot," he said, and started to cry.

Julia gathered him into her arms as she had done before when he was a child. She was not so given to emotional display, but she understood very well how he felt. She offered him what comfort she could, but judging by the hollowness she felt herself, she knew it was ineffectual.

Julia had no practical solution to offer to Harry, but the result of their talk was a strengthening of her resolve to speak with Dominic. It was the only hope she could think of to help them all. Even if he truly did have no feeling left for her, she needed to express her feelings to him to cleanse herself of them. What would be the result of it, she had not the least idea, but she refused to be daunted. In some remote spot in her heart, she could not believe the love he had professed for her at the old Dower House had so quickly and completely died.

It hadn't, of course. Dominic was not of the constitution to take to his bed and mourn any more than was Julia, but he was prey to feelings similar to both Julia and Harry. His offer of marriage to Sophia was sincerely meant when he had made it, but he had regretted doing so almost from the moment she had lowered her pretty eyes and shyly accepted his hand.

He had wondered ever since what had made him do it. He had known for months that Lady Amberly was pulling out all stops to push him into parson's mousetrap, and he had nimbly avoided every snare. He did not want to think that he had been so foolish as to ask for Sophia's hand merely in response to Julia's announced betrothal, but he feared it might be so.

He had buried the pain Julia had caused him when she had rejected him at the Dower House, and he nearly had convinced himself that it was nothing more than physical desire he felt for her. That day in the maze when he had made love to her, he had been deliberately insulting to her, not, he had thought, to hurt her in return, but to make it clear to her in what manner he still felt interest in her. Had she been compliant instead of insulted, he might well have mounted her as his mistress.

In spite of her telling him that she had refused Tallboys' first offer to her, Dominic had not been unduly surprised when he had read the announcement of her betrothal to Sir Royden, for he guessed that ultimately she would have him. But the stab of pain he had felt was greater than he had expected, and was more difficult to deny than were the other feelings for her that he refused to acknowledge.

He was not even certain exactly when he had decided to offer for Sophia, but he knew he had had no such intention before Julia's announcement. Yet he had convinced himself that it was what he wished to do. He liked Sophia; she did not have conversation the way that Julia did, and there was neither empathy nor a shared sense of humor and delight in the absurd, but he told himself that these lackings were the result of Sophia's youth and would be remedied with maturity. Sophia was not without intelligence and wit, and very much to her credit she was young and moldable.

Sophia Sutton was no sophisticate and she had confided in him that she did not really enjoy the parties and gaieties of the city. She looked forward to returning to Amberly, and was sorry that the Amberlys intended to spend a month in Brighton before doing so. Dominic could not imagine himself sharing rides and his interests with Sophia the way that he had with Julia, but at the least she would never complain when he left her to pursue his avocation and would likely be quite content to remain at home happily engrossed in domestic affairs and the children they would doubtless have together. With Julia, he had no doubt he would have had to reorder his entire life.

So at first he had counseled himself that he was behaving with great sense and foresight to offer for Sophia and that he had had a lucky escape when Julia had refused him. But the reality of it was something else. No amount of Sophia's gentle compliance could quite compensate him when he saw Julia with her fine eyes sparkling, her smile intimate, but not for Dominic.

Then he knew he had made a mistake, but he knew also that he would have to live with it, literally for the rest of his life. For him to have retracted his offer of marriage would have been dishonor to him and disgrace to Sophia. Another man might still have made that choice rather than condemn himself to a lifetime of regret, but Dominic could not. He had been bred to the gentleman's code and he would not dishonor it now to his own convenience.

He was dressing to go to Amberly House for luncheon when Taret came into his bedchamber and with a discreet cough informed his master that he had a visitor waiting in his study.

"Who is it?" he asked when the valet lapsed into silence without producing a visiting card or giving a name for the guest.

"A young woman, my lord," Taret said repressively.

The fact that he had not used the word "lady" was significant, but since Dominic had struck up no convenient alliance with any of the muslin company since coming to town, he could not imagine who could be visiting him. "Did you think to ask her name?"

"Yes, my lord," Taret said with a wounded expression. "I am afraid she declined to give one."

"Forgive me," Dominic said with an air of self-deprecation. "No doubt it is my understanding that is at fault. But why, pray, is an unknown woman who refused to give her name in my study, then?"

"She was most insistent and refused to believe me when I denied you, my lord," Taret said, very much on his dignity. "She refused to go away and threatened to pull the bell incessantly until I permitted her entrance and informed you of her presence. She said you would see her if she had to wait on the doorstep the full day and night. I did not think your lordship would care for that."

Dominic suppressed a faint smile. "No, I would not like that." He was reasonably certain of the identity of his caller now. Though he could not imagine why Julia would risk her reputation to come to him, he could think of no other woman with the bravura to outmaneuver his manservant. But Taret was familiar with Julia and should have known her by sight. "What does this lady look like?" he asked curiously.

"It is difficult to say, my lord. She is wearing a cloak and is heavily veiled."

"On a day in early June," Dominic said, his eyes amused. "That is determination."

"I am always ready to do what I must," a voice said from the doorway.

Both men turned, and a woman, robed exactly as Taret had

described, came into the room. Dominic recognized Julia's voice, of course, and his expression changed. It was bad enough that she had called on him at home without a chaperone; for her to actually come into his bedchamber was taking the impropriety of her visit to the limit.

"That will be all, Taret," he said curtly.

The valet bowed correctly, and without even allowing himself to glance at Julia, he passed her and left them.

Dominic went over to her at once and, taking her by the arm, led her firmly out of the room. He moved with purpose, ignoring her protests until they were in the study and the door shut.

"Are you lost to all propriety?" he said savagely as he closed the door.

"If I had sent you a note telling you that I needed to speak to you in private and asking you to call," she said tartly as she removed the veil and heavy cloak, "you should probably have said the same thing."

"It is not the same thing, and you know that as well as I do." His eyes scanned her from head to toe as if he could fathom her reason for coming by sight. "What is it now, Julia? Have you nothing better to do than to plague me?"

It was hardly a propitious beginning, but Julia let the insult glance off her and said simply, "No."

He gave a short, reluctant laugh. "Well, that is honest."

"We must talk, Dominic. We cannot let matters go on in this way."

"By all means, since you think it important enough to risk your reputation," he said, and invited her to take the nearest chair.

But Julia, who never had the least trouble speaking her mind, found that she could not sit calmly and express feelings that were so intense to her. She ignored his offer and walked a little away from him before turning again to speak. "I know what you think of me," she said quietly, "and I can't really blame you."

"No. You can't, can you?" he said coolly, and sat.

His words and manner were daunting to her courage, but not much worse than she had expected. She grasped the back of the chair he had offered her, and closed her eyes for a moment. "I wish with all my heart that I had understood what I felt for you when you asked me to marry you.'' She looked up at him, but his eyes studied a point somewhere on the Turkey carpet. ''I believe now that I loved you then, but I didn't want to love you and I refused to believe it could be possible.''

His eyes flicked to hers. ''So it proved, since you found my offer quite resistable.''

She would not let him put her off, and continued as if he hadn't spoken. ''I was so certain that I knew exactly what I wanted in my life, so sure that life could be tailored to my ordering. It never for a moment occurred to me that I might fall in love with someone who did not fit in with my plans and would set them awry. The principal reason I agreed to rusticate at Dumphree was because Royden seemed to dislike the notion of it. I thought that if he found he missed me, he might be prepared to offer me marriage instead of the *carte blanche* that I think he originally had in mind when he first began his attentions toward me.''

''And so he has,'' Dominic said levelly.

''Yes. But I find that what I was so sure I wanted in February is not what I want now.''

He raised his eyes to hers. ''So you intimated when we spoke at Cannabray. Yet you accepted Tallboys' offer and are to marry him in two months' time.''

Julia shook her head slowly. ''I am not going to marry Royden, after all.''

''Once again your heart has played you false?'' he said so scornfully that she winced.

''I have never been in love with Royden,'' she said, finally sitting. ''I have always known that.''

As she sat, Dominic stood and went over to a table where a decanter and glasses stood. He was not in the habit of taking wine so early in the day, but her words, unwelcome to him and disturbing to his peace, made him feel the need for it.

''It is rather remarkable,'' he commented as he returned with a glass of amber liquid without offering any to Julia, ''that you repeatedly claim to know your mind and yet change it again from moment to moment. Constancy, it would appear, is not your forte.''

''Until I met you, I was rarely plagued with doubts about what I wanted in my life.''

He gave a short, mirthless laugh. "Should I be flattered, or was that a hint for an apology?"

"It is I who apologize," she said solemnly.

This time his laugh was far more genuine. "Cut line, Julia. This mantle of nobility doesn't suit you." He drank deeply from his glass. "What is all this bother about, in any case? We met in Wiltshire, we fell, if not in love, then in lust and were lovers, at least for one morning. Because the attraction between us was so strong, I confused it with a warmer emotion. You pointed out to me my error and I came to see the correctness of it. When I came to town, it was obvious there was still an attraction and I thought it would be pleasant to renew our relationship, but you didn't care for the notion and there is an end to it."

On the surface, everything he said was true, but the emotional reality was something quite other and Julia had no doubt that he knew it as well as she, however much he might choose to pretend otherwise. "Is it the end of it, though?"

"It is for me. Like you, I have formed another connection, but unlike you, I intend to see it through."

Julia could not bear to hear him say so. "You are not in love with Sophia Sutton," she said in flat statement.

He shrugged. "In our class love matches are the rarity, not the rule. You just said you have never been in love with Tallboys."

"And I doubt I shall marry him."

He smiled slowly and sardonically. "Still hedging your bets, Julia. A moment ago you knew it, now you merely doubt it."

Julia rose again, her agitation too great for stillness. "You are the only man I want to be with, but you don't want me. Royden cares for me in his fashion and would be kind to me."

"You do him no kindness."

"Do you do Sophia a kindness?" Julia demanded baldly.

Dominic did not like her question. He did not want to examine it. He finished off the wine in his glass and rose to pour another. "My relationship with Miss Sutton is my own concern," he said coldly.

Julia followed him to the sideboard. She placed her hand on his arm to stay it as he reached for the decanter. "I think it is mine, too," she said very quietly.

He said nothing, but he remained quite still, his eyes meeting hers but so shuttered she could not even guess at his thoughts. Julia failed to find the encouragement she sought, but she would not allow herself to be craven.

"It may be that I believe you have not changed toward me as much as you say because it is what I want to believe," she conceded. "But you have not the character of a man with a fickle heart. I know you are not in love with Sophia any more than I am in love with Royden, and that we would both be making dreadful mistakes if we go through with our weddings as planned, even if it is not possible for us to make something between us."

He was still silent. They stood very close, her hand still on his arm. Dominic felt the warm contact between them, and though it was a simple touch in no way overtly erotic, a sexual current passed between them. He still did not trust her; he was afraid to believe her, but his need for her, which was more than physical and which he had tried so hard to ruthlessly deny, was all the more potent for being bottled and was beyond his ability to control. Without hurry or heat, he gathered her into his arms and she molded herself willingly to him.

The passage of time was indistinct for them both. All that mattered was their physical closeness, the taste and feel of each other. It was some time before Dominic finally loosened his embrace and they stood a little apart, though still touching.

Although he spoke words of love no more than he had at Cannabray, Julia knew that this time it was not merely desire; more had passed between them than that. She gently touched his face. "I am in love with you, Dominic," she said softly.

He took her hand from his cheek and kissed her palm. "And I with you," he said quietly.

Julia let out her breath as if she had been holding it. "Thank God we have recognized it in time. What a wretched coil if it had happened after we were both married to others."

Something changed in his expression. Julia saw it at once, and it was underlined by a physical withdrawal. He released her completely and turned away to pour himself more wine. Julia stood very still, watching him.

"What is it, Dominic?" she said evenly.

"It still is a wretched coil," he said with a mirthless laugh.

"Not now. We need only be released from our promises and then we may be together."

He took a bit of his wine and walked back toward the chairs. "You know it isn't that simple. This is your world, you know the rules that apply. You may cry off from your promise to Tallboys with no dishonor to you and no more than a bit of humiliation for him. It is not the same for me."

Julia did know that it was considered bad *ton* for a man to withdraw from a betrothal, but she knew of those who had done so, and they were not so condemned that they were no longer received. "It will make scandal, of course," she acknowledged. "But what is that to ruining our lives because we have been foolish enough to entangle ourselves with the wrong persons."

He stopped and turned. "It is worse than scandal, Julia. If I cry off, I do myself great dishonor. I might be able to accept that, though it would be difficult, for my honor is important to me. But more than that, I would seriously injure Sophia. Innuendo and rumors are always rampant when such a thing happens, and even Sophia's virtue would be in question. It could well be enough to preclude her from ever contracting another respectable match."

"With her connections and dower? I promise you she will not want for offers."

"But of what sort?" He sighed and his voice became almost weary. "What we have done to each other is one thing, and we must live with it. But Sophia is innocent and she trusted that my offer was sincere, which it was—at the time, at least. I doubt I would be able to live with myself if she received any hurt at my hands."

Julia could scarcely believe what she was hearing. "Sophia is not in love with you. If she knows what love is at all, it is Harry she loves. You needn't fear that she will languish on the shelf, for Harry wishes to marry her above all things and claims that she would feel the same if only the Amberlys had not pushed her into accepting your offer."

"Is that what he thinks?" Dominic said curiously. "How flattering! But he is misinformed. Lord Amberly is not without conscience despite his wife's machinations. Whatever Lady Amberly's objections to Linton, Amberly fears that Harry is too volatile to make a good husband for Sophia and that is why he will not countenance the match. After the sheltered life that Sophia has lived, a man like Linton, with his air of dash and recklessness, must indeed seem like one of the heroes from the novels and poems she reads with great relish. But I think even she—for she is not without a practical streak—realizes that he would make a difficult husband at best. In any case it is moot. Even if I were to cry off, I doubt Amberly would feel any softening toward your nephew's suit.''

''They—and you—do Harry a great injustice,'' Julia said, for a moment forgetting her own interest. ''I admit that he is volatile and that his past experiences with females does not precisely recommend him to a mother or an aunt as a husband, but there is his age to consider. He has tumbled in and out of love a few times, but it was calf love or lust as the case may have been. There must always be a first time where the emotions are sincere, and I believe that Harry's for Sophia are. I feel that it is different this time and that he is genuinely in love with her.''

His smile was condescending. ''Do you judge this on the basis of his claiming to love her for such a short time?''

''That is what I base my feeling for you upon,'' she said plainly.

It did silence him for a moment. ''It doesn't matter what I think,'' he said after a bit. ''The match is set and I could not cry off and allow scandal to fall on people who are innocent.''

Julia felt a wave of anger born of frustration. It was incredible to her that now that they had confessed their love for each other, there could be any impediment to their being together, especially one that to her seemed so unnecessary. She knew he spoke the truth about the scandal and gossip his ending the betrothal would cause, but she, who knew her world so well, thought his concern for his honor and Sophia's reputation excessive. ''Then what are we to do?'' she said acidly. ''Allow all of our lives to be made wretched?''

''We have made our beds, have we not? But it won't come to that, at least for Sophia. I shall see to it that she doesn't suffer for my mistake.''

''Oh, how wonderously noble,'' Julia said scathingly as her anger finally overtook her. ''And what of you and what of me? Are we to live our lives wretched and hollow, or perhaps to fall into an affair at some later time when we can no longer control our need for each other? What scandal will that bring? Who will be hurt then?"

"Don't you think that I feel this too?" he said with heat. "Don't you think that I would undo this if I could?"

Julia could not be moved by his words when she felt that it wanted so little for it all to be quite unnecessary. "It is not a question of cannot, it is a matter of will not."

He wanted to tell her what she wanted to hear, but he could not reconcile it with his conscience. His values were, if anything, more precious to him since he had taken his place in society and seen how many supposedly respectable persons merely gave lip service to the concept of honor. He closed his eyes and sighed wearily. "Whatever."

Julia could scarcely credit her ears. "And that is it? You say you love me and yet it is not enough for you to do what you must for us to be together. What manner of love is that? Do you care so much more for Sophia than for me that you would condemn me to misery to avoid wounding her in any way?"

"It has nothing to do with how I feel about you. It is just what I must do to live with myself. There is no fault in this except our own."

"And I am the victim of your honor," Julia said bitterly. "Do you suppose I wish the girl to be hurt in any way, or Royden, for that matter? But what would their pain be to ours, who love each other? It is absurd to blight both of our lives for the sake of an intangible virtue."

For him, it was clear the pain had already begun, for it was plain in her eyes. "You don't understand, Julia," he began, but she would not let him finish.

"I understand well enough," she said coldly. "If it is still revenge that you seek, your work is complete."

"That isn't my intent."

"But it is the result." She redonned her enveloping cloak and veil. He went to her and reached for her as if to take her in his arms again, but she moved away. "There's nothing else to say then, is there?" she asked sadly, her anger dissipating into resignation. "I'd rather you didn't see me to the door. This is hardly the occasion for a lingering good-bye." She turned and left, leaving Dominic prey to his own unhappy thoughts.

10

But Julia was not so completely resigned to Dominic's decision, after all. For the remainder of that day her humor fluctuated from rage to despair. She could not accept the finality of a course that seemed to her so absurd. Her anger and frustration almost made her imprudent enough to discuss her conversation with Dominic with Harry, but she was too sensible not to realize that her hothead nephew would take even greater exception to the notion that Dominic was marrying Sophia unwillingly and Harry might again talk of calling him out or decide on some other course equally foolish.

In the end she decided that there was no one with whom she could comfortably discuss her predicament. Her relationship with her brother was hardly that of confidant and her two closest friends, Elizabeth and Fanny, would doubtless feel only as she did, that Dominic was being noble to a fault. Julia had always prided herself on understanding such things as honor better than most women, who did not hold honor in the same regard as did most men, but now that it was put to the test, she knew she understood not at all. She was not certain what it was she needed to do, but she knew that she would not allow Dominic to marry Sophia without putting up a fight for him.

Julia was not the sort of woman to remain closeted in her bedchamber brooding over her predicament. When Tallboys came to escort her to dinner with a party of friends, she went without hesitation and enjoyed a pleasurable evening. That was not to say that she was able to put Dominic and their problem from her mind, but nothing in her outward demeanor gave any hint of this.

Julia had had every intention of telling Royden at once that she could not marry him, but the occasion seemed inappropriate to her and she put it off to the following day, when they were to drive to Hounslow to visit his aunt. It was during their drive back to town that she finally broached the subject.

"There is something we must discuss, Royden," she said when they were well along the road to London. He turned an inquiring look on her and she went on. "I have something to tell you that is very difficult for me, but I have no choice." Taking a breath, she rushed her next fence to get over it. "I am in love with Dominic Sales."

There was a long silence and Julia fretted to hear his response. When it came, it was completely unexpected. "I know," he said succinctly.

"I'm sorry. I wasn't aware that I was so transparent."

"Only to someone who knows you well," he said with a brief smile. "You have been in love with him since you met him at Dumphree, I suspect."

Julia laughed unsteadily. "Then you know me better than I know myself, for I did not realize it until a few days ago. I'm sorry, Royden," she said again. "I do think we might have suited each other very well. If I had not met Dominic, I would have been very content as your wife."

"Is Sales in love with you?"

"Yes."

He bent an unreadable glance on her. "Are you crying off, Julia?"

Julia was surprised by the question. "What else can I do? I only wish I had known my heart before I accepted your offer, then I would have spared us this."

"But Sales is to marry Miss Sutton. Does he intend to cry off as well?"

Julia admitted that he did not. "He feels that he could not so dishonor himself and injure Sophia."

Royden gave a nod of approval. "There are not many men with the character to live their convictions. I admire him for that."

"I do not," Julia said with feeling. "Or at least, I admire it in the abstract, but not in the reality."

"Then what it comes down to is that even though you won't marry me, you can't marry Sales either. Is that right?"

"Yes," Julia admitted reluctantly, though she was still far from abandoning hope.

"Then why not marry me?"

Julia stared at him for a moment. "You would still wish to marry me knowing that I loved another man?"

Royden laughed. "A man of such integrity that he will deny himself the woman he loves for the sake of his honor is not very likely to hand me my horns. I know you have never been in love with me, Julia, but you can't marry Sales. What has changed, then, between us?" He saw her uncertainty, and added, "Unless you wish for an excuse to cry off?"

Julia was not sure what she felt about his very generous offer. She had never doubted that Royden would take her news like the gentleman that he was, but she had not expected him to still want her once she had made her confession. Her conscience told her that it would be wrong for her to continue with the betrothal, especially since she meant to do all she could to find an honorable means for Dominic to be free of his entanglement, but her practical side chided her for wanting to abandon what she had worked so hard for, if she could not marry Dominic in any case. If she was honest with Royden, there was no deception involved. "No. It isn't that," she said at last, and told him that she would still marry Dominic if he were to find himself free. "It would be very unfair to you for us to continue, in the circumstances."

He transferred the reins to one hand and took her hand in his and brought it to his lips. "Allow me to look after my own sensibilities, Julia. I still wish to be married, but I shall leave the choice to you. If you want me to release you from your promise, I shall, but I beg you to give it thought. I am content with our arrangement even as it is."

He could not say fairer, and Julia agreed to continue their betrothal, at least for now. But she felt a faint pang of guilt, for it was as if she were hedging her bets, as Dominic had accused her of doing.

If she could not have the man she loved, if she had to live the rest of her life knowing that Dominic was married to someone else, it hardly mattered that she too was married. If anything, her motives for quitting the single state would be stronger than ever.

But she refused to believe yet that it would come to that. When she met Dominic at the Ponsonbys' that evening, she saw a wariness in his eyes that she interpreted as an expectation that she would snub him or subject him to her icy anger again. She did neither.

"I thought you wouldn't wish to see me again," he said candidly as he led her onto the floor.

Julia flashed him a quick smile. "I thought about it—you know well my wretched temper—but I won't allow any further misunderstandings to come between us." She saw a guardedness come into his expression and laughed. "Did you suppose I would not be tenacious? I have thought a great deal since yesterday."

"So have I," he said with feeling.

Julia felt a surge of hope. "To what purpose?" she said quickly.

But he shook his head in warning and did not answer her as they took their place in the set. They were too surrounded by the others in the set to say anything they would not want overheard. But he did not wish to answer at once, in any case.

Julia might have felt a certain satisfaction if she had known of the turmoil that his thoughts had been in. It was one thing for him to know what was the right thing to do, and quite another to do it. When Julia had left him, it had been all he could do to prevent himself from running after her. Just as Julia had done, it was not until he had believed her lost to him that he had acknowledged that he was in love with her. His reluctance to believe himself in love was, if anything, greater than Julia's, for he had been deeply hurt by her and did not want to give her the power to wound him again. But ultimately he could deny it no more than she could, and the fix they were in now was nothing more than the result of their own headstrong and willful natures. They were, indeed, well-matched.

His resolve to do the right thing was still strong, but had weakened a bit the moment he had set eyes on Julia again. To be so close to attaining happiness and have it just out of his grasp was unendurable. Julia's arguments that he had no right to blight her life as well as his own had also affected him powerfully. On the previous evening, which he had spent in the company of Sophia and the Amberlys, he had found himself more than once nearly beginning to say the words that would free him from his betrothal. But against this was his belief that he would find it almost equally insupportable to live with himself knowing he had behaved so dishonorably and out of his own selfish needs. Like Julia, he hoped for some miracle to free them from the coil they were in.

The dance brought them together again and Julia, less concerned with being overheard than he, said, "We must talk. There has to be some solution. I can't believe it could be otherwise."

"I am to take Sophia into supper, but afterward we might have a few minutes together."

Julia nodded her agreement and then turned to other topics. She could be content to wait knowing she had to endure only two more sets before supper. Julia took supper with Royden and Fanny and Andrew Montgomery, but she knew where Dominic sat with Sophia and the Amberlys.

She did not go out of the supper room with the others, but paused to speak with friends, letting them return to the ballroom without her. She knew that Dominic would find her and she was not surprised to feel a touch at her elbow and see his eyes smiling into hers. Her heart leapt within her, a sensation she had heretofor supposed to be nothing more than the exaggerated sensibilities of schoolroom misses. They left the supper room together, which was hardly remarkable since it was well-known that they were friends, but Julia, glancing to her left, saw Caroline Amberly looking daggers at her as they passed through the doorway.

They walked in the direction of the antechambers that were set aside for cards and conversation, and he took her to the farthest of these, which was empty.

"We shan't have more than a few minutes if we are not to be interrupted," he said.

Julia noted that he left the door just ajar for propriety's sake and smiled. She meant for this to be a calm and sensible discussion, but in a moment they were in each other's arms, the attraction irresistible. It was seductive in more than the physical sense. She wanted to be with him like this, wrapped in his embrace for the rest of her life.

"Do you see how absurd it is for us to even consider marriage to anyone but each other?" she said when he released her. "Being married to others won't keep us apart, and then what will happen? Surely adultery is a worse dishonor than ending a betrothal.''

''It won't come to that,'' he replied. ''After Sophia and I are married, we shall seldom be in town.''

Julia had had the unacknowledged hope that Dominic had realized that he had to end his betrothal made stronger by his comment during the dance. She felt this hope snatched away from her and said crossly, ''Neither of us is married yet. We might be married to each other if you will concern yourself with now and not some distant future. We must find some way now that your precious honor is satisfied and yet you are freed from your promise to Sophia.''

''I should be delighted if matters were to fall out in that manner,'' he agreed. ''I have thought of little else in the past two days and have found no solution.''

''What if it were Sophia who cried off?''

Dominic looked at her in obvious puzzlement. ''That would be unexceptional, you know that. But why should she?''

''You might be able to persuade her to do so if you attempted it,'' Julia suggested.

''By what means?'' he asked, his brow creasing with suspicion. ''I would not use trickery or subterfuge to gain my own ends.''

Julia sighed with annoyance. ''It is wonderful the opinion you have of me, my lord. I wonder that you would wish to marry me in any circumstances.''

''So do I,'' he assented with a quizzing smile. ''But it is an absurd hope.''

''It isn't,'' Julia insisted, an eagerness coming into her voice.

''What would you have me do, abuse the child?''

''If you would just listen,'' Julia said with mild exasperation. ''I have no doubt that one of the factors that has made your suit acceptable to her is that you prefer life in the country to life in town. Sophia is shy and retiring and has said repeatedly that she longs to return to Amberly. She would hate it if she thought you had taken a liking for town life and meant to live here most of the year.''

''So should I,'' Dominic said dryly. ''You pointed out yourself how ill-suited it made a match between us.''

''We shall compromise,'' Julia assured him, not allowing

there to be any doubt of their being together. "If Sophia believed that you expected her to set herself up as a fashionable hostess and entertain on a grand scale, she should probably be terrified at the prospect and might even find her courage to cry off."

Dominic's expression was clearly skeptical. "You don't find that theory a bit farfetched, Julia?"

"Do you have a better plan?" Julia demanded with asperity. "If she doesn't care for you in the first place and is only reconciled to marrying you because she thinks you will give her the life she wants, then there is every reason for her to stand up to her aunt and uncle when she realizes that she will not only find herself in a loveless marriage but one that will make her wretched as well."

"What an attractive prospect! But it is still absurd, Julia, and you know it."

"At least it is a beginning," she said with heat, her temper beginning to flare at his unwillingness even to make a push to help them. "You might at least see if it would answer to some degree. If she is at all in love with Harry, as he claims, it might be just enough to make her realize she would be making a mistake."

"And it might be just enough to make me seem like a raving lunatic," he said tartly. "You don't think Sophia and the Amberlys would wonder at such a sudden change in character? Perhaps you are right, after all; they would force Sophia to withdraw from her promise for fear of insanity in the family."

"I only wish they might," Julia replied, equally caustic. "You could begin by starting the renovations to Sales House that you spoke of, and by hiring a house in Brighton instead of going into Sussex as you planned. You might even begin entertaining at once with Sophia as your hostess, which is perfectly acceptable now that you are betrothed. All of these things would give credence to your change of preference from country to town life."

He understood the real cause of her anger and did not permit himself to match the ire. "If I truly believed it would work, I would do it," he said simply. "The Amberlys have decided against going to Brighton, after all, and have asked me to return to Wiltshire with them. I have thought of suggesting that we go as soon as possible, even before the Season is ended. I think it might be best for us if we weren't to see each other anymore."

There was such finality in his tone that it chilled her. "We can't avoid each other for the rest of our lives."

"I think we shall manage well enough. We need only be true to ourselves; you continue to live your life in town and I'll go on with my pursuits in the country. It is unlikely that we will meet often, if at all, unless Sophia and I happen to be visiting Amberly at a time when you are at Dumphree."

Julia had a horrible frightened feeling, like nothing she had ever experienced before. This, she thought almost abstractly, must be what terror is. She knew she could not allow the only thing in her life that mattered to her to slip away from her. "Couldn't you at least try what I ask?" she said, almost pleading.

He ignored her question because he had no answer for it. "The die is cast, Julia, however much we wish it were not. Whatever the cost, I must do what I know to be right."

"I do not call it right," she countered, her frustration lashing out in anger again. "I call it foolish and pigheaded." She saw an answering spark of anger come into his eyes, and suddenly laughed. "Do you see how perfect we are for each other? We should have the most glorious fights."

This won a reluctant laugh from him. "How could I resist such temptation?" he said with a sad smile that tore at her heart.

Julia did not wish to feel sympathy for him. If she acknowledged his pain, she would have to acknowledge her own, and despite his apparent willingness to accept their fate as unalterable, she still believed they would find a way to be together as husband and wife. "Apparently that presents no difficulty," she said icily. "Do you really believe we shall either of us be able to go on with our lives as we did before? I was a fool that morning at the old Dower House, but you are the greater fool now."

She felt a tightening in her throat and knew that treacherous tears born of rage and disappointment were about to betray her. He moved toward her, but Julia turned abruptly and left the room, not trusting herself to speak rationally any longer. She could not help wondering if these would be the last words she would speak to him in private, but at the moment she was too upset to care.

She found her way to the ladies' robing room and found it blessedly empty. She sat undisturbed for several minutes until gradually her pulse steadied and her more usual calm returned, at least to the surface. Several other women came into the room as Julia was thinking it was time for her to return to the ballroom, and Fanny was one of these.

She cast Julia a curious look, but said nothing, continuing her conversation with Lady Barbara Audley. When Julia got up to leave, Fanny excused herself and went out after her friend. "Are you well, Julia?" she asked. "I have not set eyes on you since supper. Have you been here all the while?"

"No. I was with Dominic," Julia said, deciding not to dissemble. Fanny made no comment and Julia said, "I know what you are thinking, Fanny."

"And I am mistaken?"

Julia gave vent to a laugh that was brief and bitter. "No. You are exactly right. Dominic and I are in love with each other."

Fanny marveled that after so many years of acquaintance, Julia still had the power to astonish her. It was not what she had expected to hear. "Are you? Then what on earth are you both doing marrying other people?"

Julia smiled ruefully. "I wish I knew."

They had reached the ballroom and there was no further opportunity for conversation, but the very next morning Fanny made a point of calling on her friend at a sufficiently early hour to be certain that she found her at home. In fact, Julia was still at breakfast when Lady Frances was ushered into the breakfast room.

Letty, who did not particularly like Fanny for no reason that Julia could fathom, puckered up to show her disapproval of someone who would call at an hour that could only be regarded as ill-bred, but her face fell when Julia quickly drank off the rest of her coffee and took her friend off to the morning room so that they could talk in private.

Though Julia naturally did not confide in Fanny the extent of the intimacy between her and Dominic, she told her most everything else, including his proposal of marriage, her rejection of it, and her subsequent realization that she did love him. Fanny was that sort of good friend who truly listened without comment or criticism, and at the end only offered advice when it was solicited.

Julia was simply in need of a confidante; she did not really expect that anything Fanny said to her would make any difference, but that did prove to be the case. When Fanny had heard all, she remarked that it was a great pity that Harry conceded the field to Dominic, falling into depression instead of doubling his efforts to win Sophia in the teeth of her guardians' objections.

Julia agreed that Harry had given up too easily when Sophia's betrothal to Dominic was announced. In spite of her timid nature, he had succeeded in persuading Sophia to meet him clandestinely in Wiltshire, risking both reputation and the wrath of Lady Amberly. If only Harry could wear down her resistance and convince her not to marry Dominic but to wait until she was of age so that they could be wed, then Dominic and Julia at least would have an end to their difficulties. She also thought it entirely possible, whatever Sophia might in her naïveté believe, that when the Amberlys saw that Harry and Sophia were so determined to be together, they would at last relent and permit the marriage. Harry might not be as fine a match as Dominic, but it was far from contemptible.

Julia did not know if this would answer any better than her scheme to make Sophia cry off, for the weak element was still Sophia herself, but she knew it was worth trying. At this point, anything was worth at least the effort.

After another day spent moping in his bedchamber with the curtains drawn, Harry had at last emerged, and if he was not his usual chipper self, at least he was dressed and shaved and went out to meet his friends. He had not yet made a showing at any of the usual *ton* functions where Sophia and Dominic might be found, avoiding them deliberately.

Impatient to speak with her nephew and give him the encouragement he needed to continue his pursuit of Sophia, she went to Morland House the next day in hopes of finding him home, but was disappointed. She left a message for him to call on her, but two days passed and she heard nothing, and even Elizabeth claimed to barely have set eyes on him in that time.

Julia ran him to earth at last entirely by chance at Hookham's Lending Library, where he had gone to return a book. "Where have you been, you wretched boy?" she said chidingly as she drew him aside down one of the high stacks of books. "I gave Tomlin a message for you to call on me."

"I know," he admitted, unrepentant, "but I haven't been about much of late."

"So your mother has told me. I gather you have been spending more of your time at Crib Parlor and Jackson's Saloon than at home or in polite company."

"I haven't felt much like being in polite company," he said gloomily.

"Well, the only company you need endure at the moment is mine," she said, linking her arm in his. "I saw your groom outside walking your horses. He can escort Midden, whom I have brought with me, home, and you may take me up for a short drive so that we may talk."

"About what?" he asked warily.

"You," she said as she steered him toward the door. "And Sophia."

He was plainly reluctant, but he did as she asked, and handed her into his curricle. He took up the reins and asked her where she wished to go, but Julia merely shrugged and said that anywhere would be fine.

"That sounds ominous. Are you going to comb my hair again about making a fool of myself over women?"

"No. I have been thinking that I have done you an injustice. I think you truly do care for Sophia."

He glanced at her sharply. "I do."

"Then you must fight for what you want. I hadn't thought you were so easily defeated, Linton," she said with just the faintest note of disappointment in her tone.

"Easily defeated!" he said, incensed. "I tried the best I know how to attach Sophia and prove to the Amberlys that I was an acceptable match for their niece, but I am no match for Sales either in title or in fortune. And he has both now, not in some distant future."

"Do you believe these things matter to Sophia?"

"Not in the least. It is her aunt who wants these things for her."

"Then it should not matter to her that Dominic is perceived by the world to be a better match," Julia said. "I expect it is as you say. Sophia is so gentle and used to obedience that she does not like to stand up to her aunt. It is a simple life that she wants, Harry, not that of a great lady. The Amberlys have probably painted you as a town fribble to her against Lord Sales' preference for country life, and that has done much to reconcile her to marrying him."

"You know that isn't true," Harry said. "I admit I enjoy the Season and my clubs and all that, but I'm as happy, or maybe even happier, at Morland as I am in town."

"But does Sophia know that?"

"What difference does that make now?"

"If you truly love her, how can you just give her up?"

"Give her up! Dear Lord, Aunt Jule, she is betrothed to Sales and they are to be married before the end of the summer."

"But they aren't married yet," Julia said, and was silent.

After a few minutes, Harry said, though in a tentative way, "I can think of nothing that would occur to prevent the wedding."

Julia shrugged. "Then you shall have to accept that your Sophia will be married to someone else because you gave up and would not make a push to change her mind. You are avoiding meeting them now, but they will be in town at least for the Season each year, and you will have to spend the rest of your life watching them together and imagining what could have been."

Harry looked as if she had struck him. He gave a shaky laugh. "I thought you wished my spirits to be raised."

"I wish you might be happy, that is all, Harry. I wish we all might be happy," she added for honesty's sake.

He pulled up his horses in front of her house and she added in a more conversational manner, "I can give you luncheon if you like."

Harry shook his head. He said nothing for a moment, apparently intent on watching the footman descend the front stairs to assist Julia from the carriage. "Thank you, but I think I would not be good company just now," he said, and then was silent again until he saluted her as he pulled away from the house.

Julia was not displeased with her effort. She had clearly given him something to think about, and that was the most she could hope for. The only thing she had to concern her now was that Dominic would not be able to persuade the Amberlys to leave town before the Season was ended, but Elizabeth had told her that Caroline Amberly had had new gowns made especially for the fete at Carlton House and was very pleased with herself for having secured invitations for it. This would at least give her precious time. If neither of her schemes came to fruition, perhaps she would think of something else. As she had told Harry, until Dominic and Sophia were well and truly married, ther was no reason to despair.

In spite of his skepticism of Julia's plan to make him seem a less desirable husband to Sophia, Dominic found himself making frequent comments about how much he was learning to love the fashionable life whenever he was with Sophia. He found he did not even have to dissemble very much, for there was some truth to it; just as Julia had learned that life in the country need not be tedious, so he began to see that many of the pleasures of the town were enjoyable and not nearly as shallow as he had always condemned them to be.

There was no doubt that his remarks distressed his betrothed, and her confusion was quite evident when he hinted that he was thinking of becoming involved in political circles and thought to have a state diner party the week before they left town for Amberly. When he suggested that she should be his hostess and plan the occasion as would befit the woman who would soon be his wife, she was so plainly shaken that he felt a pang of guilt and would have retracted the suggestion if he could have done so gracefully.

He felt every sort of monster for using Sophia so, but the stakes were high and desperate, for he had begun to fear that, honor or no, he might not be able to go through with the wedding. If there had been the least question in his mind whether or not Sophia were in love with him, he would not have even entertained such behavior and would have found some means of reconciling himself to his marriage to her. But he was certain that she was not, and keeping in mind what Julia had said to him, he made note of his betrothed whenever Viscount Linton was present. He agreed with her that Sophia was probably just as besotted with Julia's scapegrace nephew as Harry was wit her.

For the viscount had taken his aunt's advice to heart. He mad it a point to discover which parties and entertainments Sophi would be present at, and if he did not already possess a invitation, he called in all past favors to secure those that h needed. He was relatively circumspect under the watchful eye of Lady Amberly, but he managed far more snatched word with her niece than that lady would have imagined possible and in a very short time he was able to persuade Sophia to begi to meet him in secret again so that he could speak with her mor privately.

Julia noted that almost immediately after their conversatio on the way home from Hookham's Linton had again begun t frequent *ton* parties. She was even actually an accidental witnes to one of their clandestine meetings when she saw Sophia sli furtively down an unlighted corridor at Lady Benchly's rou and a few minutes later saw her nephew do the same. By th end of a sennight Julia was in expectation that she would soo hear that Dominic's betrothal to Sophia had been brought t an end.

A degree of distance was maintained between Julia and Dominic. They were civil and even friendly whenever they met but Dominic made no attempt to meet her privately and Julia was equally circumspect, knowing instinctively that it woulc be a mistake to push Dominic. She had no doubt that he lovec and wanted her as she did him, but she would not throw hersel at his head. She believed that they would be together in the end, and she was willing to be patient, at least for now.

But matters were coming to a head at a more desperate pace than she realized. It was on a sultry evening in the middle of June at Lady Sefton's grand ball, meant to rival the Carlton House fete for being the capping entertainment of the Season, that the erosion of peace for everyone began.

It was the sort of ball to which far too many people are invited and yet there are still many who scramble after invitations, willing to be squeezed into an inadequate ballroom for the social distinction an invitation would mean. Lady Sefton's immense ballroom was filled to capacity, and even hallways and ante-rooms were constantly filled with guests that evening. It was also an excellent opportunity for a quiet meeting, for in such a crowd it was easier to slip away undetected than in lesser company.

Julia and her sister-in-law, at Elizabeth's suggestion, left the heat of the ballroom, which not even all windows open to the night air could properly ventilate with so many people there, and strolled about the hallways, where it was relatively cooler. They wandered down a side hall onto which several antechambers opened, and were attracted to one of these by the sound of raised voices.

Elizabeth would not have gone too close to the door, which stood open, but Julia's frank curiosity led her to at least peek into the room to see the participants in the altercation. As soon as she had done so, she wished she had not, for she could not prevent Elizabeth from entering the room in defense of her only son, who was being informed by Caroline Amberly that he had neither character nor morals.

It was easy enough to take in the scene and guess that once again, Harry's secret rendezvous with Sophia had been discovered. Sophia sat huddled on a nearby sofa sobbing quietly into an already drenched handkerchief. Julia followed Elizabeth into the room and took it upon herself to push the door shut behind them. It was really none of her affair, and the proper thing would have been for her to have gone her own way, but she had her own interest in what would happen and she would not be denied.

Lady Amberly, like Julia, had noted that both Linton and Sophia seemed to disappear from gatherings at the same time, and this time she made it a point to follow her niece to see if her suspicions were correct. She had not only found Harry and Sophia together, she had actually caught them in an embrace that could not in any way be misconstrued.

Sophia's incensed aunt then proceeded to castigate the viscount as a libertine without a shred of honor, and though Elizabeth herself was upset that her son was so lost to propriety, she could not let him be so maligned.

"I think you forget, Lady Amberly," she said frigidly, "that your niece was also a willing participant. She is the one who is promised to wed another and yet trysts with Linton and allows him to make love to her."

The viscount would not even allow his mother to say anything against his beloved. "There is nothing wrong with what we have been doing," he said belligerently, his color high with the strength of his emotions. "Sophia and I love each other, and the only reason we are not together as we should be is because this she-dragon has forced her into a betrothal with Sales. I have finally caused Sophia to see that she cannot go through with a marriage to Sales when she is in love with me."

Lady Amberly was highly flushed as well, and at these words her color turned almost a purplish hue. "How dare you fill her head with such nonsense! If you think for even a moment that either I or Lord Amberly would ever countenance a match between Sophia and a man of your character, you must be unbalanced. I would sooner consign her to a nunnery."

This was too much for Elizabeth, who roundly informed Caroline Amberly that she had always suspected there was bad blood in the Amberly line and that neither would she nor her husband approve of a match between Linton and Sophia. Lady Amberly responded in kind, Linton continued to look murderous, and Sophia's sobs increased in both volume and intensity.

Julia, knowing that the uproar must be heard in the hall even through the closed door, sat down beside the distraught girl and began to do what she could to comfort her.

The viscount said suddenly and explosively, "The devil take all of you. This is none of your affair. Sophia and I love each other and none of your petty schemes or prejudices matters a damn." He walked over to the sofa and held out his hand. "Do you come with me, Sophie?"

The girl was sobbing and shivering in Julia's arms and she looked desperately from her aunt to Linton and then to Julia as if for guidance.

"For God's sake, Linton," Julia said dampeningly, "the girl is in no state to even leave this room just yet."

Linton glowered at his aunt for a moment and then his brow cleared as if his sense had finally told him that he had chosen the wrong moment to force Sophia to make a stand. Without further comment or even a backward glance at his mother or Lady Amberly, he turned and left the room, shutting the door behind him with a small snap to at least partially ventilate his feelings.

A cold, uncomfortable silence fell over the room when he quit it. Finally, giving Lady Morland a scathing look, Lady Amberly went to the sofa and informed Julia that she would see to her niece. Julia disentangled herself from the still-weeping girl and rose without comment. Lady Amberly took her place but Sophia turned away from her and buried her face into a pillow at the end of the sofa instead.

Elizabeth stood before them until Lady Amberly finally looked up. "You may choose to think that I excuse Linton because he is my son, but you may ask anyone who knows him well. He may have gained a reputation for wildness, but this was merely the excess of youth. There has never been any vice in the boy and there are many with far more right than you to look high for a match who would not disdain Harry for their daughters or wards. But I doubt that matters to you. You care for nothing but your own ambition and pride. I doubt you have even considered your niece's feelings."

"My niece has neither the years nor the experience to know what is best for her," Lady Amberly snapped. "She will marry Lord Sales and he will soon enough school her to contentment. He is a brilliant match for her and the day will come when she will thank me for bringing it to pass."

"Or curse you," Julia said bitterly. Her spirits were as low as they had been the morning she had read the announcement of Dominic's betrothal. There was no doubt that in future Sophia would be closely guarded from seeing Harry, and without him to give her strength, she doubted the girl would have the bottom to withstand her aunt's determination to see her wed to Dominic. She wished with all her heart that it had been Dominic who had been with her in the hallway. If he had witnessed this scene, he would have been completely justified in withdrawing his offer. If he would have . . .

"That is far more likely," Elizabeth said. She touched Julia's elbow. "We had best leave. It is pointless and demeaning to argue with anyone with such a closed mind. I am only sorry that two innocent people must be hurt by this woman's foolish pride."

Four people, Julia thought, but she made no comment and followed Elizabeth from the room. Nothing further was seen that night of Sophia, the Amberlys, or Linton, and if Dominic were present at all, Julia caught no sight of him in the crush of revelers.

11

Julia's spirits remained very down the following day. The last thing in the world she wished to do that afternoon was to go to Madame Céleste's for fittings for her bride clothes, but she and Letty had planned to meet Elizabeth and Lady Frances afterward to shop and to go to Gunter's for ices, and she supposed it was better to have something to do besides make herself wretched with her own thoughts.

Julia always enjoyed shopping for lovely new dresses and gowns, particularly when the bills were being taken care of by her usually clutch-fisted brother out of his own pocket. What manner of peal he would ring over her head if she did end her betrothal to Royden, she could only guess, but even if she did, she knew he wouldn't send the bills to her, so she made up her mind to enjoy the gift even if the purpose of it would never be fullfilled.

To her surprise, it proved to be a particularly enjoyable afternoon. Julia put her troubles from her mind with determined effort and they were a very jolly party at Gunter's, even skirting impropriety by drinking wine in public with their luncheon.

Since most of their purchases had been sent on with a footman to Morland House, the ladies went directly there to sort out their treasures before carrying them home. In the drive to Morland House they were quite merry, with much laughter and even singing. Julia was the first down from the carriage, still laughing at something droll Fanny had said, and it was she who first stepped into the front hall to discover Tomlin trying desperately to keep a very upset Lady Amberly from rushing into the hall from the receiving saloon.

Julia's laughter was instantly banished when she saw that lady's thunderous countenance, and she went over to her at once. "Whatever is amiss?" She placed her hand firmly on Lady Amberly's arm and, with Tomlin on the other side, steered her back into the room as the other ladies came into the house. "Surely we need not discuss whatever it is in the hall."

Very naturally, curiosity led the others to follow, but Julia, already guessing that her nephew had fallen into some scrape because of his passion for Sophia, had the presence of mind to say at once, "Fanny, this appears to be some sort of family matter. Would you mind very much taking my things and going with Letty to my house? I think I have too much for her to manage alone."

There was no need to give Fanny the hint twice. "Of course. Come, Letty, we'll see if we can manage all of my purchases as well in the carriage without having to ride on the roof ourselves."

A mulish expression was on Letty's face; it was obvious she knew she was being deliberately excluded and wished to stay, but where she might have given Julia an argument, her breeding would not allow her to do so in front of Lady Frances and Elizabeth, so with a petulant sniff she allowed herself to be led away.

It was clear that Caroline Amberly was bursting with whatever it was she had to say, and Julia followed her and Elizabeth into the room and quickly shut the door, then she turned around and leaned against it, almost as if she wanted to prevent any possible intrusion.

"I should have known this would happen," Lady Amberly said, at last exploding into speech. "Sales wanted us to retire to Amberly before the end of the Season, but Sophie begged me to remain until the Carlton House fete and I was foolish enough not to wonder at it. The girl detests great parties that are crushes. It was to continue to meet your unprincipled libertine son that she did so."

Julia groaned inwardly. The last thing she wished was to have to endure another round of last night's altercation, but she would not leave Elizabeth to Lady Amberly's mercy. She said quickly before her sister-in-law could speak, "Nothing is going to be served by name-calling, Lady Amberly. I fail to see why you place the entire blame on my nephew. Unless your niece has been forcibly kidnapped by him, it would appear that she wishes for his company, or she would not meet with him."

"He has filled her head with a great deal of romantic nonsense and this is the outcome of it." She opened her reticule and with a dramatic flourish withdrew from it a folded and crumpled piece of paper. Elizabeth would have taken it from her, but Julia was a bit closer and quicker.

It was a letter written by Sophia to her aunt in a copperplate hand, crossed, recrossed, and spotted here and there with water stains, possibly tears had fallen. It was difficult to read both in appearance and in content, for it went on at length in a rambling way speaking of gratitude and justifying ingratitude, but the gist of it was a confession that Sophia, though she admitted that her guardians had only her best interests at heart, had realized at last that she could not honor their wishes and marry Lord Sales. She begged pardon—repeatedly—for not having the courage to tell her aunt this to her face and then used this as justification for what she meant to do.

Julia was almost as horrified as Lady Amberly must have been when she reached the end of the letter. Sophia and Harry had eloped and were even now well on their way to Scotland. For all her hopes and schemes, Julia had never wanted this. The very young, such as Harry and Sophia, might not realize what a scandal and social stigma such a course would result in, but Julia did. Not only would their own reputations be forever tarnished, Dominic, to whom his honor was so precious, would be greatly and publicly humiliated.

It was this last that disturbed her the most, and she felt the weight of it descend upon her shoulders. If she had not spurred Harry to press his suit and force Sophia to acknowledge her love for him, this wouldn't have happened. It was hindsight to castigate herself for not realizing that Sophia would never have the courage to face up to her forceful aunt and that this must have been inevitable if Harry's suit was to succeed. Julia knew it, but she still felt wretched that she had been instrumental in bringing it about.

She wordlessly handed the letter to Elizabeth and crossed the room to one of the windows overlooking the street, wanting, for a moment, to be alone with her troubled thoughts. Her fertile imagination could well conceive Dominic's stricken expression when the news was carried to him. It would free him, yes, but at what cost? The public humiliation, the blow to his pride and his honor, were surely worse than if he had merely allowed his inclination to overcome his principles and had cried off himself from the betrothal to Sophia.

Julia felt a sudden wave of anger that he had remained so adamant and had forced them all to desperate measures, but she banished it at once. Dominic would not blame her for the elopement; he probably would not even guess that she had played so strong a part by spurring Linton on to continue to press Sophia, but she felt sufficient blame without his condemnation. She guessed, too, that Hal would suspect her of complicity, for he always said that she encouraged Harry in his excess, though this was far from true.

It was not so much to alleviate her guilt or to avoid estrangement with her family that made her decide that she had to go after Harry and Sophia and bring them back to town before any scandal could erupt. It was far more to save Dominic the pain and humiliation of a public jilting, and to make it up to him for helping to bring it about in the first place.

Elizabeth finished reading the letter and she let out a cry that was both exasperation and despair. "Oh, you foolish, foolish boy," she said as if Harry stood before her.

"This goes beyond foolishness, and well you know it," Lady Amberly said belligerently.

Elizabeth merely nodded. There was frankly nothing to argue. Not even the fondest of mothers could imagine that the timid Sophia would have been the one to persuade Harry to elope. "I don't understand how he could do such a thing," she said, still speaking more to herself than to Julia or Lady Amberly.

"I have no such difficulty," Lady Amberly said with a snort. "This is precisely the reason I have always deemed Linton an unsuitable match for my niece."

"Perhaps it need not come to that," Julia heard herself say. "The situation might still be saved, and there need be no scandal or even a marriage."

"There is nothing that will alter events now," Lady Amberly said in a flat statement. "They have been gone since before luncheon and must be well on their way to the border. If Sophia's maid, who is as foolish as her mistress, had not been weeping and carrying on, Mrs. Carry, my housekeeper, would not have become suspicious and had the story out of her so soon. I returned from visiting earlier than I planned, and was at first told that Sophia was in her room with the migraine. I would doubtless have left her undisturbed until dinnertime if Mrs. Carry had not come to me."

"Have you told Amberly?" Elizabeth asked.

"No. He is from home, and the servants are uninformed as to his whereabouts," she said with a certain dignity. It was so commonly known that Lord Amberly had a mistress whom he kept in the City and that he spent the majority of his time with her and their children that it had ceased to be scandalous for years.

"And Morland is at that wretched prizefight at Hounslow," Elizabeth put in.

"Have you sent word to Lord Sales?" Julia asked Lady Amberly.

Both other women looked at her as if she had gone mad. "No, of course not," Lady Amberly replied. "Amberly shall have to speak with him when he returns and is apprised of the situation."

Julia was silent for a moment, biting at a finger while she thought. "Lord Sales did mention something about the prizefight also, but I am not certain if he meant to go. I suppose the only thing to do is to send a sealed message to his house and hope that he gets it in time to follow me."

Lady Amberly and Elizabeth exchanged puzzled glances. "Why on earth would you write to Lord Sales, Julia, and where is he to follow you?"

"I am going after Harry and Sophia," she said with finality as much to convince herself as the other women. She had no intention of allowing herself to be dissuaded.

That of course is what immediately happened. "By yourself?" Lady Amberly said incredulously, and "Don't be absurd," was said simultaneously by Elizabeth.

After casting a quelling glance of dislike at the viscountess, Elizabeth held the floor. "You know you cannot do such a thing, Julia. It would be most improper. We hardly need you adding more scandal to what we already have."

"If I am successful, we may not have any scandal at all," Julia said calmly but firmly. "This is not a time for argument. No doubt Harry has rented a chaise; he would not take his curricle on such an errand. I shall drive my phaeton, which will be much faster than the chaise, even if he has had four horses put to it."

She went to a small desk across the room and took out paper and ink. "But first I shall send a note to Sales. If he can join us, it will give us countenance and help to divert any scandal."

Their protests continued, but Julia ignored them. She wrote rapidly and without pause, sprinkled sand hurriedly across the paper, and folded and sealed it. She made no response, even though she also heard a comment made about her entire family being mad or depraved or both. She allowed Elizabeth to take exception to it instead, for in the ensuing altercation she was virtually forgotten.

Julia went to the bellpull and finally advised them that it would be best to cease arguing until after the servant left. She gave the footman who came into the room her message for Dominic along with instructions not to wait for a reply.

"If you think you can prevent a scandal," Lady Amberly said, addressing Julia with greater civility, "it would be better if Sales never had to know of it at all."

"If Lord Sales is with me, we shall have an even better chance of getting out of this wretched mess unscathed," Julia answered. "What could be more exceptional than the four of us having gone on an excursion into the country. Lord Sales' tastes for such things are well known and it will not be wondered at."

"It is also well known that your nephew has been making a cake of himself over my niece since we have come to town," Lady Amberly said. "Do you think anyone will believe that he and Sales would go on such an outing together?"

"Let them wonder at it," Julia advised. "I shall be there to give them countenance as well."

"And if Sales does not choose to follow you?" said Lady Amberly skeptically. "Has it occurred to you that after this, he will almost certainly cry off?"

Julia lowered her lashes to veil the hope that she doubted she could conceal in her eyes. "I suppose that is likely," she said guardedly. "But it will be much better if it can occur without scandal or humiliation for him or anyone else. I wonder that you criticize my decision," she added frankly. "You should be grateful that someone is making the effort to save the name of your silly niece, who need not have brought herself to this pass if she had had the courage to tell you to your face that she did not wish to marry Lord Sales."

"Why are you doing this?" Lady Amberly asked with sudden suspicion. "The one who will bear the least brunt of shame for what has happened will be Linton, who deserves it most. He already has the reputation of a scapegrace—to be kind. He will not be subject to ridicule like Sales or have a stigma attached forever to his name like Sophia. Why should you make such an effort and even put your own reputation at some risk just to save him from his share of the consequences?"

"I am very fond of Linton," Julia said repressively, and went immediately to Elizabeth, taking her hands. "I had best go to Half Moon Street and change so that I may be off as soon as possible to try to catch up to them. Please try not to worry more than you need. I promise to do my very best. Some way we shall bring this thing off without disaster."

"I don't think I should let you go, Julia," Elizabeth said, giving her sister-in-law's hands a squeeze. "But I doubt there is anything I could do to stop you. Thank God Hal won't be back until quite late. Even if all is not resolved by then, it will be too late for him to do more than rage about it." She drew Julia close to her and kissed her cheek. "God speed you, love."

Julia returned the pressure of Elizabeth's hands and quit the room. She had Tomlin hail her a hack and in little more than a quarter of an hour she was dressed in her light linen habit and ready to begin the chase. But as she was about to descend the stair, the front doorbell resounded throughout the house. With a whispered expletive, Julia quickly withdrew down the corridor so that she would not be seen when the footman opened the door and denied her to whomever it was who called.

Julia hoped it would not be Royden. They were engaged to dine that night at Morland House, and Julia wondered if Elizabeth would have the presence of mind to send a note around to put him off. She knew she should write something herself, but every minute that escaped her now concerned her and she chafed at even the delay of having to wait until her unwanted caller was gotten rid of.

But it was not Royden or some acquaintance on a social call. It was Dominic, and he flatly refused to be denied. The footman tried valiantly, but Dominic demanded to see Julia, raising his voice ever so slightly that it carried to her. The moment she heard and recognized it, she came down the stairs at a run, gathering up the train of her habit in a hoydenish heap that was certain to leave it creased.

"It's all right, James," she said to the footman, and herself drew Dominic into the hall. She led him into the nearest room so that they could speak quickly without being overheard. "I am so glad you were at home. I have my phaeton ready to be off. Do you come with me?"

He placed a restraining hand on her arm, as if she meant to escape him at once and said, "There is not the least need for you to go anywhere, Julia. This is my affair and you may trust me to manage it myself."

"Of all the ungrateful creatures," Julia said, outraged. "Lady Amberly was too shamed to tell you and would have presented you with a full-fledged scandal if I had not insisted that there was hope to save us from that."

"I agree there is, and I am grateful that you had the presence of mind to send me word of what was afoot, but I stopped only to tell you that I prefer to take care of it myself. I promise I shall apprise you of the outcome as soon as I return."

"I don't want to be apprised of the outcome," Julia informed him roundly, shaking off his grasp. "Linton is my nephew and it is my affair as well as yours. If I am there, it will give added countenance to the situation."

"If anything goes awry, it will only endanger your reputation as well," he insisted.

"I suppose I might have guessed you would see it differently. Nothing shall go awry," she said confidently. "I am off at once, whether you are with me or not."

"I want you to remain here, Julia. I go alone."

"You have not the ordering of me, my lord," she said frigidly. "My carriage is doubtless ready for me at the door."

"It was. I told your man you would not be needing it, after all."

Julia let out a small gasp of outrage. "You had no right to countermand my order."

"None," he agreed, unconcerned by her anger. "I'll see you when I return."

Julia was furious, but the knowledge that her encouragement

of Harry was much to blame for what had happened kept her temper in check. She said quite levelly, "If you have sent my carriage back to the mews, I shall simply order it prepared for me again. My determination in this is equal to yours, my lord, and since you will shortly not be here to prevent me, I shall follow."

"You can't go alone, Julia."

"But I shall."

Blue eyes held hazel eyes in a locked stare as their wills battled for supremacy. Julia's determination proved the stronger.

"Very well," Dominic said with obvious reluctance. "As you say, I cannot prevent you. But you won't go chasing after them alone in a high-perch phaeton like some hoyden. I have my curricle and four outside, and that will cover the distance as well."

Julia was about to protest that her carriage was lighter and would be faster, but instinct told her to concede the point. It was still likely that by setting a good pace they would overtake a heavier chaise in good-enough time. "Very well, let us be off."

Conversation between them was desolutory. At first Dominic was preoccupied with guiding his team through the traffic of the city with all possible haste and then his attention was taken by the need to drive to an inch at a pace that could only be described as dangerous. Dominic had claimed not to be her equal as a driver, but he was clearly a first-rate whip who knew how to drive to an inch. The pace he set was one that even she might have been leery of, and she gripped the edge of the curricle beside her on turns that seemed impossible but were somehow navigated. She did not realize how tightly she was holding the edge until after a time when the muscles in her arm began to ache. She relaxed her hold and put her hand in her lap, discreetly massaging the throbbing in her arm.

Dominic cast a glance at her and a faint smile touched his lips. "I am not going to pitch you out of your seat, Julia. The road is in fairly good condition and the traffic is blessedly light. We'll be coming up for our first change soon, probably at the Red Doe."

"I only hope the next team may not be slugs," she said acidly, annoyed at being caught out.

"Very likely they shall be," he replied, "but we have made excellent time and surely have gained a bit on them by now."

Julia hoped this was true. The team from the Red Doe were far from breakdowns, but it was virtually impossible to get a matched team like the steaming grays that were led away from the curricle in the courtyard, so the next stage was necessarily not accomplished at quite the pace of the first. Yet it was unquestionable that they were traveling at a rate far greater than a chaise and four could have managed, and Julia was still sanguine that they would catch them up before dark.

At both stops Dominic made discreet inquiries about a chaise with a young man and woman having passed through, and at the second inn he was successful. "At least, the information is good if it is truly Linton and Sophia," he told her as they pulled out of the courtyard of the second posting inn. "They are being drawn by only a pair, and they made the change at about two, which means they are no more than an hour and a half ahead of us. If we make equally good time this time, we should cut that in half by the next change."

But fortune did not smile on their chase again. The left wheeler threw a shoe scarcely a half-hour after they were on the road, and they were forced to slow to a trot until they could find another inn. Julia swore under her breath and Dominic cast her a glance that was at once disapproving and amused.

"There is no need to look at me like that," Julia said coolly. "You know my tongue is unguarded when I am upset."

"Only too well," Dominic commented dryly. He sighed. "But you only voiced what I am thinking. I am wondering if we should even go on. There is no posting inn along this road that I am aware of for another twenty miles. Instead of shortening the distance, we shall likely lengthen it. If we do not find them and bring them back before morning, this will be nothing more than a fools' errand, with your reputation in tatters as well. I wish you had listened to me and stayed at home." He saw the spark come into her eyes and laughed. "No, don't rip up at me. I know you would not."

"No, I would not," Julia said firmly. She gave him a long look through her lashes and said leadingly, "If I am to be utterly ruined by this, there is only one solution that I know of."

He grinned. "I shall have to marry you, I suppose."

Neither of them had said anything for the entire journey about what all of this would mean to them. Each waited for the other to say something, almost dreading what they would hear for fear that there had been some change of heart. Julia looked at him, the laughter suddenly banished from her eyes. "Do you still wish to?"

"With all my heart."

To her astonishment he pulled up the team in the middle of the road and gathered her into his arms. His kiss was long and sweet and Julia felt truly at peace for the first time in a very long time. He finally released her, when the sounds of an approaching cart made it clear that they were no longer alone.

"Are you aware that we are making a spectacle of ourselves?" she asked, her voice bubbling with happy laughter.

"Quite. But since I intend to make an honest woman of you as soon as I can procure a special license when I return to town, it is of no consequence."

"Do you know," she confessed as he lowered his hands and they began again down the road at a trot, "when I read Sophia's note, which was barely legible, I nearly hooted with joy when I realized that she and Harry had eloped. Then, of course, I realized what it would mean and that it must be prevented if at all possible. But there was still a part of me that was afraid, I think; that almost wanted me to let them go for fear that if it were too hushed up, you would still feel obliged to honor your commitment to Sophia."

He shook his head. "I felt a similar elation and return to reality when I read your note. I'm not even sure that if you had not told me of your intention to go after them, I wouldn't have let them fend for themselves and hang the scandal."

Julia laughed. "Never say that I have more of a care to the proprieties than you do. You were ready to blight both of our lives for the sake of them."

"No," he admitted. "It wouldn't have come to that. I had already realized I couldn't go through with it, whatever the consequences. I was screwing up my courage to speak with Sophia and tell her about us and that I knew about Linton. I hoped we might come to some amicable agreement to mutually release each other. My principal concern was Lady Amberly.

If Sophia hadn't the nerve to face her, then it would be my task and there was no saying that she wouldn't publicize my wish to cry off for spite."

"Has it occurred to you that she would have stood to you in the relationship of mother-in-law?"

"Forcefully. Actually, it was that that convinced me I would rather be married to you. You are a witch too, Julia, but you are also an angel and I am in love with you in every guise."

Julia found this odd compliment very comforting. It was something that he had no illusions about her and loved her anyway. She felt the need, though, to tell him the worst of her latest excesses. "Do you know why I was so insistent on going after Harry and Sophia myself?"

He gave her an arch sideways glance. "Because you are an officious female who cannot bear to permit others to manage their own affairs?"

She refused the bait. "Because it is probably at least half my fault that it happened. When you refused to cry off from your betrothal, I had the notion that if Harry could convince Sophia to stand up to her aunt and refuse to marry you, it would be the answer to our difficulties."

He digested this without comment for a moment and then said, "Sophia is no match for her aunt. Elopement was a logical conclusion to that strategy. If you gave it thought, you must have realized that."

"I see it now," she acknowledged, adding with a return of her usual spirit, "but at the time I saw nothing but that I would soon lose you forever if some sort of push was not made to prevent your marriage to that wretched girl. Did it occur to you that you would likely have been making a far greater mistake marrying that pretty widgeon than if you married me. She would have bored you in a twelvemonth however much she would have permitted you to live like a hermit studying plants and insects or whatever it is that so fascinates you."

"I have already begun to find her a bit tiresome." He gave her a hurt look. "You really weren't listening when we took our morning rides in Wiltshire. I told you then in great detail what it was that interested me."

"I heard every word," she said demurely, "but retention is

difficult when one is so distracted by the attractiveness of the speaker."

"Ah. Then lessons shall have to begin again as soon as we are married."

"I shall be too busy planning routs and balls," Julia countered.

In this light manner the distance to the next posting inn was covered much quicker than either expected, and at last the courtyard of the Hare's Nest came into view. It was not the inn that Dominic would have chosen for a change, as it catered more to stagecoach and job horse trade than to the quality, and it was not likely that he would find cattle that would meet with his approval, but the next inn beyond was another good ten miles and in addition to the slow pace they had to set, it was likely that the shoeless horse would be dead-lame by then.

This inn was even more bustling than the other two at which they had stopped. A stagecoach sat waiting while the traces were done up for the change, and the passengers were milling about outside waiting the word to reboard. There were two other hired chaises in the yard, one also in the process of having the horses changed and the other with empty traces pushed off to the side. One or two other smaller vehicles were also present and Dominic had to maneuver about them with some precision.

An ostler who had just finished with the stagecoach came bustling over to them to run to the leaders' heads. It was clear from his expression that the equipage pulled by a team impressed him and was not commonplace at the inn. Dominic jumped down and spoke to him about the horses as he had done at the other stops, but this time it seemed to Julia to be more of a conversation than instruction and continued for several minutes with much nodding and gesturing from the ostler.

Dominic walked around to Julia's side of the carriage and held out his hand to her. "I think our journey ends here."

Julia did not understand him at first. "Haven't they a team to spare us?"

"It isn't that. If I am not mistaken, we will find Linton and Sophia inside."

Julia looked at his hand as if she had no idea why he offered it to her. His expression was grim and his voice deliberately even and she was more puzzled by this than enlightened, for she thought it should please him if they had caught them up so soon.

"I don't understand," she said plainly. "Why would they be here? They can't have thought to stop for the night so soon, and why would one stop when flying to the border in any case?" A thought occurred to her. "Has there been an accident?"

"Not that I am aware of," he said in that same level tone. "The ostler told me that the chaise over there came in about an hour ago with a young gentleman and lady fitting the description of Linton and Sophia and that they have not yet emerged or given instructions about readying the chaise. The post boys and coachman have been cooling their heels in the taproom and likely will be half jug-bitten by now."

Julia's color faded. An ugly possibility occurred to Julia and she knew it was a similar thought that was affecting Dominic. Julia's color faded. "My God. Do you think . . . ? I can't believe Harry would have only seduction in mind to force Lady Amberly's hand."

"If it is they, we shall soon see," he said grimly.

She at last placed her hand in his and he assisted her to the ground.

The building was low and sprawling, with only a few mullioned windows to allow light inside, and there was such a contrast to the brightness outside that it took several moments for Julia's eyes to adjust when they entered the inn. Even a quick skimming of the room was enough for her to see that neither Linton nor Sophia was there. But this brought greater anxiety rather than relief. Since there was no other couple who might have been the ones from the chaise, she could only suppose that they were in a private parlor.

Dominic went at once to a prosperous-looking man in a clean white apron behind the tap whom he rightly took to be the landlord. "I am Lord Sales," he said at once, knowing that this was an occasion to flaunt his title. "My wife and I have been traveling with our nephew and niece, and due to an unfortunate indisposition my wife suffered at our last stop, we were separated from their carriage but are to meet them here. Can you tell me if you have a young man and woman who arrived an hour or so ago and have taken a private parlor?''

There was no cloud of suspicion on the landlord's brow. An obsequious smile spread over his countenance as his eyes scanned Dominic's perfectly cut coat and buckskin breeches and Julia's elegant carriage dress. He did not question their veracity for a moment but informed them at once that just such a pair was to be found in one of his parlors and personally escorted them there. Dominic carelessly dropped a gold coachwheel into the man's hand and ordered a bottle of the inn's finest Madeira to be brought to them.

What would have occurred if the parlor had contained complete strangers was not to be discovered, for when the door opened, Harry turned quickly away from the window where he was standing and looked at them with a hunted expression. His shoulders sagged with obvious relief when he saw them, causing Dominic and Julia to exchange puzzled glances.

It was far from a scene of desperate seduction that they were presented with. To their right, on a sofa near the hearth, lay Miss Sutton, a damp cloth across her brow and a thin blanket pulled up to her chin. She opened her eyes at the sounds of intrusion, moaned softly, and then shut them again.

''I know,'' Harry said with a lopsided half-smile, ''I should be horrified that you have found us, but the truth is, I was never dashed happier in my life to see anyone, Aunt Jule.'' His eyes flicked to Dominic, and a wariness came into them. ''You shall want an explanation and you shall have it, but I think we had best go outside to discuss it, my lord. Sophia is already sufficiently overset.''

There was no denying this. Her color was a pasty white and she looked utterly wretched.

''Carriage-sick, I suppose?'' Julia said without inflection.

''It isn't her fault,'' Harry said quickly. ''If she hadn't been so anxious about what Sales and her aunt would do when they found out about us, I'm sure she wouldn't be half as bad off.''

''No doubt,'' Dominic said dryly.

Julia went over to the sofa and sat on the edge beside Sophia. Harry and Dominic watched her speak softly to the girl for a few moments, each occupied with his own thoughts.

Then Dominic said, "I think the time for explanations is now. Shall we walk out in the courtyard for a bit?"

"Shouldn't we be more private in another room?"

"What is more private than quiet conversation in the middle of noise and bustle?" He laughed at Harry's wary expression. "Don't look so concerned, Linton. I don't mean to ask you to name your seconds."

Harry raised his chin. "If you do, my lord, I shall be pleased to oblige you."

Dominic put a hand on his shoulder. "The last thing I want is to put a bullet through you."

Encouraged that Dominic was not going to demand that his honor be satisfied at once, Harry agreed, and they made their way outside.

Dominic and Harry walked toward the rear of the courtyard near the stables, deftly maneuvering around ostlers, horses, and carriages. Dominic allowed Harry to make his explanations in his own way, which the latter did by detailing the history of his love for Sophia.

Dominic might have wished that Harry had begun a bit further along, but he listened patiently and attentively as Harry finally reached the point where Lady Amberly had followed them into the antechamber and declared that she would never countenance a match between them whether Sophia was to wed Dominic or not.

"You see," Harry said at this point, "I had just persuaded Sophie that she had to face you and tell you the truth, that we are in love and mean to be married even if it means waiting until Sophia is of age and no longer needs her aunt's consent. Then Lady Amberly comes bursting into the room, demanding to know what we think we are about."

He sighed. "Sophie was quite brave at first. She told her aunt that she was not going to go marry you and that she wished to marry me instead, and then all hell broke loose. Lady Amberly made a great scene, even though she knows how delicate Sophia's sensibilities are and that Sophia becomes vaporish whenever anyone raises his voice in her presence. Of course Sophie could not stand up to that—I always knew that, which is why I convinced her to tell you before her aunt because

I knew that you, whatever else you might do, would not scream at her or shake her."

"I should hope not," Dominic said, horrified at the image of himself as an abuser of women.

They were wandering aimlessly and were near the back of the rambling stables. Harry stopped and turned to face Dominic. "I must say, Sales, you are taking this remarkably well."

A faint, ironic smile played on Dominic's lips. "Actually, I have a confession to make to you as well. I would not necessarily do so, except that Julia is your aunt and you will likely guess at the truth yourself soon enough."

The viscount gave him a swift, keen look. "Perhaps I already do."

"I think it likely," Dominic agreed. "The truth is that you have done me a service in a way, though I deplore your means of doing so."

"What choice had I? After that blowup at the Seftons', Sophie was ready to give up completely because she was in a quake at facing her aunt if she ended your betrothal. The only thing I could do was convince her that it would be best if we married first and faced the dragon together."

"From what I know of Morland, he would be another obstacle to clear."

Harry nodded. "But after Lady Amberly, even his bark will seem worse than his bite. And what can he object except for the manner in which it was done? Sophia is an heiress and of impeccable birth. But I needn't tell you that."

"Hardly."

"You mean to marry Aunt Julia, don't you?"

"Ah, you do know."

"I thought it even when we were at Dumphree, though Aunt Julia kept telling me I was queer in my attic. I didn't even think you were a threat to me with Sophia; I thought you were just kind to her because of your friendship with the Amberlys. I couldn't believe it when Sophia told me you had offered for her. I wanted to call you out then," he added with a brief laugh. "But Aunt Julia told me that I was a fool and that what I should do is not give up with Sophia."

"She did that? When?"

"A few days after your betrothal was announced. I was in a sorry state and she told me that I should not despair. Until you and Sophia were actually married, there was still hope. I was too wrapped in my own misery at the time to think of it, but I suppose she meant it for herself as well."

"I suppose."

They resumed walking again. "Why did you offer for Sophia if you were in love with Aunt Julia?" Harry asked as they headed back toward the inn.

"Why not?" He gave a self-mocking laugh. "You are right that there was something between Julia and me at Dumphree, but we have had our differences from the beginning. We quarreled in a manner that appeared to be final, and within the week her betrothal to Tallboys was announced. After that it made little difference to me whom I married. Caroline Amberly had been storming the citadel since the day I came to live at the old Dower House at Amberly. Now that I have the title, I have an obligation to be married. It seemed to me at the moment that marriage to Sophia would answer. I am fond of her and I think she will make an excellent wife for the right man. The difficulty was that I very soon realized that I was not that man. But then it was too late. I could not in honor cry off and expose her to ridicule and me to dishonor."

"And then you and Aunt Julia made up your difference."

"Yes."

"Was that why she was so encouraging to my hopes for Sophie?" Harry asked suspiciously.

"I expect. She wanted me to convince Sophia that I had changed my mind about living in the country and meant to open my town house year 'round and entertain in state."

Harry gave a bark of laughter. "No wonder Sophia turned to me again as her savior. She would hate that."

"The question is, will Julia be content with the other? It will mean compromise, of course, for both of us."

"Aunt Julia loves to be in the first stare of fashion, which deplores all things provincial, but I think her real inclination is quite different."

"It will not always be the most comfortable of marriages, I fear," Dominic said, but his smile was one of pleasurable anticipation, not concern.

They returned to the parlor to find Sophia sitting up on the sofa in a far better state than that in which they had left her. Julia sat beside her and she gave them an encouraging smile when they came into the room.

"Sophia is feeling far more the thing now," she said brightly. "She even thinks she is well enough to travel again. I have sent instructions for both carriages to be made ready so that we may be off as soon as possible. With luck we should be in town again by dinnertime."

Sophia rose and went to Dominic. "I am sorry," she said in a very quiet yet firm voice. "I never meant to use you so. I should have had the courage to tell you honestly that I was in love with Harry, but I could not."

She addressed a point about midway down his chest. He cupped her chin in his hand and raised her face. "I am very fond of you, Sophia," he said gently, "but I should have realized as well that we would never suit. If you are in love with Linton, I wish you both very happy."

At these words, Sophia started weeping again, as if she had endured a reproof. "You are so kind," she sobbed. "I deserve that you should hate me."

Harry took her hand and drew her into an embrace, letting her cry against his shoulder.

Julia walked over to stand beside Dominic. He looked down at her, an enigmatic smile playing on his lips. "Arranged everything to your satisfaction, have you?"

Her expression remained grave, but her eyes danced. "Yes, I think so. You may drive Sophia in your curricle and I shall ride in the chaise with Harry. That way she won't be carriage-sick and it will give us better countenance, since she is still your betrothed in the eyes of the world."

"Then, if you can separate our lovebirds," he said with a nod toward Harry and Sophia, who had stopped crying again and was gazing lovingly into Harry's admiring eyes, "we had best be off. The sooner this is settled for all of us, the better."

Julia heartily concurred with this and she called Harry to order while Dominic left the parlor to settle any charges with the landlord.

12

The return journey to town was thankfully uneventful. Julia had more than a few choice words to say to her nephew about his volatility, and she scolded him roundly for so nearly casting them all into a wretched scandal, but she did so in a far milder way than she might have if she were not cognizant of the encouragement she had given him to pursue Sophia.

They made the decision that Dominic would take Sophia directly to Amberly House while Julia would go to Morland House with Harry to help soften the wrath of his father, who was doubtless home by now and apprised of all that had occurred.

When the chaise pulled up in front of Morland House, it was lit up inside, as if there were a party going on. Julia and Harry went in to an empty front hall and Tomlin informed Lord Linton that Lord and Lady Morland were to be found in the principal drawing room. The servant's accents were so repressive that Julia knew he knew some great storm was about to break.

Heaving a small sigh for the scene she knew they would have to endure, she started up the stair followed by her nephew. She had little doubt that she would come in for her share of the blame in all of this.

The sight that met them when they entered the room was more alarming than Julia had even imagined it would be. Not only was Morland there standing near the hearth and looking thunderous, both Lord and Lady Amberly were seated on a sofa near to him and in the chair next to Elizabeth's was Royden. Julia had to repress a sudden urge to giggle. It looked so like the ending scene in a farce. And so in its way it was.

Predictably, it was Lady Amberly who stood and spoke first. "What have you done with my niece?" she demanded when she saw that Julia and Harry were alone.

"Dominic has taken her home," Julia answered quietly in deliberate contrast to Lady Amberly's tone.

Morland was not one to give precedence in his own home; he strode past Lady Amberly and confronted his sister and son both verbally and physically. "What the devil have you to do in this, Julia? I suppose you have been filling his head with nonsense. And you," he said, rounding on his son, "haven't the sense you were born with. You were never raised in this house to be a damned libertine. I have had to endure nearly two hours of listening to you being described as such without being able to make any justifiable defense of my own son because of your actions. You have shamed not only yourself but me and your mother and the name of Marchant as well."

The color had drained from Linton's face and his eyes took on a cold glitter. Afraid that his temper would overcome his repentance, Julia laid a hand on Harry's arm and said to her brother. "Of course, he should not have done such a thing, but he is in love with the girl and felt desperate. But Dominic and I have brought them back before it could come to scandal, and now we need only sort this out and no one need suffer any injury at all for it."

"Hiding behind your aunt's skirts won't avail you, Linton," his father said, too furious to listen to any reason. "I shall have more to say to you later."

Harry's white cheeks were suddenly suffused with color. "You may say it to me now, if you please," he said, his voice tight with suppressed rage. "I may not have had a thought to the proprieties, but I have done nothing of which I am ashamed. I love Sophia and she loves me, and if other people had not interfered to keep us apart, none of this would have been necessary."

The earl's expression was one of icy fury and Julia feared that he was about to forget the presence of everyone else. She would have spoken again to prevent it if she could, but before she could do so, a voice said behind her, "Take a damper, Linton. You're in the suds deeply enough without adding filial impiety to your list of sins."

Julia turned and looked gratefully up at Dominic. To her surprise, Sophia was with him as well. As soon as Lady Amberly saw her niece, she let out a little cry and rushed over to take her in her arms. "My poor girl," she said with tenderness that surprised everyone. "What an ordeal you must have been through."

Sophia's ready tears rose to the surface, and her aunt led her over to the sofa to seat her between her and Lord Amberly. It was left to Dominic to sort out the chaos and make explanations that were comprehensible to everyone. Such was his air of command that even Morland was quiet and allowed him the floor.

Julia thought with pride that Dominic did superbly. It was not to be supposed that neither Lady Amberly nor Morland allowed him to speak without questioning his story, but he handled them firmly and with unruffled aplomb.

The only thing he made no mention of at all was himself and Julia. Though Royden sat so quietly and self-effaced that he almost might not have been there, Julia, at least, was very aware of his presence, and she was grateful to Dominic for his tact. He made it appear that it was no more than that she had gone with him to bring the eloping couple back for Harry's sake and never hinted that Julia had her own stake in the matter.

When he had finished, it was Lord Amberly who spoke first. "I must say, Sales, you have taken this handsomely. Another man would not be so generous."

"There is no cause for me to be mean," Dominic replied. "I am very fond of Sophia and wish only for her happiness."

"My dear," Lady Amberly said to her niece, "you must be very grateful for Lord Sales' goodness. You are very fortunate that he is understanding and forgiving, and you must never again give him the slightest cause to reproach you after you are wed."

A strained silence fell over the room. Julia cast a quelling frown at her nephew, but he had already been silenced by a similar glance from Dominic.

"Perhaps I have been a bit ambiguous," Dominic said into the breach. "While I truly do wish for Sophia's happiness, I don't believe that it lies with me, Lady Amberly. Sophia has asked to be released from her promise to me and has returned my ring. But you must not chide her," he added, quickly seeing the older woman's expression. "In the circumstances, if she had not, I must have done so myself."

"If you think for a moment," Lady Amberly said, rising and addressing Harry, "that as the reward for your outrageous behavior I mean to countenance a match between you and my niece you are sadly mistaken, my lord."

"For God's sake, Caroline," said Amberly, standing also and taking her arm. "Have the grace to know when you are defeated. What else can you do but countenance a match between them now? Even if they were brought back before they had spent the night together, her maid knows that she meant to elope with Linton and has likely whispered it in confidence to her friends, who will whisper it to theirs. There is no keeping a thing like this completely quiet."

"Do you want Sophia married to a man whose reputation for wildness is only exemplified by what he has done?"

"My son would be a superb match for any young woman he chose to honor with his attention," Elizabeth said, entering the fray.

Morland was leaning against the hearth and he straightened and said to Amberly, "I think it is you and I who should talk at this point. If you like, we can do so now in my study."

Lord Amberly nodded. "Caroline, take Sophia home at once, if you please. We shall discuss this when I return."

There was an implacable note in his voice that made it clear that however much Lady Amberly might rule the roost, there were times when her lord was quite capable of asserting his authority. She asked for a footman to send for their carriage and this was done with alacrity by Elizabeth, who was not only closest to the bellpull, but who would be only too happy to see the Amberlys out of the house.

Dominic, too, took his leave of them, stopping only to say a few quiet words to Harry. Not even another glance was exchanged between him and Julia before he left. Within a quarter-hour, only Julia, Harry, and Royden remained in the drawing room, the latter had not yet spoken so much as a word and only rose as Elizabeth followed Lady Amberly from the room.

Harry looked from Julia to Royden as if surprised to find them together. A bit awkwardly he said, "I'd best change. Might go 'round to the Daffy Club for a bit." He received neither comment nor argument from his listeners and hastily made his exit.

Julia and Royden stood facing each other several feet apart. "Well, Julia," Royden said at last, "where exactly do you and I fit into all of this?"

"Do we fit at all?"

"I begin to fear not. There is no longer any impediment to your marriage to Sales, is there?"

"None," Julia averred. "I am so very sorry, Royden."

"Not sorrier than I, Julia." He saw her stricken look and gave a faint laugh. "No, no, love. Don't imagine that my heart is blighted. Though I am gravely disappointed, I assure you it is not as bad as all that. Ours was never a love match, but I think we might have done very well together and I regret that it was not our fate to be together, nothing more."

"You are very generous to me, Royden," she said with feeling.

"We shall continue to be friends, Julia, I am certain of it." He lifted her face to his and kissed her gently and platonically. "Marry Sales and be happy with him. You will make it work if you want it badly enough."

"I do."

"Then remember me at the christening of your first brat," he said with a laugh. "I may not choose to dance at your wedding, but I shall be delighted to celebrate with you then." He kissed her again in much the same manner and then left.

A few minutes after he had gone, Elizabeth came into the room again. "I thought you would not wish me to intrude," she said plainly. "Have you settled matters with Royden?"

"Yes." Julia sighed. She picked up her reticule from the table where she had cast it on entering the room. "He accepted it like the good man and gentleman that he is. Oh, Elizabeth, I feel the worst sort of wretch," she said on a plaintive note. "Why did I embroil him in my affairs just to hurt him, which I knew I must have done from the day I accepted his offer? I should have stood by the decision I made at Dumphree."

Elizabeth gave her sister-in-law a quick hug. "If Royden bears you no ill-will, you must not punish yourself for feelings you could scarcely help. We all do things from time to time in the stress of the moment that we wish we had not. It is not like you, Julia, to be so maudlin."

Julia laughed. "How true. In fact, I have not been like myself for some time. I wonder if that is good or bad."

"It depends on what form that takes. I have noticed some very positive changes in you since you returned from Dumphree. You are gentler, and less brittle, for one thing."

"Goodness, was I such a cold fish before?" Julia asked, alarmed.

"No. But you were very self-protective after Tony died. Even though your papa and Hal pushed you into marriage with Tony, I think you loved him after a fashion, and missed him. And then, you were so determined to establish your independence. You may have been afraid that softness would make you vulnerable to further disappointment in your life."

"Do you think that I am risking that again? You know that Dominic and I are so very different that it will not be easy for us to adjust to each other's preferences. We are equally strong-willed as well." She gave a rueful laugh. "At least we shall probably never be bored. I only hope we don't mutually throttle each other in the throes of an argument."

Julia began to walk from the room and Elizabeth escorted her into the hall. She shook her head. "I don't think so. You are not a green girl and Dominic is a man of both sense and sensibility. If you never lose sight of the fact that your love for each other is more important than any matter outside of that part of your friendship, then I believe you will deal extremely. Hal and I do, you know, and that is how we manage, for we are really quite unsuited in temperament."

"Thank goodness," Julia said as she turned at the top of the stair to give Elizabeth a brief hug. "I should never be able to cope with two of Hal. Do you think he will dislike this match?"

"He will grumble because it was not of his choosing, as Royden was, but there is no real reason for him to dislike it, after all. Does it matter to you? It shouldn't."

Julia shook her head. Her smile was content. "Not at all," she said, and finally left to return to her own home.

Elizabeth's own town carriage took Julia home. During the

short drive her thoughts returned to all the events of the day. As she entered the house, she was thinking of Dominic and wishing that he hadn't left Morland House so that they might have been together to talk about their own hopes and plans for the future. But she understood why he had felt it necessary to do so, and she chided herself for her impatience. If it was going to be a lifelong relationship between them, they would have all the time in the world to discuss and sort out all that had happened between them.

She felt a tiny twinge of anxiety, as if now that there was finally no impediment to come between them, one or the other of them might suddenly discover that it was not love, after all, but merely the chase. It had happened to her before, though not to such a degree, and she knew perfectly well that her interest in Dominic had first been piqued by his lack of interest in her.

"Good evening, Davies," she said to her butler as he opened the door to her. "I know it is shockingly late, but do you think you might ask Mrs. Fletch if she could make up some sort of tray for my dinner. Anything will do. I find I am not dining out tonight, after all."

The butler cleared his throat portentously, "Very good, my lady. You have a visitor—a gentleman—awaiting your return in the library. Do you wish me to deny you?"

Julia looked at him in surprise and then the likelihood that it was Dominic occurred to her. "No. I shall go to the library at once."

She saw by a quick flicker in Davies' usually impassive expression that he disapproved, though whether of her guest or of her decision to receive him alone, she didn't know or care. The whole world was welcome to think her a loose woman if it were Dominic who awaited her.

Julia was not disappointed. When she came into the room, Dominic, who was standing at one end leafing through a book he had pulled from one of the shelves, looked up, and the smile he gave her made her heart swell and set to rest any lingering fears. This was the man she loved, and he loved her. Nothing else truly mattered.

"Has the dust finally settled?" he asked as she approached him.

"Barely." He took her hands in his and she put her head against his chest, just enjoying the comfort of his closeness. "Amberly was still with Hal when I left, but I doubt there will be any real difficulty about the settlements. Harry's fortune is not as fine as yours, and he will be a mere earl, but I think Lady Amberly will be reconciled to the match in the end."

"She has little choice now." After a pause, he said in a more guarded tone, "What of Royden?"

Julia moved a little away from him. An imp of mischief stirred in her and her expression became very grave. "That was not so pleasant. I am afraid he took it in very bad part, Dominic. He feels that you deliberately set out to alienate my affections and have impuned his honor. I am not certain, but I think he means to ask you to name your seconds."

Dominic was very still for a moment and then he said, "I shall, of course." He turned away from her. "Damn," he said forcefully. "What can I do but accept?"

"And let him put a bullet through you?" Julia said, marveling at the lengths he was prepared to go for the sake of his honor.

"Can I deny that I love you and would more than once have enjoyed putting a bullet through him in a far less honorable manner when I thought of you being his wife. No. We shall meet, and if it is in the cards that I am to die at his hands, then so be it."

Julia was horrified. "Dominic, you could not be so stupid."

He suddenly laughed. "Certainly I am not stupid enough not to know when I am being quizzed. Royden hardly gave the appearance of a man suffering under a grievous injury tonight."

Julia relaxed, hardly aware of how tense she had been. "You are a wretch."

"My only real concern is your highly dispeptic brother. If one could be slain by a look, I should have been laid out on the floor of his drawing room tonight. Does he guess about us?"

"He does now, and of course he does not yet approve because, as Elizabeth said, it was not his idea, but he shall come around quickly enough. He won't be at all dispeptic with you. You have too large a fortune. He shall, however, drive a hard bargain with the settlements."

Dominic smiled and shook his head. "We shan't wait for the

lawyers. I intend to get a special license tomorrow and we shall be married before the day is out. Since our marriage will already be a *fait accompli* by the time settlements are discussed, he won't have a great deal of leverage."

"What has made you think that I am so eager to wed you that I would do so in such a hurly-burly fashion?" Julia said haughtily. "I am very expensive, you know, and Hal will drive a hard bargain for fear that he might someday find me cast back in his care."

"You may have the whole of my fortune, if you please," he said magnanimously. "But wed you shall be no later than tomorrow."

"Truly, Dominic, you know we cannot. First you must publish the end to your betrothal to Sophia, and then we must wait a decent interval before announcing ours."

"Tomorrow," he said in a voice that brooked no argument. "We shall leave it to your very proper brother and Lady Amberly to see to the proprieties. We shall be gone from town by the end of the day."

"The end of the day! You are either mad or drunk," she said roundly. "I couldn't begin to be ready in so short a time, and I don't even know where we are going."

"The Hebrides."

"Never."

"I'll teach you to love it."

This last was said in such a caressing way that Julia felt a small thrill of anticipation. Not even the isolated reaches of the kingdom would be intolerable to her with Dominic beside her. "I may come to like it," she conceded.

"And I may come to like Lady Jersey's routs, though it will take some schooling."

Julia put her arms about his neck and smiled, her eyes half-closed and her lips very close to his. "Then let the lessons commence," she said huskily, and kissed him with the fervor of a longing finally satisfied.